"There is no friend as loyal as a book."
– Ernest Hemingway

Crazy for Home

Book Two – Texas Ghost Stories

By

Karen Sue Burns

Copyright

ISBN 978-0-98960-275-4

Credits

Editor — Lori Leger (Cajunflair Publishing)

Cover — The Killion Group

For all the readers who enjoy a good old-fashioned love story with a sweet ghost thrown in for good measure. We all understand that a spirit in the house increases the fun and the romance.

Chapter One

October 19, Monday

It's an accepted fact that a child's toy left in the middle of a kitchen floor does indeed have the potential for disaster. Maggie Todd held a freshly made apple pie in her hands and turned toward her oven. She stopped short at the miniature soccer ball directly in her path. "One mess avoided," she mumbled, kicking the potential for disaster out of her way. She placed the pie on the preheated oven's center rack, closed the door with a satisfied sigh—one pie down, one to go.

Without fanfare, she turned from the oven, took a couple of steps, and tripped over the very same ball. She hit the floor hard, simultaneously releasing a string of mild curses.

"Are you hurt?"

She looked up from the humiliating position of flat on her butt. An extremely handsome man stood in the middle of the kitchen, one masculine hand stretched toward her.

"I saw you go down." He leaned in to extend his hand even further. "Please, may I help you?"

She reached for the broad palm and muscular forearm. His fingers closed around hers and she felt the warmth and security of a Rocky Mountain fire in the middle of a long winter. He pulled her upright.

"Thanks." Maggie rubbed her hands together to keep from massaging her slightly sore backside.

"No problem." An amused look graced his face. "No one was up front so I came back here when I heard you fall. I'm Alex Brady, I have a room reservation."

She blinked as the realization hit her. *This man* was the six-month guest reservation and three hours early? This man, with his gorgeous blue eyes and dark wavy hair, was her newest guest? She brushed hair back from her face, wishing she hadn't left the front door unlocked. She hated that he'd caught her unprepared and appearing unprofessional. She wiped her hands on her jeans and immediately jumped into the role of innkeeper and hostess.

He circled a hand over his chest and pointed an index finger at her. What? She looked down then turned her back to him. The top button of her blouse had come undone, displaying the plunging pink lace on her bra. She sucked in a breath, corrected the situation, and turned around, determined to ignore the adorable grin on his face.

"Mr. Brady, welcome to The Blue Barn Inn." She untied her "Kiss the Cook" apron and hung it on a hook inside the pantry. "If you'll follow me, I'll show you to your room then we can get your luggage."

"Lead the way."

She exited the kitchen and walked through the dining room to the entry foyer and the second floor stairway. As she walked up the stairs, with Mr. Brady behind her, Maggie realized she had on her oldest pair of jeans—the ones with a red heart sewn on the right cheek, covering a four-inch hole. He'd have to be blind not to notice. As a professional, she'd ignore it. If everything worked out the right way, she wouldn't be dealing with Inn guests for much longer. She'd taken enough time off from her much preferred life and marketing career in Los Angeles to manage the Inn after her dad's illness.

She led him down the hall and opened the last door on the right.

"This is the Pecan Room, our largest guest room," Maggie explained. "Since you'll be here for several months, I thought this one would make you the most comfortable. There's also a small sitting area."

He moved a few steps into the space, frowned, and looked at her.

"I thought the room I rented was attached to the library. Where is it? This room isn't at all what I expected or want for six months."

"The library suite?" Panic peppered along her spine. Oh, shit. Had they booked the wrong room? "I'm sorry for the confusion. I need to check the reservations on my computer. Would you mind waiting while I check?"

"No problem."

"Great." Relief swept through her. She could salvage this reservation. "Let's go back downstairs."

She settled him in the living room with a cup of coffee, a plate of cookies, and the morning newspaper. She rushed to the office behind the kitchen.

It took seconds to access the online reservation system. It was worse than she first thought. Sure enough, Mr. Brady had both the Pecan Room and the Brazos

Library Suite reserved. How the hell had this happened? Sunny, of course. She'd deal with her little sister later.

He seemed to be set on the library suite and that was fine. The daily rate was forty dollars more than the upstairs room. She'd ignore, for now, how much business they'd lost with both rooms booked for one reservation.

Maggie stepped into the bathroom and leaned over the sink toward the mirror. Damn. She rubbed a smudge of flour off her chin. Since she'd by-passed make-up that morning, she took the time to apply a little mascara and lip-gloss before grabbing the suite's key out of a basket on her desk. She hurried back to her guest.

"Mr. Brady—"

"Alex."

"Okay, Alex." A faint smile tickled her lips. "We do have the Brazos Library Suite reserved for you. Again, I'm sorry for the confusion."

"No problem." He lifted the remainder of a cookie. "These are delicious, by the way."

Maggie grinned. He liked her cookies. Why did she care whether this handsome man liked her chocolate chunk coconut bar cookie? Well, because she did.

"The Brazos Suite is just down the hall."

She knew he liked it by the way he walked around the space, poked his head in the closet, ran a hand over the desk, and sat on the bed.

"This will work," he said. "The library is through the door by the bathroom?"

"Let me show you." Maggie led him to the library. "Your key locks both doors. So keep the library door on your side locked when you're not using it."

From the doorway, she watched him move slowly around the room and survey the dark oak shelves that were packed with books of all sizes. A small rectangular oak table with two chairs sat near a wide window covered in white sheer curtains. A leather chair sat tucked away in a corner with a nice pole lamp behind it—a perfect spot for reading. An antique desk that had belonged to Maggie's grandmother graced the one wall not covered with bookcases. The room had always had a studious feel to it.

He turned to her, wearing a satisfied smile. "Is the library available to the other guests?"

"When we have a guest in the suite it's open from ten in the morning to three in the afternoon. Frankly, it doesn't get a lot of use. Most guests are out during the day and prefer watching a movie in the evening."

"That'll work." He pulled out his wallet and handed her a credit card. "Go ahead and charge six month's rent. I'll probably forget to pay you once I get working."

Maggie accepted the card and handed him the key. "Once we get you unloaded, you may park in the back, under the carport. I'll get your luggage."

She walked toward the front door. Alex caught up with her.

"Hey, I'll get my stuff. Not on your job description." He strolled out the door and bounded down the front steps.

She watched him open the back of his black SUV. Well, okay. She could deal with a gentlemanly guest. And, six month's rent in one pop—a nice boost to the Inn's cash flow. She hurried to her desk thinking about

her new guest with his quick smile and his friendly
demeanor. Hmm, his looks weren't bad either.

~~*

Alex hung the last shirt in the closet then stowed his
suitcase on the floor. He turned back to his home for the
next few months. It wasn't all that bad, except for the
green striped wallpaper with little pink roses and
matching pillows on the bed with larger roses. No way
could he stand pillows with roses for any period of time.
He shoved them into the corner of the closet's top shelf.
Now he had the perfect location for completing his work.

The library was a huge surprise. It contained a
number of books on Texas history, several on his
research list. This was fortunate as it would reduce the
number of trips he'd have to make to Texas A&M's
library in College Station. He'd be able to save both gas
and time.

He placed his laptop on the desk. The Inn had
wireless Internet so he was set up in less than five
minutes. Internet access was one of the main reasons
he'd chosen The Blue Barn Inn for his work. He'd
already prepared outlines for several topics that were
appropriate for his Ph.D. dissertation. The tedious work
of writing it was yet to come. But right then, he needed
food before he could even think about opening a book.
He stuffed the room key in his pocket and headed out the
Inn's front door.

Maggie, the cute-as-hell innkeeper, was nowhere in
sight.

What was her story? He hadn't expected to find a
woman who looked like a Hollywood starlet in a small

town B&B. God, that long dark blonde hair and the green eyes presented one fine package. Her face had the cutest chin, like a heart. But whatever—he was done with relationships and had no interest in women. His only goal was to write his dissertation and obtain a university teaching job. Women were off his radar for the next couple of years.

He didn't need a distraction as he was on a tight schedule. He couldn't screw this up. He'd made a big deal of changing careers, going from the world of high tech video games to studying American history with an eye on the classroom. If his paper wasn't approved he'd look like a fool and his stress level would once again elevate.

On the sidewalk, he ran a hand through his hair and looked from one end of the street to the other. He had no clue as to the direction that would lead him to food, but in a small town it couldn't be all that far. He turned left, trusting that his instincts would prove correct.

After fifteen minutes and a couple of turns, he found Alamo Street, the main drag in the historic section of Brenham. He soon found the Farmer's Market Diner and per the sign on the door, it was open for breakfast and lunch until two in the afternoon. He pushed on the door and entered the lunch domain of small town USA.

Light blue vinyl booths lined the walls to his left and right while square tables were scattered in no apparent pattern in the middle. The walls were covered with Texas travel posters, old black and white pictures of farms, and several years of Texas A&M football schedules.

Alex found an empty table with a pebbled grey

Formica surface near the "Daily Specials" white board. A petite waitress with long brown hair streaked with gray and wearing a Texas A&M maroon tee shirt approached him.

"Welcome to the Farmer's Market. I'm Fran. Our lunch special is on the board over there or you can order off the menu." She slapped a plastic-coated cardboard on the table then smiled. "I'll be back in a jiff."

Alex perused the list of lunch options, confirming he wasn't dining in downtown Houston. And that was just fine. He liked the feel of this diner and its smell—earthy and sweet—no doubt due to the gallon-sized bottle of pancake syrup on the table and a miniature potted African Violet.

Fran returned with a pencil and an order pad. "I haven't seen you around here before."

"It's my first trip to Brenham."

"Welcome, again. This is a great little town. Are you going for the special or do you want something off the menu?"

"I'll have the tuna melt with sweet potato fries and iced tea."

"Sweet tea or regular?"

"Regular."

"Coming right up."

Fran left with the menu and a swish of her hip.

Alex checked the e-mail app on his cell phone. He responded to a message from his mother saying he'd arrived in Brenham and yes, his room at the Inn had a decent bed. She continued to worry about his back after a bad fall in sixth grade.

Fran returned to the table with his tea.

"Here you go." She stood by the table with one hand on her hip. "Pardon me for being nosy but are you passing through or visiting someone here?"

"Actually, neither." He figured he might as well tell her. He knew how small towns and gossip percolated together. "I'm finishing up a college degree and staying at The Blue Barn Inn for a few months."

Her brown eyes widened and she leaned toward him. "I love the Todd's, always have. But you be mighty careful at that inn, especially after dark."

"Why?" He couldn't imagine that Brenham would have much of a crime problem, day or night.

She leaned even closer and kept her voice low. "Because it's haunted . . . with the ghost of Rob—well, let's just say the ghost is male." She stepped back from the table and bobbed her head. "That's all I'm saying, just ain't safe to talk about it." A bell dinged and she hurried to the back.

Now, that he hadn't expected—a ghost at the Inn. The Inn's website said nothing about it, at least when he did his research for a place to stay in Brenham. Hmm, this might be an interesting twist. He'd loved ghost stories as a kid and had developed a series of ghost video games in his prior business life.

A ghost at a well-known and established business had to have some type of story. If the ghost actually existed, he might create one last game to finish off his series in style.

~~*

Maggie perused the pantry shelves and made a note on

the grocery list. The back door banged. "Sunny, is that you?"

"We're back."

Maggie stepped out the pantry door. "Where'd you go?"

Sunny entered the kitchen holding her two year-old son's hand. "We heard a nice story at the library and checked out new books."

"That sounds fun. How'd Tyler do?"

"Pretty good considering he wouldn't get off my lap during the story."

"That's because he loves his mama." Maggie ruffled the brown curls on his head. "How about some lunch?"

"My thoughts exactly." Sunny placed Tyler in his blue booster chair at the round oak table and gave him milk in a Sippy cup and a graham cracker.

While Sunny prepared his lunch, Maggie made two plates with tuna salad, apple slices, and butter crackers.

"Our new guest arrived this morning. You had two rooms reserved for him."

"Not again, I'm sorry," Sunny said, making duck lips. "I don't know why I can't get the hang of that reservation system."

"Don't click so much."

"Yeah, that's it or maybe it's the fact that I'm allergic to computers."

"Don't be so hard on yourself." Maggie knew her little sister didn't enjoy working on the PC but it was a necessity in running the Inn. Maybe she needed another lesson.

"I'll get the hang of it, eventually." Sunny spooned

macaroni and cheese onto Tyler's favorite green plate then added blueberries and carrot sticks. "What's the guest like? Isn't he the one who's staying for a while?"

"That's the one. He paid for six months, which helps the bank account. He said he'll be busy once he starts working." Maggie set the lunch plates on the table and poured glasses of iced tea.

"Working, huh? Maybe he's a writer since he was insistent on having the library suite. Sounds boring to me." Sunny placed the plate in front of Tyler who immediately went for the blueberries.

"Maybe so, but he doesn't look boring." Maggie remembered his easy smile and the humor in his eyes as he'd pulled her from the kitchen floor.

Sunny raised an eyebrow as she sat next to Tyler at the table. "Really?"

"Uh-huh." Maggie jotted on a note pad as she chewed on an apple slice.

"What are you writing?"

"Things I don't want to forget." Maggie checked her watch. Yikes, she didn't have much time. "I have an appointment at the bank this afternoon."

"What for?"

"I told you yesterday." Maggie laid her pen across the paper. "Come on, you need to keep up with this stuff. I'm asking for the loan to renovate the Barn."

"Right, I remember." Sunny scooped spilled blueberries from the table onto Tyler's plate. "Have you talked with Mom and Dad about your idea?"

"Not yet. I need to find out if we can get a loan." Maggie had never talked with a banker about a loan and she wouldn't admit her nervousness about the meeting to her little sister. She'd do her best not to blow the opportunity and tell her parents once the deal was done.

"They won't be happy you didn't talk to them first."

"I'll handle it when I need to." Maggie picked up the pen and tapped it on the table. "You know we need to sell the Inn, right? I don't want to be a permanent manager and who knows where you'll move to next. Having the Barn fully functional for weddings and parties will only increase its value."

"You've told that me a million times." Sunny placed her petite hand over Maggie's to stop the tapping noise. "But still, I wish we didn't have to sell. The Inn has been in our family for years. I suppose you're right, but it seems like an awful lot for you to take on."

"Don't worry. Jim Evans has drawn up preliminary plans with cost estimates for the construction. If we get the loan, he'll be doing the hard work."

Sunny rose and used a wipe to clean Tyler's face and hands. "Jim has been friends with Dad for years. How do you know he hasn't spilled the beans?"

"I don't, but Dad hasn't called so I figure Jim hasn't talked."

"I'm putting Tyler down for his nap. Good luck at the bank."

Maggie cleared the table then changed for her meeting. She wanted to look professional but not like a city girl so she dressed in navy slacks, low heels, and an ivory short-sleeved sweater set. She grabbed the file of Jim's plans and her notes and climbed in her car.

Ten minutes later, a secretary ushered her into the

loan office at Brenham National Bank.

"Mr. Lamb, I'm Maggie Todd."

A man rose from a large leather desk chair and came around the huge oak desk. He stood in front of Maggie.

"Yes, you are." He grasped her out stretched hand and squeezed it. "Do you remember me?"

Maggie disengaged her hand and studied the man. He looked about her father's age and gazed at her with kind blue eyes.

"You do look familiar. Please forgive me, I've been away from Brenham for a number of years."

"Your dad and I went to high school together. Plus, we were poker buddies." He patted a chair in front of his desk. "Have a seat." Oh no, would he contact her dad about the loan?

"I remember now." She sat and placed the file folder on her lap. "Mr. Lamb—"

"Please call me Larry." He smiled slowly. "Now, tell me why you need a loan."

"It's about a remodeling loan for The Blue Barn Inn."

"What part of the property would you be remodeling?"

"I'm the new manager of the Inn and it's the Barn's building that needs to be remodeled. I want to turn it into a venue for weddings, meetings, and parties."

"What kind of parties?"

She nearly giggled. "I'm not talking about fraternity keg parties but weddings and birthday, anniversary, and retirement parties . . . family events."

"I see. Do you have any plans drawn up?"

"Yes, I do. Jim Evans did these for me." She opened the folder on her lap and spread his plans over the desk.

She fidgeted while Larry looked at them. Now that she faced him, her stomach rolled and she was unsure of how to convince him that The Blue Barn Inn deserved a loan. The ideas she'd jotted down earlier seemed childish. Apparently she'd forgotten everything she'd learned at her job in Los Angeles about marketing and selling an idea.

"Maggie, this looks interesting. Have you done a study as to the need for this type of venue in Brenham?"

"Not a formal study, but we've had so many calls the last few months asking about our event facilities. It got me to thinking we needed something like this." She swallowed and went on. "With the right advertising we could draw clients and guests from surrounding towns."

He leaned back in his chair, a hand stroking his chin. "Yes, you may be right about that. Having B&B rooms and a party facility together would add to the attractiveness."

"That's my thinking as well," she said, a bit of relief floated over her.

"So the primary projects are the kitchen, restrooms, bar/dining room, and an entry hall-reception area. What loan amount are you requesting?"

"Seventy-five thousand," she said. She'd increased the amount she really needed, figuring banks never loaned what you asked for—reverse psychology, right?

"Okay. I'll make copies of these documents and I'll need to tour the Barn. Would tomorrow morning at ten be suitable?"

"Oh." Maggie hadn't expected he'd want to look at the Barn, but of course he'd want to. Damn, she should have considered that. She'd give him a million dollar tour if that's what it would take to get the loan. "How about we push it to eleven and then you can stay for lunch, get a taste of our menu, and tour the property."

"That sounds fine. I'll bring your plans back, too." Larry stood. "By the way, what do your parents think about your renovation plans?"

Crap. The question she prayed wouldn't be asked.

"I've not been able to contact them. They're so busy since they moved to Florida after Dad retired." Maggie's parents had assumed the Inn's management over ten years ago after Grandma Todd had finally turned over the reins. Maggie became innkeeper less than a year ago, after her father's heart attack and then retirement.

"Give them my best." He walked her to the door of his office. "I'll see you in the morning."

She shook his hand and stepped to the door. "Thanks, Mr. Lamb. I'll see you tomorrow."

As she walked back to her car, Maggie's stomach twisted. Why had she asked him to lunch? Damn. Would he contact her parents? She'd ignore that worry and dazzle him with her menu and her tour guide skills.

Chapter Two

October 20, Tuesday

"Wake up. Come on, you sleep like a log."

Maggie heard a voice far in the distance then her shoulder shook back and forth and the voice became closer. She rolled to the other side of the bed to get away from the noise but it followed her.

"Maggie, wake up . . . wake up, now."

She opened an eye and found Sunny, holding a sleeping Tyler in her arms, leaning over her.

"What are you doing?" Maggie whispered, going from zonked out to wide-awake in two seconds.

"It's the ghost. He's here, in our room."

"What?" She sat up and patted the middle of the bed. "Put Tyler down before you drop him."

"You're right." Sunny placed her son on the bed and pulled the blanket to his chest. "He could sleep through a hurricane."

"Guess he gets that from his aunt. Let's go to the kitchen. We'll hear Tyler if he wakes up." Maggie shuffled behind her sister out of her bedroom. "How about I make tea?"

Sunny opened the refrigerator. "No way, I want a glass of wine."

Maggie shrugged a shoulder. "Fine. I'll get the

glasses."

They settled at the table with the wine.

Maggie looked at her watch—twelve-thirty. "You said the ghost was in your room. Are you sure?"

"Yes, he stood right next to the bed and stared at me. His eyes were dark and transparent and so very sad."

"This is the first I've heard about him being inside the Inn." Maggie had always been skeptical about the existence of ghosts, especially since she'd never seen one up close and personal. The possibility of one named Robert Grant haunting their Inn did seem farfetched, but then again, their grandmother had talked to him more than once. Maybe it wasn't a simple story to entertain her easily bored granddaughters.

"I know, he's supposed to be outside or in the Barn."

"Did he say anything?"

"He mumbled and swayed around a bit. I don't think ghosts are supposed to talk."

"Says who?" Maggie asked.

"Geez, I don't know."

"You're sure it was this ghost, Robert? Maybe you were dreaming."

"No, I wasn't dreaming. I saw the darn ghost. I know it was Robert Grant."

"How can you be so sure?"

"I've seen pictures of him. It was definitely Robert Grant."

Maggie didn't doubt that Sunny believed the ghost had been in her bedroom. But that didn't mean he'd actually been there. On the other hand, Sunny was practical and stable and not prone to being scared by "things that go bump in the night."

Maggie sipped the wine, gazed at her sister over the rim of the glass. "Maybe we should look into the history of this ghost. I can't even remember the stories that Grandma Todd told us." She had managed the Inn for forty-five years before their parents took over.

"Me either." Sunny twirled her glass, staring at its contents. "I was what, five years old at the time?"

"And I was a teenager more interested in boys than a ghost story."

"Guess we, no you, should make up for not paying attention."

"Yep, that's why we have Internet access here." Maggie winked at her sister. "I'll do a search on Robert Grant tomorrow."

~~*

The next morning, Alex strolled eagerly into the dining room at nine o'clock, anticipating his first breakfast at the Inn. He sat at the only empty table and poured coffee from the carafe in the middle. It was strong and black, just the way he liked it.

The dining room reminded him of his grandmother's house with a mahogany china cabinet and lace things on the tabletops. Of course, the surround sound in the ceiling wasn't in his grandma's house. He recognized the music playing as new age, soothing and invigorating at the same time.

An older man approached his table.

"Good morning, mind if I join you?"

"Please do," Alex replied and offered his hand. "I'm Alex Brady. I just arrived at the Inn yesterday."

"Nice to meet you, Alex, I'm George Brown. This is my last morning. I'll be heading back to Austin."

A young woman carrying a pitcher entered. She stopped at the other tables first, poured from the pitcher, and then approached Alex's table.

"Good morning, I'm Sunny. May I pour you a glass of orange juice?"

Both men nodded and she poured into stemmed glasses. "I hope you're hungry. We have a delicious meal this morning."

Alex looked around the room. "Is Maggie around?"

Sunny nodded. "She's in the kitchen finishing breakfast. I'll bring it out in just a minute."

In less than five minutes, Sunny arranged a series of dishes on a sideboard along the wall next to the kitchen. She turned to address the diners.

"Good morning, everyone. Our menu today includes a delightful and hearty mix of dishes." She pointed to each dish as she stated its name. "Please help yourselves and enjoy."

Alex and his companion made small talk while the other guests filled their plates. He was the last to visit the buffet and take advantage of the food. He studied the menu board.

Today's Breakfast
Herbed Eggs & Sautéed Arugula
Crème Brule French Toast
Mixed Fresh Berries
Cheese Grits
Cinnamon Pear Scones

The breakfast was exceptional. Maggie obviously knew her way around a stove. The next six months were looking up if he'd have food like this every morning. He wanted to tell her he liked her cooking but she hadn't yet appeared.

He decided to wait for her with a third cup of coffee. Soon, he was alone in the dining room. Sunny started to gather dishes.

"Mr. Brady, can I get you anything else?"

"No thanks, having one last cup of coffee."

She smiled then went into the kitchen and seconds later Maggie appeared.

"Oh, Alex, I didn't know you were still here. Did you have a good night? Was the bed okay? Do you need anything?"

He laughed. "Yes, yes, and no. By the way, your breakfast was fantastic. I'll have to run every day to work off the calories."

"I understand. I'm out the door at six every morning. I like my own cooking too much."

"Hmm, maybe I'll join you."

She gathered dishes from the sideboard and turned back to him. "That would be nice."

Sunny walked into the dining room carrying a little boy. "Mr. Brady, you're still here. Is there a problem?"

"No," he replied quickly. "I wanted to tell Maggie how much I enjoyed breakfast. This place is great." He rose from the table.

"My big sis is a great cook," Sunny said as she nudged Maggie in the side. "And this is Tyler who is sweet most of the time. But just in case you hear a toddler crying, you'll know it's not a ghost."

"Nice to meet you, Tyler. I better get to work, lots to do."

"Have a good day," Maggie said. "If you need me during the day, my cell phone number is in the notebook in your room or you can always check the kitchen."

Alex returned to his room, energized and ready to work. In fact, he had so much work ahead of him, he didn't know if six months would be enough time to complete it all. He had to stay focused.

Of course, thoughts about the innkeeper at the other end of his temporary home might rattle his concentration. He'd simply have to deal with the distraction like an adult and ignore Maggie as best he could.

~~*

Maggie blew out a controlled breath. Larry Lamb should arrive at the Inn any minute. She had an enticing lunch started and had worked hard on her pitch for the loan. She'd show him the Barn and the grounds and do her best to paint a picture of the event venue she envisioned. That shouldn't be hard. She believed her ideas were on target and the end result would be worth her efforts to sweet talk the banker.

She stirred the squash soup on the stove and lowered the heat. It was the perfect accompaniment to her chicken salad and herbed biscuits. Providing lunch to the banker now seemed like a stroke of genius and hopefully, it would seal the deal. That is, if he hadn't contacted her father about the loan request. Fingers crossed that he hadn't made that call.

Sunny entered the kitchen and stowed her cleaning

supplies in the broom closet.

"Beds are stripped, dusting done, bathrooms cleaned."

"Thanks, sweetie. It sure is nice having you here," Maggie said. "I don't know what I'd have done when Delores retired if you hadn't offered to move here."

"Nah, I'm the lucky one. This is the perfect spot for Tyler and me while Jason does his last overseas tour. It keeps him from worrying about us."

"I agree, it's a win-win for all of us. Don't forget the banker will be here in a few minutes and that he's an old friend of Dad's. I plan to dazzle him with my charm and plans for the Barn."

"I'm sure you'll be sizzling."

"Very funny." Maggie stuck out her tongue. "When Tyler wakes up, you and him come to the Barn and agree to all my plans. I want Mr. Lamb to understand that this is a family business and we're all on board for this remodeling."

"I never looked at the plans," Sunny admitted.

"That's okay. Just agree to whatever I say."

Sunny saluted her. "Aye, aye, captain."

The doorbell chimed.

"That's Mr. Lamb." Mandy untied her apron, handed it to Sunny. "Would you taste the soup? It might need more salt." She hurried to the front door.

Mr. Lamb stood on the porch, looking like a friendly grandfather, a smile on his face. Maggie shut the door behind her and stuck out her hand. "It's good to see you again, Mr. Lamb."

"You as well, and remember, it's Larry."

"Yes, of course." Maggie walked down the front steps. "I thought we'd walk to the back so you could get an idea of our parking and the layout of the Barn and the house."

"Good idea."

They walked on the gravel driveway to the back of the house and the site for the remodeling Maggie proposed.

"As you can see we have a large parking area for our guests."

"Yes, it does look adequate," Larry said with a wave of his hand. "Let's tour the Barn."

He seemed awfully nice but she still worried he'd contact her parents. She needed him to approve her loan request without doing that—she'd deal with her parents later. She turned to him and exhibited a million-dollar smile. "Please, follow me."

They walked over the gravel lot to the front of the Barn. Maggie pulled keys out of her pocket then unlocked the red door. Larry walked behind her into the great room.

He stopped in the middle and turned a slow circle. "This room is huge . . . and a bit dreary."

"I agree. Now you understand why a renovation of this entire space is needed."

"I certainly do. Show me the specific areas your plans mentioned."

"Let's start with the kitchen."

For thirty minutes, Maggie showed him every corner of the Barn she hoped to update—new bathrooms with separate dressing areas, a new foyer with a sofa and chairs, and a built in bar with a long line of leather stools in the dining room that would seat one hundred people for meals.

Larry asked several thoughtful questions, which gave Maggie hope that he would approve her loan. The last stop on the tour was her plans for the yard between the barn and the house. She hoped this would illustrate her overall vision for the Inn.

"Larry, let's go outside and I'll show you the last part of my proposal."

He motioned with his arm. "After you."

Maggie moved out the door to the straggly yard. She stopped halfway to the house.

"I envision this space," she circled her arms in front of her, "as an outdoor option for weddings and receptions. I'd like to build a gazebo by the fence and add a flagstone walkway from the barn to the patio and a second walkway from the parking lot to the gazebo. At the cross of the two walks, I want a small fountain surrounded by a flowerbed."

"Good use of all the space you have here."

Maggie walked toward the cracked patio. "Thanks. The new terrace will open up more space for guests to enjoy the outdoors."

"Seems like you've given this a lot of thought."

"I've been thinking about the project for quite some time." She glanced at her watch. "Why don't we go inside for lunch? I can answer any other questions." Maggie placed him in the dining room with a glass of iced tea.

She stirred the soup with a wooden spoon as Sunny

arrived with Tyler.

"Why didn't you come outside?" Maggie whispered before kissing Tyler's cheek. "I needed you."

"Sorry, Tyler just woke up. I started on the laundry."

Maggie put a finger to her lips. "Quiet, he's in the dining room."

"How did it go?"

"Okay, I want you and Tyler to eat lunch with us."

"Not a good idea, Tyler will be a distraction."

"Exactly. I want Mr. Lamb to realize the Inn is a family business and that you and I are on top of things."

"Gotcha. I'll get Tyler in his booster seat then serve the soup while you get the salad plated."

"Thanks, Sis."

Tyler clutched his brown teddy bear, George, as Sunny led him to the dining room. Maggie watched them with a lump in her heart. With her brother-in-law, Jason out of the country, she was responsible for her small family.

Sunny had taken on the housekeeping duties for the Inn like a real trooper. She and Tyler had made this place feel like a home. She'd proven to be vital in the team effort of running their family business. Maggie couldn't help but wonder how long it would last. She shrugged off the negative thought. It was time to concentrate on the tasks at hand—lunch with Mr. Lamb and securing the bank loan necessary for the Barn's renovations.

Sunny returned and loaded the soup bowls onto a tray and carried it out of the kitchen. Meanwhile, Maggie set up the salad, red leaf lettuce under the chicken/red grape/walnut mixture with carrot sticks on the side. She placed the biscuits in a basket lined with a green ivy napkin and set it on a dark oak tray with the salad plates.

"Thank you for joining Sunny, Tyler, and I for lunch." Maggie watched Larry's face as she sat across from him. He grinned at Tyler and winked.

"Mr. Lamb, I work here at the Inn with my sister. What can I do to help you understand why we need a loan to expand our business?" Sunny cocked her head to the side.

Maggie noticed the surprise on his face. He needed to understand that Maggie and Sunny were a team. A team dedicated to securing what was best for the future of the Inn. Perhaps another approach might work with the banker.

"Larry, have you attended the Halloween Festival in Chappell Hill?" Maggie queried.

"Of course, many times. My grandkids love it."

"I plan to take Tyler this year," Sunny said. "He's too young to understand the correlation of pumpkins with Halloween ghosts and goblins."

"We go for the food and the shopping," Larry said. "I don't believe in ghosts."

"But some people do," Sunny countered. "In fact, I saw one last night."

Larry's fork clattered on the tablecloth. "Sorry. It's true then? The Inn is haunted?"

This conversation had taken a wrong turn. "Larry, my sister is teasing you," Maggie said. "I'm sure you have additional questions about our loan request."

He chuckled. "Yes, of course, I do have more questions. A loan request for this sum of money isn't a slam dunk."

"We understand," Maggie said. "Let's enjoy our lunch then Sunny and I will answer all your questions." She softly kicked Sunny on the shin under the table and Sunny glared at her.

Tyler provided the lunchtime entertainment with reciting the ABC's and the naming of barnyard animals based on the sound they made.

Maggie watched in awe as her sister and nephew turned a business lunch into a laughter packed lunch. Mr. Lamb seemed charmed by Tyler and his cute-as-a-button toddler antics.

Once they finished lunch, Mr. Lamb had a couple of questions about the renovation. She'd expected him to have tons more, so it was a pleasant surprise.

He complimented the chicken salad, said he'd be in touch, and left. Maggie crossed her fingers, hoping for the best. Once the renovation was completed and business increased, she could list the Inn with a business broker and get back to her life in Los Angeles.

After lunch, Sunny took Tyler to their room for quiet-time so Maggie cleared the table and worked at straightening the kitchen. As she filled the dishwasher, she heard a knock. She straightened and looked around. The source of the knock stood in the doorway between the kitchen and dining room.

"Alex, hi, how are you?"

"Stretching my legs and off to get lunch."

"Lunch? Oh please, I have squash soup and chicken salad. Sit down at the table here and I'll serve it right up."

"But lunch isn't included in my room rate."

"That's true. Let's just call it my treat."

"Okay, but I'll take you to dinner one evening in payment."

"That sounds like a fair exchange." She'd have no problem eating dinner with this man.

"Which reminds me. I want to ask if I could make a special arrangement with you."

"Special arrangement?"

"Could I get dinner here every evening? That way I won't have to spend extra time going out, waiting, etc. I'd think at least an additional twenty dollars a day would be in order."

He looked at her with pleading eyes. The man needed to eat and how could she refuse him. She stuck out her hand and he shook it. "Okay, Alex, we have a deal, I'll prepare you dinner every evening. Hope you don't mind if it's what Sunny and I eat."

"That's fine with me. What time?"

"Um, around six, that works best with Tyler's schedule, or I'll bring you a tray. We'll see how it goes, okay?"

"Great."

"By the way, six is also cocktail hour."

Chapter Three

October 21, Wednesday

Alex needed a break. Four straight hours of working, hunched over his computer, had his back muscles screaming for relief. A ten minute walk should put him right again. He let himself out the front door of the Inn and set off down the block, destination unknown.

He loved a small town and Brenham was no exception. The quaint houses had him imagining families, human events, and hopes for the future. He could almost picture himself living permanently in a town like this—one with history and character. The historical background was one of the reasons he had decided to write his dissertation in Brenham.

Of course, he had to finalize his topic and its historical element soon—real soon or his schedule would go to hell. His indecisiveness on the topic was so unlike him. Usually he was a quick decision kind of guy after he studied a carefully prepared logical analysis.

He rounded the corner onto Alamo Street and the array of old storefronts turned into trendy boutiques and restaurants with at least one antique store on every block. He meandered along, window-shopping to a degree, as most of the stores were geared toward women. He hadn't passed one sporting goods store.

Just as he got to the end of the block to turn back toward the Inn, Alex came to a children's store, The Purple Cow. A couple of child-sized mannequins dressed in winter coats and hats filled the front window, along with books, soccer balls, and trucks. He liked the look of one yellow truck. It was the perfect size for Tyler.

He entered the store and immediately felt out of his element. He felt like a giant around the small clothes and accessories. His discomfort must have shown on his face as a sales clerk approached him after a minute.

"Good afternoon, may I help you?" The older woman reminded him of Mrs. Claus without the red dress and white hat.

"Yes, thanks, I want to buy a truck for a little boy."

"Okay. What type of truck?"

"Hmm…"

"How old is the child?"

"Two."

She wiggled a finger. "Follow me."

And he did, like a lost puppy following a bone.

After much deliberation, Alex selected a wooden fire truck with black rubber wheels and a white ladder screwed onto either side. It had nothing that Tyler could pull off and put in his mouth. He also bought a book titled *The Ugliest Fire Truck*. The Mrs. Claus look-a-like assured him it was perfect for a two year old.

Now carrying a purple shopping bag, Alex resumed his walk back to the Inn. He felt good. His first purchase of a children's toy wasn't half bad. Of course, if he wanted children of his own, he'd better get on the stick. He wasn't getting any younger, as his ex-finance had recently told him. She and his ex-dog should be moving out of his Houston condo on Saturday.

At least he'd realized what a mistake he'd made during the engagement. They weren't right for each other, and marriage would have turned their lives into a living hell.

Within fifteen minutes, he was back at the Inn and used his key at the front door. The house was quiet. He longed to see Maggie and give her the truck for Tyler. But his guest status held him back from looking for her or calling out her name. The Inn was her home and he had to respect the boundaries that represented.

He went to his room and for the hundredth time reviewed the outline for his dissertation. Which way should he go? The history of Brenham and Washington County was extensive, with many characters and events spanning over nearly two hundred years. He had to make a decision. Unfortunately, he was interested in each and every topic. *Damn it, focus Brady*. He threaded his hands through his hair then paced the room—desk to window to bed and back to the desk.

He snapped his fingers; he'd make a decision using the scientific method.

He sat at the desk, pointed an index finger at the computer monitor. "Eenie, meenie, miney, moe," he recited as his finger circled over the monitor's screen then touched the list of topics. He had his dissertation topic—"The cultural, economic, and social perspectives that led to the first tax supported school system in Texas."

Shit, that was a mouthful and typical for a

dissertation. He sent an email message to his graduate advisor with his decision. Now that he knew his topic, he could get his ass in gear for the research.

Actually, he loved doing research. The search for facts and knowledge turned his brain on in a big way. The process comforted him, reminding him that there was order in the world, and yes, history did repeat itself. He liked that, the sense of security that man had no surprises up his sleeve, merely a new angle on an old problem.

Now that he had his topic, he wanted to celebrate. The decision had hounded him for almost two months. And he felt ridiculous for making it into such a big deal, especially after using such a simple method to make his final decision. Oh well, it was over. He picked up his keys and left the Inn in search of a liquor store for a bottle of whiskey. Funny how this place felt like home after only two days.

~~*

"Thank you for calling, Larry," Maggie said, tamping down her excitement. "Yes, I'll be at the bank at nine tomorrow morning to sign the loan documents." Once she heard him say The Blue Barn Inn had been approved for the full amount of the loan, it had been impossible to concentrate on the rest of his message.

She quickly called Jim Evans and arranged a meeting, also the next day, right after her return from the bank. Although this was both exciting and scary, she knew in her heart that good times, good events, and good guests were in the Inn's future.

Maggie poured a glass of iced tea before gathering

the day's mail off her desk. She turned on a Victorian table lamp and plopped into the yellow easy chair in the corner of her bedroom.

She felt wonderful. Her plans for the Inn were on target and she'd soon have it in tip-top shape as the premier wedding venue in Brenham. She was absolutely certain a buyer would view it as a fantastic investment and snatch it up. She could then return to her life in LA and Sunny could rejoin her husband after his deployment ended. Renovating the Barn would be good for everyone.

She sipped her tea, glad for the chance to kick back and relax. She pulled a thick envelope off the top of the pile of mail. The return address said Adams & Smith, PC. She slipped her index finger under the flap of the envelope and drew out a thick stack of papers.

"What the hell?"

"Maggie, please." Sunny scolded as she and Tyler walked through the door. "Tyler came to say good night."

Maggie set the papers on her lap then placed her arms around the sweet two-year-old standing before her. "You ready for night-night?"

Tyler nodded then hid his face behind George, who he held tightly in his arms.

She whispered in his ear. "Sleep tight, little pumpkin."

He nodded with a sly smile and she kissed his cheek.

Sunny swung Tyler into her arms. "I'll be back once he's asleep."

Maggie tossed the papers on the floor next to the chair and rose to peer through the window that faced the

Barn. Moonlight flooded its front. The paint definitely needed to be refreshed. She hoped to find a new blue color—something on the dusty side yet with a richness that popped through. Color wasn't one of her strong points so she'd need Sunny's help when she went to the pick it out.

She pulled back the lace curtain for a better view and pressed her face to the glass. Something moved by the side of the Barn next to the parking lot. She grabbed her keys off the desk and ran to the back door. Teenagers had better not be hanging out back there and smoking. She'd had the problem a couple of times over the summer.

She ran down the steps to the yard and swore. She'd forgotten to get a flashlight. The barn was nearly dark on the right side. She walked slowly, heading toward the glow from a flood light on the covered parking lot.

"Who's there? Come out, right now," she demanded.

Silence. She shouted louder. "Come out, now."

A figure moved from the corner of the Barn closest to her.

Maggie's eyes widened while her heart sped into over drive. "Oh. My. God."

"Finally, we meet."

She could only stare at the ghost—hold on, was she admitting that a ghost stood not five feet from her? He was tall and young and transparent.

"You're Maggie, right?"

Holy shit, ghosts could talk . . . and in English?

"Who are you?" Dumb question, she knew his name.

He laughed, a hollow rumbling sound. "You know who I am. I'm Robert Grant."

"I guess you're real then."

"Real is a relative term. Let's say I do exist although I realize you've never believed in me."

"How do you know that?"

He pointed to his head. "I was considered quite intelligent, even graduated from business school. I've always had the gift of foresight. Things come into my mind and they're always the truth."

"Why are you here? At the barn, I mean."

"This is where I was murdered."

Maggie backed up a step. "M . . . murdered?"

"That's right, by that bastard, Herbert Adams."

"How do you know he killed you?"

He looked at her through transparent eyes, a half smile teasing his mouth. "I know because I was there."

She bristled then realized the silliness of her question. "Yeah, I guess you were. Sorry. Can I help you with something?"

"Yes, I want to talk with Grace."

"Grace?"

"Yes, Grace Edwards."

"I don't know her."

"Of course you do, she's the woman with the little boy in the bedroom over there." His arm raised and a long finger pointed above her head.

She followed the line of his finger and realized he was pointing at the back of the house. He was talking about Sunny.

"You're referring to my sister, Sunny, and my nephew, Tyler. We don't know, nor do we have a Grace Edwards at the Inn."

"Miss, I believe you're mistaken. I saw the woman last night. It's Grace, although I was taken by surprise at the presence of a child. Where did he come from?"

Maggie swallowed a giggle. This ghost was kinda cute. "Mr. Grant, the boy is Sunny's son. I can assure you the woman is my little sister and not Grace."

He looked at Maggie for a moment, raised his arms to the darkened sky and cried out, "Where's my Grace? I had planned on proposing to her." He repeated the words over and over as he turned from her and walked into the shadows at the side of the barn. His voice held such anguish that Maggie wanted to follow him but stopped herself after two steps. Following him in the dark was not a smart idea.

She returned quickly to her bedroom and found Sunny with her legs draped over the side of the easy chair.

"You comfortable?"

"Yes, ma'am." Sunny raised a wine glass. "Where were you?"

"You will not believe who I just spoke to." The ringing of her cell phone interrupted Maggie.

"This is Alex Brady. I was wondering about dinner. The dining room is dark."

"Dinner?" Then she remembered. "I'm so sorry, I totally forgot our agreement. Let's meet in the kitchen and I'll prepare your meal right now." She stowed the phone in her pocket. "Come on Sunny. I'll make dinner for you and Alex Brady."

Maggie pulled a container of tomato basil soup from the freezer and set it in the microwave on defrost.

"Sunny, would you pour me a glass of chardonnay?" She noticed Alex walk in the kitchen. My, he was a handsome man.

"Alex, good evening. I'm sorry for my memory lapse. Would you like a drink before dinner?"

"What are we having?"

Sunny waved a wine bottle she'd retrieved from the refrigerator. "We have red or white wine or a vodka tonic."

"I'll take the vodka," he said. "Anything I can do to help with dinner?"

Maggie turned from the counter by the sink. "Good heavens, no. You're our guest."

Alex rubbed a hand over his face. Opened his mouth, shut it, opened it again. "Yes, I realize I'm a paying guest. But surely, we can dispense with the guest-host formalities since I'll be staying at the Inn for such a long time."

Maggie considered his suggestion for all of two seconds. Why not? He seemed like a nice guy and it was pleasant to have a man around since it had been two women for over six months.

"Okay, Alex, consider yourself an informal guest of the Inn." She handed him a knife and a cutting board. "Make yourself useful and cut carrot sticks while I make your drink."

"Yes, ma'am."

An hour later, over cups of coffee, Sunny questioned Maggie. "You never did tell me who you talked to."

"When?"

Sunny rolled her eyes. "When I was putting Tyler to

bed."

Maggie narrowed her eyes. "Sorry. I actually spoke to Robert Grant."

Sunny's coffee sloshed onto the table. "I thought you didn't believe in our ghost."

Alex sat forward in his chair. "I've heard about him. Fran mentioned him."

"Fran at the diner?" Sunny asked.

Alex nodded. "How long has the ghost been at the Inn?"

"The original building was built in 1915 so it's been a while," Sunny replied. "I'm sure Mom and Dad know about him."

"Whatever. Do you want to hear my story or not?" Maggie said.

Sunny and Alex nodded so she continued.

"I saw something out my bedroom window and went to investigate. That's how I found Robert."

"Interesting," Alex said. "What does he look like?"

"Like a ghost," Maggie put a hand over her mouth to hide a giggle.

Sunny punched her in the arm. "Be more specific. I'm curious to know if he looks the same to both of us."

"That's right, he was in your bedroom. He was tall and wearing old-fashioned clothes and I could see right through him."

"Sounds the same, like a Hollywood-type ghost," Sunny said. "How did he sound? Was he nice?"

"He seemed pleasant enough and he can read minds or something like that. Plus, he told me he was murdered by Herbert Adams."

"Hmm . . . I wonder if Herbert is related to the folks who own Adams Nursery?"

Maggie leaned forward in her chair. "Wouldn't that be something? I wonder if Herbert went to prison."

Alex waved a hand. "Wait a minute, back up. Robert can read minds?"

Maggie shook her head. "I don't know. He said he has the gift of foresight and things come into his mind that end up being true."

"Ooh, spooky," Sunny teased.

Maggie laughed at her sister. "Don't be a smart ass. He wants to talk to you."

"Me? Why me?"

"He thinks you're someone named Grace Edwards."

"I bet that's why he came into my room last night."

"Hold on, he was in the house?" Alex's tone registered a cross between alarm and fascination.

"Yes, and it scared the bejesus out of me. I woke up in the middle of the night and found him bending over me."

"That's incredible," Alex said. "How'd he get in your room?"

"Geez, Louise," Maggie said. "He's a freaking ghost. He probably walked through the wall or the door or flew in the window."

Sunny scrunched her face. "That's not something I want to even think about."

"Sounds like he has some kind of attachment to you since he thinks you're this Grace person," Alex said.

"I told him you aren't Grace." Maggie tapped a finger to her chin. "I have an idea."

"Like what?" Sunny said, narrowing her eyes.

"I know," Alex said. "You want to find out who this Grace person is and her connection to the ghost. Right?"

"Well, yes, that seems like the logical thing to do."

"Good." He rose and placed his mug in the sink. "This sounds interesting so I'll take care of it. Thanks for dinner."

Maggie jumped from her chair. "Wait a second. The Inn's ghost has nothing to do with you. Sunny and I will take care of this."

He turned back to them at the door to the dining room. "No need. I'm really good at scouring the Internet and databases for research purposes." He saluted them and walked out the door.

Maggie looked at Sunny, throwing her hands in the air. "Do you believe that man? Who does he think he is?"

"That did seem a little weird. But let him do the research. You have enough to do around here."

"Ya think?" Maggie crossed her arms over her chest. "Well, I'll show him anyway."

"How and why?"

"Why? Because . . . because it's none of his business. He's a guest here."

"A guest who paid in advance for six month's rent," Sunny reminded her.

"True. But still, it's none of his business. We shouldn't have discussed Robert in front of him."

"What if he brings it up again? Aren't you fixing him dinner every night?"

"I'll fix a tray for his room," Maggie said. "No more eating in the kitchen, it's inappropriate anyway since he's a guest. Mom would have a cow if she found out."

"I'm not telling her. You cook and I'll deliver the tray every evening."

"Sounds like a plan."

Chapter Four

October 22, Thursday

After signing the loan documents, Maggie huddled with Jim Evans over his blueprints for the Barn's renovation. Excitement bubbled in her chest and threatened to explode. She couldn't wait to get started.

"First thing we do is some demo then an asbestos inspection," Jim said. "Because of the Barn's age I'm certain we'll have to do a treatment."

"I remember. How long will that take?"

"At least a week for everything."

"Okay, that's reasonable." Maggie was relieved it wouldn't take longer.

"In the meantime, you need to pick out the kitchen appliances."

"Sounds like fun. Where should I go?"

"Head over to Brazos Appliances and talk to Joe. They have a decent showroom and can do the ordering. Just ask Joe to fax me what you select so I can make sure everything fits."

Maggie rubbed her hands together. "Ooh, this will be cool."

Jim smiled and shook his head. "Just pick out what's on the list."

Maggie soon went into the house and found Sunny and Tyler dusting the living room.

"You interested in a little shopping?"

"For what?" Sunny held a feather duster in the air like a sword.

"It's shopping. Does it matter?"

"Nope. Let me get Tyler to try the potty then we can go."

Thirty minutes and one experimental potty session later, they strolled along the aisles of Brazos Appliances pushing Tyler in a stroller and scoping out stoves, dishwashers, and refrigerators.

Maggie could barely absorb the smorgasbord of choices before her. "This is like a candy store for cooks," she whispered to Sunny.

"You're so weird," Sunny said, playfully shoving her sister's shoulder. "What do you need first?"

"Everything." Maggie stopped next to a double wide, zero depth refrigerator-freezer combination. It was magnificent. She opened both doors and stuck her head into each side. "This is so cool and the freezer will give me extra storage." She turned, intending to gain Sunny's opinion but she and Tyler had moved over to the stoves. They were standing next to Mildred Adams.

What a perfect opportunity.

Maggie sauntered over to the stoves. "Mrs. Adams, hello. How are you?"

"Just fine."

"I hope you know we love the flower arrangements the nursery provides for the Inn."

"Of course you do. Our work is always excellent," Mildred said. "Sunny here tells me you're remodeling the Barn."

"We are. It will be a wonderful venue for weddings and parties."

"Aren't you afraid of that old ghost scaring people," Mrs. Adams snickered.

Maggie laughed, the old biddy. "Now, Mrs. Adams, why do you think there's a ghost at the Inn?"

"Because Grandfather Herbert told me all about that mean old man who ended up as a ghost there."

"Seriously?" Maggie did her best imitation of an offended B&B manager. "That's why you think a ghost is haunting us? Because years ago some relative in your family made up a ghost story?"

Mildred wiggled a finger in front of Maggie's face. "Don't you dare patronize me, young lady. I know exactly who your ghost is. Grandfather Herbert did not lie." She nodded at Sunny. "Teach your sister some manners."

Maggie watched Mildred waddle away. "What the hell is wrong with her?"

"Maggie," Sunny pointed at Tyler in his stroller.

"Sorry," Maggie whispered. "I bet this Herbert is the same man that Robert mentioned last night."

"I agree, too much of a coincidence. He obviously didn't tell her the truth, probably due to his guilt. Robert Grant is not an old man ghost."

"I think we need to do a bit of research on this uncle. I mean, what's his story?"

"No, enough with the research," Sunny laughed. "Aren't we supposed to be looking for appliances?"

"You're right. I wonder if we could use this ghost thing to our advantage. Add some mystery or excitement to the Barn. Maybe we could re-name it."

"No way, Mom and Dad may not be doing the day-to-day management of the Inn, but they still own it. I don't think they would allow it."

"They don't have to know. We could use it for marketing, maybe—"

"Stop." Sunny raised a hand. "I will not be involved in anything that Mom and Dad won't like."

"Okay, okay, but I still plan to think about marketing with a ghost angle."

Sunny shook her head. "Whatever."

~~*

Alex was having a bitch of a time getting his head into his dissertation. He had his topic related to the establishment of the first tax public supported school system in Texas, but he couldn't get motivated to begin the initial research. Maggie's face came into his mind and his semi-rude words to her that he was better at Internet research than her. Well, it was true.

He'd had fun eating with her and her sister last night, too much fun. She was cute but definitely not his type. Hell, that was if he even had a type. Based on recent events, he was toxic when it came to women. His ex-fiancé had told him more than once he was boring and insensitive. She was probably right. Thus, he had no business even thinking of Maggie as anything other than an innkeeper.

He rubbed a hand over his face. He'd stay away from her, that's exactly what he'd do. Since he had a brain block on his own research, he'd look into the Inn's history and find out if it included a person named Grace

Edwards. He figured the local public library would be the best bet for finding the resources he needed.

After entering the Nancy Carol Roberts Memorial Library, he headed to a computer and the online catalog to search for local high school annuals and books on Brenham history since 1900. He lucked out and found annuals starting in 1920. He pulled out the first five and took them to a table along with a couple of books on Brenham history.

The student list in the back of the 1920 annual included Grace Edwards as a sophomore. She appeared the next year as a junior but wasn't listed in the 1922 yearbook when she would have been a senior. He chewed on the end of his pen, something must have happened during the summer of 1921 or the next school year. Hmm, who were her parents?

Almost two hours later, Alex jotted the last note on a yellow legal pad then snapped the book shut. Damn, he was good. He knew the identity of Grace and her list of school activities, even had a picture of her. She did look a bit like Sunny. He couldn't wait to tell Maggie. She'd be . . . whoa, stop.

Yesterday he'd declared to himself that he'd stay clear of Maggie and now he wanted to tell her what he'd discovered about Grace. More than that, he found himself imagining what it would be like to kiss that pretty mouth of hers. Where the hell had that come from? He had no intention of kissing her and he sure as hell wouldn't think about it again. He needed lunch—low blood sugar was affecting him in strange ways.

On the way back to the Inn, he drove through the

outside order lane of a fast food burger joint. He carried a supersized diet drink and a bag containing burger and fries to his room. The Inn was quiet except for the hum of a vacuum cleaner on the second floor. Sunny was working. Before he could stop the thought from taking shape, he found himself wondering what Maggie was doing. He forced it from his mind. How she spent her days was no concern of his.

He tossed his backpack on the bed then set his lunch on the desk. His cell phone rang, the caller ID read "Mom."

"Yes, I'm eating my vegetables."

"Very funny, Alex," his mother said. "Have you settled in and started working?"

"Yep, the Inn is nice and I finally nailed down my dissertation topic. Now it's research and writing."

"Good. You can give me all the details in person."

"Mom, I won't be able to get to Houston until Thanksgiving."

"Not to worry. I plan to drive over to Brenham on Friday. I need to talk with you about something."

"Talk to me? About what? Is everything okay?" Alex's bad news radar activated. "What's going on?"

"Nothing is wrong. I simply need to talk with you. I've already made a reservation for Friday and Saturday nights."

"Okay."

"We're going to the Scarecrow Festival on Saturday so clear your schedule. I know you have a hard time being spontaneous so that's why I'm telling you now."

"Geez, I'm not that bad."

"Yes, you are. I'll see you Friday."

He looked at the phone. Did he have a hard time being spontaneous? True, he liked planning his schedule well in advance. Did that make him inflexible? That's probably what his ex-fiancée meant when she said he was boring and no fun. Well, hell, he was fun. Hadn't he made millions designing video games? You couldn't do that without having some fun. He tore the paper off his burger and chomped down. *He was fun, damn it.*

~~*

Happy, sad, or indifferent with her life, Maggie found contentment and pleasure with cooking. Thursday afternoon was her scheduled time to try new breakfast recipes. Sunny functioned as the official taste tester and she was brutal. If she didn't like a dish she had no problem saying so and explaining in detail why it wouldn't work on their menu.

Today Maggie was making a tomato pesto tart and pear brioche bread pudding. Her breakfast menus tended to be more brunch than straight breakfast so the dishes were more "exotic" than bacon and eggs and a lot more fun to prepare. Cooking was her creative outlet, and the Inn provided the perfect opportunity to try new recipes.

She'd miss the fun when she went back to Los Angeles. She'd never had enough time for cooking with her ultra-busy marketing job. Of course when she returned to LA she'd have to find a new job as she gave hers up to move to Brenham. But that shouldn't be a problem as she had tons of contacts.

She gathered the ingredients for the tart and set to work. First, she placed a tart pan covered by a piecrust in the oven. While it baked she set slices of bacon in a sauté pan. She shredded mozzarella, chopped basil, and grated Parmesan cheese. She hummed as she worked and wondered if anyone else thought grating and chopping were fun—maybe Rachel Ray or Paula Dean.

After the crust baked for a few minutes, she sprinkled shredded mozzarella over it and set it aside to cool. She drained the bacon on paper towels and began to slice beautiful red tomatoes.

Cooking wasn't work to her, more like pure enjoyment. She'd gotten hooked at ten years old shadowing her mother in the kitchen and learning the basics of cooking and baking. After a few years, Maggie even prepared the family meals when her mother worked the three to eleven shifts at the hospital. She'd loved nursing and would fill in wherever she was needed.

Trudy Todd was one of those mothers who had a practical approach to child rearing. She'd admitted as much shortly before Maggie's college graduation. Maggie thought back to their conversation as she layered tomatoes over the mozzarella.

"Maggie, I'm so proud of you. In one week you'll be a college graduate and headed to Los Angeles." Trudy had hugged her oldest daughter with a fierceness she rarely displayed, tears slid down her cheek.

"Mom, you've known for three months I'll be moving to LA," Maggie squeezed her mother's hand. "Are you worried I can't take care of myself?"

"Oh no, I taught you how to take care of yourself. You're an excellent cook, you know how to keep an apartment in order, and you can balance your checkbook."

"Then why are you upset?"

Trudy rose from the kitchen window seat to open a bottle of wine, poured two glasses, and waved Maggie over.

"Sweetie, let's toast."

Maggie accepted a glass. "Toast to what?"

"To your graduation, of course, and to you having turned out so well."

"Turned out so well? I think I understand what you mean. I've made it through middle school, high school, and four years of college without seriously disappointing you and Dad." Maggie grinned over the top of her wine glass. "Admit it, I'm a good kid."

"Yes, you are, even though you can't wait to get out of Texas."

"I want to see something new, spread my wings, experience life outside of Houston and Brenham."

"I understand and you are well prepared for living on your own in the big city."

Maggie laughed. "How can you be so sure?"

"Because I raised you as a level-headed, responsible adult, who uses a practical approach to your life."

"Maybe too level headed," Maggie muttered.

"What did you say?"

"Nothing. Your practical approach to raising me paid off. No worries with me."

Maggie remembered the ache in her stomach after that conversation. It hadn't eased until she reached the LA city limits a week after her graduation. The drive from Houston had given her too many hours to think about her life and her motivation for leaving Texas. She'd been scared to death of what lay ahead.

Pushing away thoughts from her past, she stirred the mixture of mayonnaise, Parmesan, pesto, and cracked pepper. She spread it over the tomatoes, sprinkled crumbled bacon and added the second layer of mozzarella. Chopped basil added the final flavor and she popped the tart in the oven. She had a feeling Sunny would like the recipe.

Next up was the bread pudding. She'd decided to revise a favorite Christmas recipe for white chocolate bread pudding. Pears would give it a fall flavor and she'd always wanted to combine bread pudding with fruit. Hmm, a splash of rum or orange liqueur would be a nice addition to the pears. Fruit and alcohol always mixed well.

~~*

Mildred Adams loved champagne and strawberries. One glass and three plump berries at six p.m. every evening had been her custom for the past five years. The ritual was a salute to her dear departed husband, Hoover, who had introduced her to the bubbly wine between bites of the berries on their wedding night. It seemed so decadent at the time and proved to be one of those habits easy to adopt, which she did. Hoover would be proud.

"Hey, Mom, you starting without me?" Hank Adams rushed into the family sitting room and kissed his mother's cheek.

"Sara will pour you a glass." Mildred shook a brass bell and nodded toward her son when her maid appeared. "My son desires a glass of champagne."

"Yes, ma'am."

The wine was soon served and Hank sat opposite his mother in a burgundy wing chair that matched hers. A low fire burned behind glass doors.

"Mother, did you have a good day? Did the Thursday sale bring in extra customers?"

"Actually, it did. We had a very busy afternoon."

Hank nodded. "That's wonderful."

"If you'd bothered to drop by your job you would have seen it yourself."

"I told you I'd be gone all day to Houston. I needed to check on those seedlings for spring and that new outlet for organic fertilizer."

Mildred discounted his excuse with a wave of her jeweled hand. "Don't forget Adams Nursery is your inheritance. If you run it into the ground after I'm gone, you'll have nothing."

"So you've told me a million times. You know I'm a good manager. I promise I'll continue as an exceptional manager once you've gone to your great reward." Hank tossed back the champagne. "Anything interesting happen?"

Mildred wiped her fingers with a linen napkin. She eyed her only son. He wasn't a bad boy—hadn't settled down yet, didn't know his own mind. But Mildred was patient. She'd had to train the father so she sure as hell could train the adult son in how to run a business, regardless of how well he thought he managed it.

"Funny you should ask that. I had a strange conversation at Brazos Appliances today."

Hank stretched his long legs in front of him, crossing

them at the ankles. "With who?"

"That Todd woman who's running The Blue Barn Inn now, I think her first name is Maggie. We talked about that ghost at the Inn."

"I wouldn't talk too much about him."

"Why?" Mildred chuckled and threw her son a skeptical glance.

"It could stir up talk about his death."

"Why in the world would that matter to me?"

"Jesus." Hank looked at the ceiling briefly then at his mother, his lips tight against his face. "Because the death of Robert Grant was never solved."

"How do you know that?"

"Grandpa Herbert told me all about it. In fact, he told me how he—"

Mildred raised a hand toward her son. "Stop right there. I don't want to hear another word. Pay no attention to the ramblings of an old man."

"Oh, I think his ramblings were quite specific as to what he did. It's not a good idea for talk around town to focus on the ghost of Robert Grant; especially since the Adams family still resides in Brenham. People can easily get the wrong idea."

Mildred stiffened at his words, itching to throw the wine glass at him. But that wouldn't do, not at all. Hank had idolized his father and loved his grandfather with no idea of the worthless pieces of garbage both had turned into years and years before their deaths. At least in death, Hoover had been released from his sins. The devil didn't care two cents how he'd hurt his wife in life. Good riddance.

~~*

"Mama, don' wanna go bed," Tyler whined.

"Now, bubba, it's past your bedtime." Sunny tucked the blanket around her son. "You are a tired little boy. Close your eyes like the sleepy man and I'll sing a song."

The promise of a song did the trick. He snuggled under the blanket, hugging George under his chin. "Song, Mama," he whispered as his eyelids closed.

Sunny loved this time of day. Tyler was so sweet and reminded her of her husband. She would sing to him along with Jason, praying the words would reach her husband across the globe. Stay safe, sweet man.

"Golden slumbers kiss your eyes, smiles wait for you when you rise. Sleep pretty baby, do not cry, and I will sing you a lullaby."

Sunny knew the minute Tyler slept. His breathing regulated and his face relaxed, transforming his features into something angelic. He'd be out until morning. She was thankful her son was a good sleeper. It sure helped her disposition and energy level.

Everyday, he looked and acted, as only a two year old could, more and more like his father. His smile and the twinkle in his eyes were all Jason. She stuffed the control for the nanny cam in her pocket and crept out of the room, content that her son would have a good night.

She found Maggie in the kitchen, no surprise there.

"Hey, sis, got food?"

"What are you, a five-second TV commercial?"

Sunny wagged a finger at her sister. "Smart ass. I'm hungry. You cook, me eat."

"You're such an annoying little sister, but I love you

anyway." Maggie one-arm hugged her. "Yes, I have food. You pour the wine and I'll fix our plates."

Sunny set two placemats on the table then grabbed a bottle of chardonnay and two wine glasses. She eyed the plates Maggie set on the table.

"Yummy, looks good. New recipe?" She placed the video monitor on the table. She'd see and hear Tyler if he made a peep.

"Yep, a tomato pesto tart with bacon and your old favorite, mandarin orange and avocado salad." Maggie sat and tasted the wine. "Perfect. I wonder if Mr. Brady liked his dinner."

"How could he not, this looks delicious."

"Thanks, sis."

Sunny munched, enjoying her salad and the tart. Maggie was a master at creating new recipes. She should open a catering business or a restaurant. "I just had the most fantastic idea. You should become a caterer."

"A caterer? No way. As soon as I sell the Inn, I'm moving back to LA to pick up what's left of my marketing career."

Sunny did not believe that for one minute. Maggie was becoming more and more attached to the Inn and Brenham. "No, you won't."

"Yes, I will."

Sunny stuck out her tongue. "No, you won't."

"I'm going back to LA."

"Ladies, I'm returning my dinner tray."

Sunny swiveled around and saw Alex standing in the doorway holding his dinner tray. A smile played on his mouth. Geez, he must have heard them talking like third graders. Sunny jumped from her chair and took the tray from him.

"I hope you enjoyed the meal," Maggie said.

"Thursday is new recipe day so we're her guinea pigs, or victims every once in a while."

"That's not true," Maggie said. "I've only had one major disaster with a new recipe."

"Yeah, and it was a huge major disaster," Sunny added, her eyes twinkling.

Alex cocked his head. "Okay, I'll bite. What was the recipe and what happened?"

Sunny shoved a wine glass in his hand. "Sit down. You need to be sitting when you hear this story."

Maggie began her tale. The plan had been to make Thai chicken for her high school boyfriend. It started easy enough but the red peppers were an issue. First, she didn't know the correct procedure to seed and dice them and nearly cut off her thumb. Next, she burned the peppers on the stove and the fumes nearly gagged her. Maggie had called to Sunny for help, who'd cried at the awful smell once she entered the kitchen.

Maggie turned and hit a knife on counter; it fell and sliced through the bottom of her right leg, which started to bleed profusely. Sunny then found their Dad in the study and he took the girls to the family doctor. Maggie got stiches and the house smelled for a week. She never did cook dinner for her boyfriend.

"The worst part of the whole thing was being grounded for two weeks for dripping blood on the living room carpet," Maggie said.

"Have you made Thai chicken since then?" Alex

queried innocently.

"No. I guess I should give it a try. I do know how to handle peppers now."

"I think you should find the perfect recipe and make it. Then we can have a party." Sunny grinned as she spoke, enjoying their teasing.

"Party? Who would we invite?" Maggie asked.

"How about Mildred Adams? We could talk to her again and discover what her husband's grandfather told her about our ghost."

"Whoa," Alex said. "Who's Mildred Adams?"

"Her family owns the largest nursery in four counties. It's been around for years. I remember someone told me they used to have a large ranch but couldn't keep it up during World War II." Maggie scrunched her nose. "Not enough men to work it."

"You don't like that reasoning?" Alex asked.

"Well, gee, it doesn't take a man to do every job. Seems to me the women in the family should have had more grit."

"Maggie, that's not fair," Sunny exclaimed. "We don't know the whole story, just what Nana told us. Maybe they were sick or . . . or couldn't ride a horse."

"That's just stupid. You do what needs to be done for the family," Maggie said. "That's what we're doing here. Believe me, I'd much rather be in LA."

"You're from LA?" Alex had a puzzled look on his face.

"I moved there after college."

"Where'd you go to college?"

"University of Texas." Maggie raised her right hand

with the index finger and little finger pointed upwards. "Hook 'em horns. Don't tell me you went to A&M."

"Nope, Stanford."

"Impressive."

"Yep, good school and I enjoyed my computer science degree."

"Computer science? Isn't your Ph.D. in history?"

"That's right. But I did use my undergrad degree to the best of my ability."

"I'm confused," Sunny said as her eyebrows squished together. "Why switch from computers to history?"

"Sunny, Alex is our guest," Maggie chastised.

"That's okay," Alex said. "After graduation, I started my own business creating and writing the code for video games."

"How cool," Sunny exclaimed, she loved playing video games. They'd entertained her while she'd been bed ridden the last two months of her pregnancy with Tyler. "I love my Nintendo DS. Any games I'd know?"

Alex grinned. "Black Sabbath, Dungeon Queen, and Demons and Angels were pretty popular. And a ghost series called Dead of the Night. I've done a few iPhone apps, too."

"Black Sabbath. Ooh, I love that game. Weren't about a gazillion copies sold."

"Not quite, but it was my best seller."

"How did you go from video games to studying history?" Maggie said, her head tilting to one side.

Sunny watched Alex run a hand through his dark hair. He was a nice looking guy and he seemed to like

Maggie. He always kept his eyes on her. They'd make a nice couple. Whoa—what a fantastic idea. If Maggie became interested in Alex, she might give up her idea of selling the Inn and decide to stay in Texas.

Hmm, Sunny would need to give this more thought and perhaps help promote the two of them getting together. The more she thought about the idea, the better she liked it.

". . . I made a lot of money and decided I wanted to change things up. Here I am in Brenham writing my dissertation. Once that's done, I'll get a teaching job."

"That's some story," Sunny said and hoping he didn't notice she hadn't been listening. "We're glad you chose our B&B for your writing. I'll do my best to keep Tyler out of your way. He can be a noisy little boy."

"Don't worry about that," Alex said. "I put on headphones when I need to concentrate."

"Okay, then," Sunny rose from the table. "I need to get to bed."

Alex and Maggie said goodnight at the same time, then laughed. Sunny glanced back at them as she left the kitchen. They were both smiling, too cute.

Yes, she needed to think about how they could spend time together, time away from the Inn, time alone. Maybe Jason would have an idea even though he never liked it when she meddled in someone else's life. No, she'd keep this to herself and have a bit of fun along the way.

Chapter Five

October 23, Friday

Early the next afternoon, Alex clicked off his cell phone, rose from the desk, and stretched. He'd been at it for five straight hours, ignoring the hunger pains over the lunch hour. His mom's arrival would be a good time for a break.

He walked out the front door of the Inn and found Maggie sitting in a rocking chair on the porch.

"What are you up to out here?"

She frowned at the question. "My job."

"Excuse me?"

"Sorry, forgive my rudeness," Maggie lowered her eyes briefly. "I'm waiting for two guests to arrive."

"That must be my mom and her friend. She just called."

Maggie pointed to the street as a white luxury coupe parked along the curb. "That must be your mother."

Alex watched the driver's door open. When had his mother purchased a new car and why wasn't she driving? He noticed a gray-haired man emerge from the car then heard his mother's voice.

"Alex, baby, we're here." Her voice carried through the open window.

Alex flew down the steps from the porch and

approached the car, sensing Maggie right behind him.

He caught his mother in a hug after she exited the vehicle and kissed her cheek. "Mom, it's good to see you. You look fabulous." Alex was surprised at his mother's strength as she squeezed his shoulders.

"Thanks, sweetie. Now, I want to introduce you to someone." She stepped back from her son and hooked arms with the man standing beside her.

The man extended his hand to Alex. "Hello, I'm Roger Dougherty, a good friend of your mother's."

What the hell? Alex had no idea his mother was dating anyone and especially a man as smooth as this Roger character.

He shook Roger's hand, adding an extra dose of pressure that didn't seem to faze the older man. "Nice to meet you, Roger."

"Same here, Alex."

"Mrs. Brady, Mr. Dougherty, I'm Maggie Todd, the manager here at The Blue Barn Inn." She shook hands with each of them. "Welcome to Brenham."

"Miss Todd, it's so nice to meet you." June Brady's gaze scanned the entrance and walk area. "I love this front yard. It's so colorful and cute."

Alex let his gaze follow hers, realizing he had never before paid much attention to the yard. Pots of flowers bordered the steps to the front door and across the front of the house, creating various splashes of color. A scarecrow in front of the bushes had his hand raised in a wave. Maggie really knew her business.

Maggie beamed at the compliment. "Thank you. Let's get your luggage inside and I'll show you to your room."

Room? Mom and Roger weren't in separate rooms? Alex rubbed his face with his hand. He needed to have a talk with his mother. She and Roger staying in the same room—he didn't know if he could handle that.

Alex trailed after Roger and grabbed a suitcase from the trunk of the car.

"Please follow me," Maggie said. She strode through the front door then up the stairs to the second floor. "You'll be staying in the Lavender Room."

The door was open so Alex walked right in. It was a large room with small purple flowers on the walls and a king sized bed—one large bed. He blanched at the thought of his mother sleeping with Roger but obviously he'd been out of touch with her much too long. He'd simply have to get to the bottom of this. It would have to wait until his she finished oohing and ahhing over the room's quaintness. Women were so good at scoping out the tiniest detail . . . brain surgeons should all be female.

Roger stood by the bed while Maggie explained the amenities to June. Alex felt a semblance of affinity with the man. They were both pawns in the dance of the women going over the room's details.

Maggie and June emerged from the bathroom, chattering like longtime friends.

Roger spoke first, interrupting their girl talk. "Is everything okay?"

June grinned at him. "Yes, this room is perfect."

Alex needed to get back to work. Plus, he didn't belong in the room his mother would be sharing with a man. "Mom, I better get back to work and let you two settle in."

"Of course, I know you have so much to do. But I do hope you can join Roger and I for dinner this evening."

"Sure—"

"Good. Maggie, perhaps you could join us. Give us the lay of the land and all."

"Well, uh, I—"

"That's an excellent suggestion." Alex turned to Maggie. "Please, join us. You deserve a night off."

Maggie seemed flustered, yet she smiled and accepted. Alex figured she didn't want to offend him or his mother. He'd make sure she had an enjoyable evening. She gave Roger and June a few more instructions about the Inn then handed over the key and departed with a smile and a promise to meet them in the living room at six o'clock.

Alex kissed his mother on the cheek, nodded at Roger, and departed as well. He could put in three more hours of work before dinner. Truth be told, he hadn't looked this forward to a meal with his mother in quite some time.

He had a very understanding mother concerning his own romantic escapades so he wondered why she hadn't told him about Roger. Surely, this was a fling for her with a fancy car driving, gray-haired, mature man with good manners. That's right, it was a fling—perfectly understandable and acceptable for a woman over fifty. At least she wasn't a cougar.

~~*

Maggie's bed was littered with clothes. She had no idea what to wear to dinner. Why was she making such a big deal out of a dinner with three of the Inn's guests?

She knew why. One of the guests was Alex, and he made her nervous.

Which was stupid.

She grabbed a red sweater from the bed and slipped it over her head. Skinny jeans and black flats completed the outfit. She turned from side to side in front, admiring her slim image in the mirror. Good enough.

In the kitchen, she made a cheese tray of Brie, Gouda, and white cheddar with red grapes for color. She added wheat and butter crackers to a basket then uncorked a bottle of pinot grigio wine. She wanted to surprise her guests with a simple happy hour before they left for the restaurant. Hospitality was now her middle name.

After the much appreciated wine and snack, the foursome piled into Alex's SUV for the short ride to the Longhorn Grill and Saloon. As is typical for small towns that shut down at five every evening, they had no problem finding a table.

"Not too busy this evening," Maggie said to their young waitress who handed out menus.

"Scarecrow Festival," she replied with a grin. "Brenham loves festivals."

Maggie watched Alex and his mother, curious to learn their reaction to small town festivities.

June placed a hand on Alex's arm. "Remember I told you we're going to that tomorrow."

"Halloween is fun in this part of Texas," Maggie explained. "The Scarecrow Festival is a huge event a few miles from here. Food, drink, and lots of shopping."

June clapped her hands gleefully. "Shopping is what attracted me."

"Sounds like a plan," Alex said. "I bet Tyler would get a kick out of the pumpkins."

"Who's Tyler?" Roger asked.

"My younger sister works with me at the Inn. Tyler is her little boy," Maggie replied.

"Wonderful," June said. "The festival will be a family affair for all of us."

"Good idea," Alex agreed quickly. "We can all go together."

Maggie shook her head in silence and ignored Alex's comment. This dinner was much too complicated and now they were all going together to the festival tomorrow. This was taking hospitality at the Inn too far. But she hadn't nixed the plan and would muddle through it with grace and good cheer.

The conversation turned from festivals to the memorabilia on the walls of the restaurant—University of Texas Longhorns versus the Aggies at Texas A&M. Brenham folks loved their college sports teams, football being king.

The waitress returned for their dinner orders. They all ordered steaks and smashed potatoes and decided on a bottle of cabernet, fitting to accompany beef. The conversation transitioned to the weather, the upcoming holiday season, and the topic for Alex's dissertation.

"Goodness," June said. "How did you decide on that?"

"Mom, it's a perfectly reasonable subject to research and write about."

"Sorry." June patted Alex's hand lying on the table. "It just sounds boring compared to video games."

"Don't worry, video games have been good to me, but I like this topic. In fact I've been toying with an idea for a game on Texas history."

"Would that be an educational game?" Maggie teased.

Alex looked surprised at the question. "I've never considered that." He leaned in close and kissed Maggie on the cheek. "Thanks for the great idea."

Maggie knew her face was flaming yet no one else at the table noticed. They were all talking about the Texas flag on the wall. What had prompted Alex to kiss her? Well, it wasn't a real kiss, being on the cheek and all. But still, it wasn't normal for a guest to kiss her nor was it normal to go to dinner with guests of the Inn. This had to be the last time. It simply wasn't proper innkeeper etiquette to socialize with guests outside of the Inn. This would be the first and only time.

Of course, Maggie realized why she had so easily agreed. She was lonely. Even with Sunny and Tyler, she was still lonely—deep in the bone, missing male companionship kind of lonely. Even so, Alex Brady was not the antidote. He was a guest and that was a line she shouldn't cross.

"What do you think, Maggie?" June's question, as well as the expectant expression on her face, took her by surprise.

"I'm sorry. What do I think about what?"

"Just confirming you're going to the festival with us tomorrow." Roger gave June's shoulder a gentle squeeze.

Mildred Adams and her son, Hank, interrupted the conversation as they stopped at the table.

"Yes, Maggie, are you attending the Scarecrow Festival tomorrow?" Mildred said, jutting her chin in the air.

"I haven't decided."

"Oh, come on, try to get out of that Todd rut of indecisiveness."

"Excuse me?"

Mildred rolled her eyes. "I hear your ghost is still around."

"Like I said, excuse me?" Maggie looked at Hank and Mildred with narrowed eyes. "You want to know if the ghost is still around. What ghost are you referring to?"

"Stop playing stupid, Miss Todd," Mildred spit out. "Hank knows all about Robert Grant and your accusations."

Maggie stood. "Mrs. Adams, what the hell are you talking about?"

Mildred jabbed an elbow in Hank's chest then gained a step toward Maggie, an index finger wagging in front of her. "Listen here, little missy, don't you play dumb with me."

Hank pulled Mildred back from the table. "Mother, enough," he hissed. "We need to go. Good night everyone. Sorry for the interruption." Hank waved a hand and pushed his mother toward the front of the restaurant.

"What was that?' Roger exclaimed, mouth open, eyes following Mildred and Hank as they exited the restaurant. "Who are those people?"

Alex rose and gazed at Maggie, "Apparently, they know the story of the Inn's resident ghost."

"Ghost," June cried. "There's a ghost at the Inn?"

Roger patted June's arm, kissed her temple. "I'm sure this is a misunderstanding. Right, Miss Todd?"

Maggie sat again and her mind reeled from Hank's words to Mildred's. Why were they so antagonistic toward the Inn? What the hell was their problem?

Alex rubbed Maggie's shoulder for a moment before returning to his chair. She enjoyed the comfort and weighed how to answer the questions about the ghost. Truth or story?

"Actually, The Blue Barn Inn does have a resident ghost. He seems like a nice guy."

"Oh, my goodness. You know him? How old is he? When did he die? Why is he at the Inn? Did he die there?" June ran out of breath from her rapid sequence of questions.

Roger folded his hand over hers. "Darlin', let Maggie explain."

June nodded, a lopsided smile on her face.

"When I was younger, my grandmother told me the story about the ghost in the barn who cried at night," Maggie said. "But no one knew why he cried."

"I'm helping Maggie look into that," Alex added.

"My goodness," June giggled. "This is quite the mystery. I love it."

Chapter Six

October 24, Saturday

Maggie needed to run. She'd been lazy the last three mornings. Today presented the perfect opportunity to get back in the groove before she began her chores. She tied her long hair back with a plastic band then made her way through the quiet of the kitchen and dining room. She had a good hour before starting the coffee for her guests at seven a.m.

After exiting the Inn through the front door, she stopped on the porch to stretch. As she pulled one calf against her quads then the other, she gazed over the front yard. The fall colors in pots of orange and yellow mums bordered the porch steps. The scarecrow and bale of hay in the middle of the yard added to the Halloween theme. She couldn't wait for the thirty-first when she'd place carved pumpkins with lit candles across the inside of the porch.

Tyler would have a blast with pumpkin carving. And toasting the seeds would be fun as well. A child certainly added to the fun of Halloween. She should ask Sunny about Tyler's costume.

Stretching completed, she bounded down the porch steps to the sidewalk then heard a sound behind her and turned.

Alex bounded down the steps.

"Good morning, Miss Todd. Beautiful day."

"Uh-huh, it's still dark."

"Right. Do you mind if I run with you?"

Yes, she did mind. Running was a solitary experience and that's why she liked it. She had nearly an hour to herself and her thoughts.

"Sure, but don't expect me to talk."

"No problem. I'm not much of a talker myself."

Maggie nodded then set off down the street. She ran her usual route stealing an occasional glance at Alex. He, of course, could leave her in the dust. But being a gentleman, he matched his stride to hers.

After fifty minutes of running they ended where they started, on the porch steps of the Inn. Maggie stretched one leg then the other against the top step. Alex did the same next to her. She finished and started up the steps.

"Nice running with you. I need to get the coffee going."

"Same here. I'll see you later." Alex folded himself into a rocking chair on the porch.

"Right." Maggie entered the house and shut the door behind her. Her focus transitioned from running with Alex to starting the coffee, taking a quick shower, and preparing a healthy and hearty breakfast. As she walked to the kitchen, she marveled at how easily she had melted into the ebb and flow of being an innkeeper. Must be a lesson from all those meetings she'd attended in LA—if you can't control it, fake it.

~~*

The Scarecrow Festival had been a local tradition, at

least since Maggie was a little girl when she'd visit her grandparents in Brenham. Each year it had grown, adding more venues and becoming more crowded with visitors. She loved it nonetheless. The group from the Inn assembled in the parking area, a field of beaten down grass, and walked toward the festival's entrance.

Sunny pushed Tyler in a travel stroller over the bumpy ground with Maggie on the opposite side of Alex and his mother. She was determined to maintain her distance and a professional demeanor around him.

Once through the entrance, the group huddled near a huge map of the festival grounds.

"Ooh," June said pointing to the map's pink colored area. "Look at all that shopping. I know where I'm going." She turned to Roger and took his arm. "Come on big boy, we're going to stroll and don't you dare make a face."

Roger shook his head as he patted her hand on his arm. "I wouldn't dream of it. Us old folks don't want to slow you kids down, so how about we all meet up for lunch in a couple of hours?"

A surprised Maggie glanced at Alex. She had expected him to tour the festival with his mother. He merely smiled, raised his sunglasses for a moment and settled them back on his nose.

"That sounds like a plan to me," Sunny chimed in, adjusting the teddy bear on Tyler's lap. "We're going to the petting zoo. You guys want to come?" She waved to June and Roger as they walked off.

"Absolutely," Alex said. He stepped next to the stroller. "Tyler can't be the only man to accompany you ladies. I'll push."

Maggie looked at Sunny, rolled her eyes, and muttered, "Whatever." She pointed to the left. "The zoo is over there."

She took off walking, stopped after a few steps, turned around, and witnessed Alex playfully bounce the teddy bear in front of Tyler. She huffed a breath and muttered to herself. "Damn, I gotta stay away from him, too perfect." She went back to them. "Are we going to find the animals, or not?"

"Right now," Sunny said and stepped away from the stroller. She leaned toward her sister and whispered. "Don't be irritated that Alex is coming with us. I think he felt weird tagging along with his mother and Roger."

As usual, Sunny summed up the situation like a three hundred dollar an hour psychiatrist. Maggie placed her hand over her mouth, feeling silly. "You're probably right. I'll play nice."

They turned at a gravel path toward a large working barn. A man in muddy boots and a battered straw cowboy hat led two chestnut horses out of the barn and down the path toward a fenced coral. The horses pranced over the gravel like royalty.

Tyler kicked his legs, pointed with his sweet little index finger, and yelled, "Horsey, horsey, horsey."

"Yeah, buddy, those are pretty horses." Alex leaned over the stroller and shook Tyler's finger. "Let's see if we can find a pony for you to ride." He turned to Sunny. "Is that okay with you?"

She nodded. "I figured we might as well give it a try but I'm warning you. He'll probably start bawling."

"Just like his mom," Maggie added, remembering when Sunny was a toddler and scared of any animal bigger than a turtle. She smiled as Sunny shook a finger at her.

They soon reached the petting zoo in back of the barn. It was surrounded by a weathered fence just tall enough to keep the animals in and provide plenty of viewing space of the children inside.

Sunny motioned for Alex to park the stroller alongside the fence. "Will you guys watch this while I take Tyler in? This is his first time so I want to go slow."

"Sure," Maggie said. "We'll watch you two from here."

"Let me know if you need any help," Alex added.

Sunny nodded and went through the gate. A teenaged boy with an earring and black eyeliner manned it and made sure it was locked.

Maggie leaned against the fence and set her arms on the top rail. She raised her eyes to the sky. It was Texas blue and free of clouds. What a perfect day. She wrinkled her nose then chuckled as the scent of manure floated by. It couldn't be helped while standing near a barn and a petting zoo.

"What's so funny?" Alex said, mimicking her pose on the fence.

"Oh, just the earthy scent of the animals."

"Yeah, don't get that in the big city like Los Angeles."

She squinted at him. "How do you know? You've been to LA?"

"Oh, yeah, met some movie producers out there a

couple of years ago. Crazy people if you ask me and traffic worse than a hurricane evacuation."

"Movie producers, huh? Sounds very la-de-dah."

"Yeah, right. It was a major waste of time. We disagreed on the film adaptation for one of my games." He stomped a foot on the packed earth. "Those Hollywood people are too high strung for my taste."

"Really?" She nodded in agreement and used one hand to hide her grin. Hollywood people, indeed.

"How long did you live there?"

"Almost ten years. I moved out right after college graduation for my dream job. I love LA and can't wait to move back."

"Why are you in Brenham then?"

Maggie didn't feel comfortable telling him her life saga right then. "Trust me, it's a long, boring story."

"Yeah," he said, squinting at the barnyard. "Let's go check out the ponies for Tyler. Sunny is waving at us." He pushed back from the fence. "Come on, wouldn't you like a ride, too?"

She rolled her eyes and bumped her fist against his arm. "I bet I'm over the age limit. But Tyler's not." She moseyed through the gate, threw a quick smile at the teenage guard and pushed the stroller toward Sunny. "How did Tyler do with the goats and pigs?"

Alex came up beside her.

Sunny brushed hair out of her eyes and patted Tyler's back as his head rested against her shoulder. He pulled up suddenly then laid his cheek back down, tuckered out.

"Looks like Tyler's not up for a pony ride," Alex

said in a quiet voice.

"Right you are. Let's go look at the shopping stalls." Sunny placed him in the seat of the stroller, tucking a blanket around his legs. "He'll be out for a while and we can look around without him fussing."

"Let's go." Maggie led them out of the barnyard, retracing their steps on the gravel walkway, and hung a right toward the open-air pavilion's retail vendors. She walked in front of the stroller while Alex hung a couple steps behind her, near Sunny. She heard them whispering but couldn't make out their words. Sunny was being polite to him, that was all. And why did she care if they talked?

A few minutes later they entered the shopping pavilion, a mammoth slab of concrete with a roof fashioned out of sheets of white corrugated steel. A straight walkway sliced it in half with various-sized stalls on either side. One step inside and Maggie sighed, ah, evergreen and vanilla. It smelled like Christmas a week before Halloween.

"I'm looking for a big wreath for the front door of the Inn," Maggie said, leaning over to Sunny. "Help me find one. Painted Christmas pots for the porch would be good, too."

Sunny nodded. "Will do, but you can paint those pots yourself."

"I know that." Sometimes little sisters were simply a pain for pointing out the obvious.

~~*

Women were weird. Maggie and Sunny quibbled about painted Christmas pots for at least five minutes before dropping the subject when wreaths came into view. Alex followed them dutifully. His logic being that Tyler needed another bro on the shopping trip—to balance things out with two noisy women.

He ended up pushing the stroller again as the two sisters couldn't keep their eyes and hands off the stockings, wreaths, candles, ornaments, etc. etc. It was exhausting looking at all the red and green stuff that covered shelf after shelf. Why did they get so excited about a baby bear ornament then scoff at his idea of miniature footballs for a tree decoration? He shook his head as he waited for Maggie to finalize her latest purchase, something red with gold ribbon.

"I think we're done." Sunny bent over the stroller, adjusted Tyler's blanket, then straightened. "We need to go to the car to stow all this stuff."

Alex surveyed all the paper and plastic bags at her feet. He shook his head. Women were like shopping robots—give them twenty percent off and they'd buy-buy-buy. But Sunny was right; they needed to lug all the packages to the car before meeting his mother for lunch.

Maggie arrived and they headed to the parking lot, all three carrying a load of shopping bags. They quickly stowed everything in the back of Maggie's SUV and headed back to the festival. The fall sun was bright and the temperature pleasant. A large crowd walked with them toward the festivities.

Maggie walked along side Alex while Sunny pushed Tyler ahead of them. "Sorry we took so long shopping. Christmas is my favorite time of year."

"No problem. I'm used to it." He noticed she looked

at him with narrowed eyes. "I am."

"Ah, I see," she said. "You must have a lot of experience shopping with a woman."

"My ex-fiancé had a black credit card and loved to use it."

"Poor you," she said and nudged his arm. "No more shopping today."

He wiped his hand across his brow in mock relief. "Whew, good thing since I've reached my quota."

Sunny turned backed to them. "I see June and Roger."

Alex sighed. He didn't know if he'd ever become accustomed to hearing his mother's name linked with a man's. He sighed again; maybe it was one of those things he had to accept.

They soon reached the couple waiting at the entrance to the festival's main street.

"Everyone ready for lunch? My treat," Roger said, displaying a friendly smile with his arm over June's shoulders. "We found a very nice barbeque café."

"Sound good," Maggie said. "Show us the way."

Within minutes they'd taken over an outdoor picnic table under a wide red tent. A waitress in a short denim skirt and a straw cowboy hat arrived with menus.

"Hi, y'all. What can I get ya to drink?"

Alex didn't have to think about that question. "I'll have a Shiner." It was his favorite Texas brewed beer. Maggie and Roger ordered the same while June and Sunny opted for iced tea.

June smiled at Tyler sitting on Sunny's lap. "I bet Tyler would like a glass of chocolate milk."

"Oh, no, not this time," Sunny said. "Chocolate keeps him awake and he'll need another nap after lunch. Regular milk is fine."

To emphasize her point, Tyler beat a spoon on the table, bobbed his head and yelled, "milk, milk, milk," in his two year-old voice.

Everyone laughed as Sunny calmly removed the spoon and replaced it with a small blue truck. "Shh, Tyler, play with your toy." She kissed his head and he immediately quieted.

"He sure does mind his mama," June commented.

Sunny grinned. "Only when he has an audience."

While they waited for their drinks, the ladies talked about the Christmas decorations they'd purchased. Roger smiled and looked at Alex. "You like college football?"

Whew, saved from more girl talk. "Sure do, although I've not played much myself. I was more of a geek growing up than a jock."

"You've done well for yourself, being a geek, that is."

Alex took a pull on the beer just delivered. "Yeah, I guess you can say that. Apparently, my mother has been talking."

"Yes, son, she has. Your mother is very proud of you." Roger drank his beer as well then raised the bottle in approval. "First time I've had Shiner. Excellent."

"What else has she mentioned?" Alex was not happy that his mother had blabbed about him to a complete stranger. What was it with mothers? Geez, they'd talk about their kids to anyone.

"She gave me little detail other than how proud she

is. I did a search on you myself."

"You what?"

Roger narrowed his eyes and cocked his head toward the women. He lowered his voice and leaned forward. "It was a basic internet search, nothing that took any effort. I was curious about June's son, nothing more."

"Okay, I'll buy that. Why so curious?"

Roger rose from the table. "Take a walk with me outside."

Hmm, what was this about? Alex rose and patted Maggie's shoulder. "Roger wants to show me something. We'll be right back."

He followed Roger down the alley with all the food venues. After walking a few steps, out of sight of their table, Roger stopped and turned to Alex.

"I had a good reason for checking you out."

"Yeah? What?" Alex was not happy with this conversation.

"I wanted to get a handle on how you'd react to . . . things."

The man was talking in riddles. "What things?"

Roger turned away from him for a moment then rotated back, his mouth set. "I guess this is as good a time as any to tell you. I had hoped for a different setting."

"Whatever. Tell me what?"

"I love your mother and I want to marry her. I'm asking you for your blessing."

Roger's words slammed into Alex's chest—his mother getting married? What the hell? "I don't know what to say, I don't know you."

"Exactly. That's why I suggested to June that we visit you this weekend. I want you to get to know me and vice versa. I already have a ring."

"A ring?" Alex ran a hand through his hair; this was one of the strangest conversations he'd ever participated in. He cocked his head at Roger and recognized determination and compassion on his face. Okay, he'd do his best. He stuck out his hand. "Let's see how it goes."

Roger shook it. "Fair enough."

~~*

Maggie balled up her napkin and placed it on her plate. The barbequed brisket and potato salad had been good. Now she was ready for the afternoon's fun.

"Who's up for the talent show? The granddaughter of our neighbor, Margaret, is one of the headliners."

"That sounds like fun," June said.

"I need to take Tyler home for his nap," Sunny said. "He won't make it much longer. Maggie, can I take your car back and you guys ride with June and Roger?"

"Sure." Maggie dug out her keys and handed them to her sister. "Do you need help?"

"No," Sunny said rolling her eyes. "Like I haven't done this a million times before."

"We'll walk out with you." Alex rose and stole Tyler off Sunny's lap, tucked him in the stroller along with George. "Let's roll, big guy."

The group walked toward the front of the festival. Sunny soon waved good-bye as she headed toward the parking lot.

"The stage area is just past the petting zoo." Maggie looked at her watch. "The talent show starts in ten minutes."

Roger grabbed June's hand and headed off. "We better get a move on. Come on you slow pokes. Try to keep up."

Maggie chuckled and elbowed Alex's arm. "Hey, slow poke, get a move on."

"You're such a comedian." Alex nudged her side and walked with her, keeping pace behind Roger and June.

They soon entered the barn-style auditorium and found seats in the bleachers near the front. Maggie waved at Margaret, a few rows away. After the two ladies sat between the men, a sense of contentment passed though Maggie. She looked around the auditorium, taking in the families anxiously waiting for the show and had the same feeling. She shook her head, fighting off the sudden sense of belonging that washed over her. She didn't—she couldn't belong here. She'd be on her way back to Los Angeles as soon as the Inn sold.

The lights flashed and the show's MC strolled to the middle of the stage. The gray-haired man looked at the audience from one side of the bleachers to the other then he opened his arms wide. "Happy Halloween, y'all."

The crowd replied with the same and clapped. The first act, an all-girl dance team from a local dance studio, was soon on stage, grooving and jiving to a rock number. The blaring music seemed to agree with the audience as hands began to wave back and forth in the air.

The enthusiasm continued into the next act, a five-member rock band, which played just as loudly as the previous song. Maggie was glad that Tyler wasn't there;

the noise would surely bother his ears.

June leaned over and spoke close. "I love this . . . it's just like a Rolling Stones concert."

Maggie nodded. June wasn't the old lady that Alex had described. She had a hunch June and Roger had a lot of fun together and a very special relationship. Her mind wandered to Michael, the man she'd dated for four years in California and who had broken up with her out of the blue. That split had been the final push for her to return to Brenham to help her parents with the Inn.

She sighed. Someday . . . yes, someday, she'd have that special relationship, too.

The acts continued, one after the other, each one better than the last. The final act was Margaret's granddaughter, Lizzie, a seventh grade comedienne. She walked to the middle of the platform as a stagehand brought out a pint-sized stool and a bottle of water.

Lizzie waved to the audience and spoke into the microphone she held. "Good afternoon, Brenham. How y'all doing?"

"Just fine," someone yelled.

"Well now, I'm glad to hear that. Me, not doing so good . . . difficult week, middle school is tough. Anyone out there go to middle school?" She waved her hand in front of her.

Most of the audience raised a hand.

"Good, y'all will understand," Lizzie said. "First, I got an 'F' on my creative writing paper. My English teacher disagrees with my theory that the school principal might be a zombie. I told her to prove it and—"

The audience roared and clapped.

Lizzie grinned, obviously enjoying the response to her story. "And she said no, I had to prove he's a zombie or write another paper. So, I did what I had to. I did not want to write another paper."

"What'd you do?" someone yelled from the front row.

"What did I do?" Lizzie replied while pointing a finger at her chest. "I set a trap for him."

The audience laughed again. Maggie wondered if Lizzie realized that her comedic timing was excellent. She dramatically opened the water bottle and drank from it. "Actually, the trap didn't work out exactly like I planned. You see, my theory that zombies can't drink coffee was blown last Monday morning. The principal . . ."

Alex's laugh caught Maggie's attention. It came from deep in his chest and floated around her. He had an easy sense of humor and wasn't so sophisticated he couldn't enjoy a small town talent show. She liked that and turned her attention back to Lizzie.

"Thanks, y'all. Yeah, I sure did have a lousy week. And I promise . . . that food fight in the school cafeteria wasn't my fault. Sure, I might have thrown an itty-bitty apple . . ."

Maggie's attention transitioned from watching Lizzie to thinking about her own teenage years. They'd lived in Houston and she'd attended the local public schools. She'd made good grades, participated in several school clubs, and had a couple of close girlfriends. Nothing too special about any of it, other than driving to Brenham every other weekend. The entire family went to help her grandmother run The Blue Barn Inn on weekends, its busiest time. Of course, those many required trips did create a problem or two.

She remembered the first time she'd really raised a fuss with her mother about going to Brenham. It was during her sophomore year in high school and she'd planned on going to her best friend's sweet sixteen-birthday party on a Saturday night. Her mother said absolutely not as helping her grandmother was more important. A huge fight ensued and Maggie vowed she'd get out of Houston just as soon as she could. No way would she be stuck in a hick town working at a lame bed and breakfast.

She'd gotten out of Texas all right but look where she was now. Brenham was okay but in her heart she felt she was a big city girl, not a small town Texas girl.

June shook her arm, dragging Maggie out of her trip down memory lane. "That little girl is adorable."

A minute later they rose, wildly clapping. The entertainers came back on stage together and the applause intensified.

"That was fun. What's next?" Alex looked from Maggie to June.

"I'm a bit tired," June said, taking Roger's arm. "Do you mind going back to the B&B?"

"I really should get back as well," Maggie said. "I have a lot of paperwork to tackle." Alex shrugged and Maggie followed him out the door of the auditorium with Roger and June behind them.

The bright sunlight warmed Maggie as they walked to the parking lot. The festival was still crowded with parents and children hurrying from one end of it to the other. Laughter echoed in the distance along with a cow mooing. Yep, this was the epitome of small town Texas—good people and noisy cows.

~~*

Alex and Maggie managed to stuff themselves into the back seat of Roger's two-door coupe. Although the space wasn't meant for two grown adults, he didn't mind it as they headed back to the Inn.

Maggie's hip and thigh brushed against his when the car rounded a corner. Roger's driving style wasn't for the faint of heart. But Alex ignored it as the physical contact with Maggie trumped poor driving any day.

He watched her as she answered a question from Roger about Brenham's history. Her face glowed with a slight blush and her green eyes crinkled as she laughed at a remark from June. Amazing how gracious she'd been in accepting his mother's request for dinner last night and the festival today. His ex-fiancé would have been put out and royally pissed at having to entertain the "old folks" as she called anyone over forty. What in the hell had he ever seen in that woman?

Maggie glanced at him and smiled. She wiggled in the seat, pulling away from him. "Sorry, I keep pushing into you."

He winked at her. "No problem."

She frowned and turned away toward the other side of the car.

Damn, bonehead move. He had no business flirting with the innkeeper. Should he apologize? No, that would make it a bigger deal. He'd act like nothing had happened.

"Hey, Mom, what are you guys doing tomorrow?"

June turned to the backseat. "We're looking at the nursery's here on our way back to Houston. I thought I might try to actually plant something in the garden."

"Isn't it too late in the year to plant stuff?"

"Actually no, son." June said began to discuss plants and flowers with Maggie. He again tuned them out.

Maggie intrigued him. He'd never expected to find an innkeeper in Brenham with her looks and her brains. Plus being so easy to talk to. If the situation were different he'd ask her out for a romantic dinner where they could relax and share a bottle of wine and get to know each other.

But that wasn't happening. He had no business even thinking about Maggie. God, his track record with women sucked at best. No need to add another bad relationship to the trail of the ones behind him. He ran his fingers through his hair, frustrated with himself at his lack of concentration on why he was in Brenham. Finishing his dissertation was his only goal for now. Period.

Chapter Seven

October 25, Sunday

Maggie rolled over and turned the alarm off before it began to buzz. Plopping against the pillow she rubbed her eyes. Damn, she hated getting up so early. But what choice did she have if she wanted to run before the day began. Running kept her weight in check considering what she ate. She did like her own cooking. She threw off the bed covers and smiled. Her cooking was worth getting up so early.

She brushed her teeth and washed her face then threw on a pair of yoga pants and a sports bra/tank top combo. Soon she'd need a hoodie as the weather turned toward winter temperatures. After drinking a glass of water she headed to the front porch to stretch.

Five minutes later she put in her ear buds, hopped down the steps, and began to jog down the street with Coldplay helping her establish her rhythm.

She followed her usual route and ran on autopilot, knowing the course so well. It was safe to run so early, unlike Los Angeles where she ran after work with a canister of mace in her hand. Regardless of that, she still couldn't wait to leave Brenham and return to her real home.

And that reminded her that the Barn's remodeling

would begin the next day. She clenched her hands and did a mini fist pump. Finally, this show would get on the road and she'd be able to list the Inn with a business broker. That part of the plan would commence right after the first of the year.

She could almost see the end of her time in Brenham and the Pacific Ocean lapping at the beach in Malibu. Not that she could afford to live there but the beach was free. Her breath hitched for a moment as she considered that she'd probably be back in LA in less than six months. And she'd make the absolute best use of her time until then. But first things first . . . make breakfast for her guests then review the remodeling plans one last time.

A figure shot past her on her left then did a slow jog back towards her. She laughed. It was Alex.

"Hey there, hard time getting up?" she teased.

He moved alongside her and matched her stride. "Nope, decided to sleep a few extra minutes. I was up late last night."

"Really? Watching chick flicks on TV?"

"No, reading and taking notes," he said, smiling. "All this research is killing me. I've never read so much in a short period of time."

"Hmm, guess its part of being a student." Maggie didn't like talking when she ran. It usually caused her to lose her groove of putting one foot in front of the other. She wasn't much of an athlete, meaning she had a serious lack of physical coordination. Alex must have gotten the message as he ran beside her and said nothing else for the next half hour.

Maggie turned toward home. "Are you continuing on or going back to the Inn?"

"I'll go with you. Lots to do today."

She nodded and headed home.

Once back at the Inn, they both stretched on the porch. Maggie reminded Alex that breakfast would be at nine then walked through the front door and headed toward a hot shower.

Thirty minutes later she was in the kitchen and turning on the coffeepot. She loaded it every evening to save precious time each morning. She pulled a large casserole dish from the refrigerator. This was a new recipe for orange glazed French toast. Hopefully it wouldn't be a bomb. Next she'd peel potatoes and—

Still wearing his Spiderman pajamas, Tyler ran into the room yelling, "Antie, Antie, juice."

Maggie bent over to gather the sweet baby into her arms. "Good morning, little man." She kissed his head and hugged him tight. "Would you like some juice?" He nodded his head vigorously.

She set him down and retrieved a cup off the drainer. Once he had his cup he made a toddler-beeline for Sunny coming through the door.

"Good morning, coffee's about ready," Maggie said.

"I'll pour you a cup. What can I do to help?"

"Nothing right now. Go ahead and feed Tyler." Maggie strapped him into his booster chair and sliced a banana to get him started. Sunny handed her a coffee mug.

"I saw you running with Alex this morning," Sunny said.

"Uh-huh, he joined me halfway through." Maggie inhaled her first gulp of coffee. Ah, the world was right once more.

"Not the first time, huh?"

"No." Maggie looked over the top of her mug. "Are you trying to make a point of some kind?"

"Me? Nope, no point. Just find it curious, you running with a guest."

"It wasn't planned." She moved to the sink and began to peel the potatoes. "We weren't really running together, more like running in the same place."

"Right."

Maggie didn't notice the smile or the fist pump that Sunny performed. In fact she had no clue about Sunny's plan to bring Alex and her together, nor the bonus to Sunny's plan that Maggie would stay in Texas and not return to California.

A knock sounded at the kitchen door and Alex poked in his head.

"Any chance I could have some coffee?"

"Of course." Sunny poured a cup and handed it to him. "You're up early for a Sunday morning."

"Yeah, have a full schedule today. What time is check out? I need to make sure I'm here when Mom and Roger leave."

"It's at 11:00 a.m. but your mother can leave later if she wants."

"Oh, no, let's keep her to the rules."

"Alex, that's not very nice," Maggie said. "There is no issue whatsoever in making an exception for your mother."

He threw a hand up. "Whatever. Thanks for the coffee." He stomped out of the kitchen.

"What's up with him and his mother?" Sunny asked.

"Who knows? I think she's great. Reminds me of our mom."

~~*

Alex walked back to his room mumbling to himself. "Yeah, go ahead and break the rules for June but for me . . . no way."

He clomped inside and landed at the window. While drinking his coffee he stared at the street. What the hell was wrong with him? Did Roger proposing to his mother really piss him off?

The fact that he wasn't sure pissed him off even more. He backed away from the window and plopped in the desk chair. His foot began to tap a steady beat on the floor.

Ever since Roger had told him about his intention to propose, Alex had been gathering a list of reasons why it was a bad idea. Of course, as a rational man, he knew that was stupid and unfair to his mother.

Why did he have an issue with her becoming a bride? She deserved a boatload of happiness.

How long had she been alone since his father died? Too many years with too many of them devoted to Alex. He rubbed a hand over his scruffy face and sighed deeply. Yes, he'd been a jerk for thinking how his mother's engagement might impact his life. This should be all about her, not him.

At the bottom of it—would it change his life? No. No, it wouldn't, other than to have a stepfather to watch sports with. And, more importantly, his mother wouldn't be spending her days alone.

He needed to talk to Roger. He rose from the chair and heard a knock on the door. No doubt Maggie to chastise him for being rude in the kitchen. He yanked the door open, ready to explain his behavior.

"Oh, Mom, what are you doing here?"

June narrowed her lips for a moment then smiled. "Good morning, do you have a minute? I need to talk with you."

"Sure. Why don't we go in the library, it'll be more comfortable."

He ushered her into the library and motioned for her to sit in one of the reading chairs. He sat across from her.

"Alex, I have something to tell you and hear me out before you say anything."

"Sure, Mom." Alex felt practically giddy, knowing what she was about to say.

"Sweetie, I know you were surprised by me arriving here with Roger and I don't blame you."

"True. But don't worry about me, Roger seems like a great guy."

"I'm glad to hear you say that. We had a long talk last night and we've come to a decision about our relationship."

"Okay." Alex knew his mother would go nuts about planning a wedding. After all she didn't have a real one the first time. He'd do whatever he could to support her.

"Well . . . Roger and I are moving in together. We're going to live in his house."

"What?" Alex jumped from the chair. Move in

together? He'd expected a wedding date, not cohabitation. "I forbid you. You can't do this. I thought Roger was proposing to you."

June laughed so hard her eyes filled with tears. "You, you forbid me? Are you living in the 1700s?" She wiped her eyes and composed herself. "Roger did propose to me and I said yes . . . well, more like yes with a 'but' attached."

"Jesus, Mom, what the hell are you talking about?"

"Good grief, Alex, calm down. This is perfectly explainable. Roger did propose and I said yes but I want to make sure we are totally compatible before we take any vows."

"And living together is the method to accomplish that?" Alex sat down again.

"Absolutely. Don't forget I'm not some silly twenty-five year old playing house. This will be a true test to make sure we can live in the same house and survive."

"I'll buy that, but is it really necessary?" Alex couldn't believe how prudish he sounded. "Don't you guys know each other well enough by now?"

"Yes we do and that's why I'm insisting on a trial run. We've both lived by ourselves for several years and quite frankly, we're a bit stuck in our ways."

Alex groaned at the understatement for any sane person over thirty. He could see that his mother was serious and hell-bent on this living together test. He might as well give her, and Roger as well, his blessing as they'd do it anyway. Silly kids.

"Okay, I understand your logic. What's the plan for a wedding date?"

"Between Christmas and New Year's. That will give us a good six weeks to experience living together. Assuming all goes well we'll plan a small wedding, or go to Las Vegas, I suppose."

Alex rose and kissed his mother on the cheek. "Your plan is excellent and Roger is a lucky man. What can I do to help you get moved to your new home?"

"Nothing. We'll have movers pack and I'll rent out the condo. Just in case." She stood and they hugged.

"It's time for breakfast so I'll get Roger. We'll start back to Houston as soon as we're finished."

He escorted her out of his room and then headed to the dining room. Every table was occupied except for one in the corner. He sat there and poured a cup of coffee from the carafe on the table.

Roger and June arrived a few minutes later. Sunny noticed the ring on June's left hand and the engagement was announced. Maggie made mimosas for everyone in celebration.

Alex was amazed at the genuine pleasure the other guests expressed at his mother's good news. It gave him hope that love didn't have an expiration date.

An hour later Alex walked June and Roger to their car and stowed their luggage in the trunk along with a couple of shopping bags from the festival. He hugged and kissed his mother then shook Roger's hand. "Congrats again. Let me know when you decide on the wedding date."

Maggie rushed down the front walk. "I'm glad I caught you. I couldn't let you go without saying good-bye and this is a thank you for staying at The Blue Barn

Inn." She handed June a small basket. "These are my apple-pecan muffins. Hopefully you'll think of us when you eat them."

June wrapped her arms around Maggie. "Ah, sweetie, thank you so much." She backed up. "When will the Barn be ready for events?"

"The plan is mid-December. Barring any disasters, of course."

"Good, I'd like to book a small wedding a couple days after Christmas. I'll call you once we have the date nailed down."

"Ooh, that sounds wonderful. I'd be honored to host your wedding. We'll make it a beautiful event for you and Roger."

June hugged her. "Perfect. I'll be in touch."

Chapter Eight

October 26, Monday

Maggie reviewed the remodeling list on her clipboard one last time before entering the Barn. Jim and his crew had been there all morning, working on demolition of the interior, phase one of the renovation.

She entered through the back door, intending to find Jim and stay out of the way. She trusted him completely and didn't want to make his job harder by inserting herself into every little detail of the remodel. Jim was in the area designated as the new kitchen. He had a crow bar in his hands, pulling away stained sheetrock.

"Jim, y'all are making good progress. When will we have the asbestos inspection?"

"Maggie, hey," Jim lowered the crow bar and a dust mask over his face. "The initial demo is going great so we should be done by this evening for the inspection tomorrow. Then we wait for the asbestos abatement."

"How long does that take?"

"Just a couple of days. We'll be building the kitchen cabinets at the shop while we're waiting. All normal."

"I'm glad to hear that," Maggie said after breathing a sigh of relief. "I'm afraid I'll be somewhat of a basket case through this whole project." She pointed at her chest. "Control freak."

Jim laughed. "I don't think I would have figured that out except for the ten page spreadsheet you provided. You must have Googled a lot."

Maggie laughed. "Busted. You caught me. What can I do to keep us on schedule?"

"Honestly? Stay out of the way until I need you. We'll most likely run into a surprise or two and that's when I'll need you."

Jim's face was set in "I'm in charge" mode and Maggie had no reason to disagree with his method. She'd already promised herself she'd not be a nuisance during construction. And it was good that Jim had been honest with her. That said a lot about his work ethic.

"I won't hang around too much but I will check the progress at the end of the day. No way I can ignore what's going on."

He chuckled. "No problem, I'll expect to see you at closing time. So far we're on schedule." He looked at his watch. "Of course we've only been on the job for four hours."

""Good point," Maggie said. "Holler when you're done for the day and we can talk again."

Jim nodded and moved off to speak to one of his workers.

Maggie retraced her steps through the Barn and exited to the yard. It, too, needed updating. She'd decided to go with her original plan of a gazebo, a fountain, and a flagstone walkway. She had a clear vision of what she wanted and prayed she'd explained it well enough to Jim.

She'd dreamed about a spring wedding at the gazebo

with flowers surrounding its base and bordering the walkway. White chiffon would drape around the gazebo intertwined with ribbon in the bride's colors. It would be an intimate wedding with the reception inside the Barn. Tables would be set up inside and outside and the long oak bar would serve just the right drinks for the newly married couple and their guests.

Maggie imagined bridal colors as she walked around the side of the Inn. She needed to decide on the number of pots of Christmas flowers to decorate the porch and along the front bed.

She studied the porch and set a picture in her mind of alternating clay pots with poinsettias and pansies on every other step. That would work. She entered the Inn through the front door and went straight to the kitchen.

Sunny came out of the utility room. "What are you up to?"

"I'll be working on a new recipe for chicken in pastry pockets."

"Yum. I still think you should go into the catering business."

She pulled puff pastry out of the freezer. "You know I don't have time for that. Plus, I'll be going back to LA once the Inn sells so why start a business?"

"You still haven't mentioned that to Mom and Dad, have you?"

"No, but I will once all the remodeling is finished. I'm sure I can convince them it's the smart thing to do for the family."

"I wouldn't be so confident if I were you," Sunny said softly.

"What did you say? I couldn't hear you."

"Nothing, nothing important."

Maggie went to the office for the recipe and the business phone rang.

"I'd like to speak to whoever books your events, please."

"This is Maggie Todd, how may I help you?"

"Oh good, my mom told me to call. She said you're remodeling that old barn space for weddings and parties."

"Yes, that's true. Who is your mom?"

"Oh, I'm sorry, Fran Walters. She owns the Farmer's Market."

Maggie knew Fran casually. "Of course, what sort of event are you calling about?"

"My wedding. Dustin, he's my fiancé, and I would like to get married on December 19th. I've dreamed about having my honeymoon in Rome at Christmas-time so that's the reason for the date."

Maggie wanted to jump up and down. "That date shouldn't be a problem. How many guests?"

"We're keeping this small so no more than one hundred."

"That won't be a problem. Can you drop by this week and look over the Barn. It's in construction but I can give you a good idea of the layout and the look we're going for."

"That's sounds great. Let me talk to my mom and I'll call you back for a day and time."

"Perfect. Also, can I have your name and phone number?"

"Silly me, of course. My name is Emma Walters and my finance is Dustin Miller."

Maggie jotted down the names and phone number then performed a hip-hop jig around the office.

"Hot damn, we're having a wedding at the Barn."

She hurried to the utility room and found Sunny folding towels.

"Guess what?"

"I'll play, what?"

"Don't be a smarty pants. Remember Fran at the Farmer's Market?"

"Uh-huh."

"Her daughter just called and wants to book a wedding. She even knows about the Barn's renovation."

"That is good news. " Sunny placed the last towel in the laundry basket. "Isn't it nice that someone wants to get married?"

Maggie gave her a sharp look. "What do you mean by that?"

"I simply think it's nice." Sunny lifted the basket and adjusted it against her hip. "I'd love to go to your wedding but," she shrugged, "I don't think it will ever happen."

"Why in the world would you say that?"

"You're more interested in going back to La-La-Land than seeing what's right in front of your nose."

"What?" Maggie had no clue why her sister was in such a mood. "There's nothing wrong with LA. People there get married all the time."

"Whatever. It's not the same as getting married in Texas." Sunny walked out the door and turned back.

"Admit it, you can't wait to leave here."

Maggie watched Sunny walk away in a huff then poured a cup of coffee and sat at the oak table.

Yes, she was anxious to leave Brenham. No, anxious wasn't quite right. She had her heart set on getting back to her life in LA and the time in Brenham wasn't going fast enough. She couldn't wait to get back to the crazy and loud California hustle. Although, she sure didn't miss driving congested freeways to get to work or to the grocery store. A lack of traffic was one of the nicest things about living in a small town.

Small towns were great for raising a family—fewer negative influences and a quieter way of life. Not that she had given one thought to having a family. That had always been in the future, the future where she was settled with her job and had fallen in love with the perfect man.

Right. She wasn't any more ready for a family today than the day she'd graduated high school. Thinking about it sure as hell wouldn't make it happen. Did she want it to happen? Now that was the million-dollar question.

She shook her head and went back to her recipe testing—that she knew how to do.

~~*

Alex loved Monday mornings. And this one, a few days before Halloween, was beautiful. He'd spent a good four hours on writing, thankful he'd reached a confident point with his dissertation that he could stay on schedule. Sure, he had more research to do but he was past crisis mode and determined to be finished by mid-March and then his defense the end of April. He'd start applying for teaching jobs after the first of the year. His mother would tell him he was being arrogant—applying before he had the degree—no way would his dissertation not result in a Ph.D. No freaking way.

He rose from the desk and stretched his back then loaded his battered messenger bag. He'd grab a quick lunch on his way to the A&M library. A smell of something delicious caught him as he closed and locked his room. Maggie must be trying out a new recipe. Might as well get a taste.

He hitched the bag over his shoulder and went straight to the kitchen.

"Hey, Maggie, what are you cooking?"

She turned from the kitchen's island work surface and looked at him, concentration on the dish before her evident in her liquid green eyes. She blinked and the look was gone.

"Alex, hi, what are you doing?"

"On my way to the library but smelled something really good. What is it?"

"Really? It smells that appetizing?"

He nodded. "Yes, ma'am, it sure does."

"Great." Maggie beamed, obviously pleased at his remark. "Hold on, let me give you a couple in a napkin. You can take them with you."

"Great." He accepted a couple of pastries from her and took a bite. "This is good, thumbs up."

Maggie grinned and blushed ever so lightly. He liked that he had an effect on her. Yeah, he liked that a lot. But he needed to get on the road. A&M was forty-five minutes away.

"Gotta go, Maggie, you're a great cook."

She raised her chin. "Thanks for being my culinary tester."

"Anytime." He saluted her and headed for the back door and his SUV. No need to stop for a burger now.

Two hours later, he sat at a table in A&M's main library. He had his stack of books for note taking.

"Oh, oh, Mr. Brady."

He turned around and his stomach rolled. Crap, the undergrad student he'd met last week. She'd nearly talked for an hour and he'd lost valuable time.

"Hi, uh . . . sorry, I forgot your name."

"No problem, it's Brandy." She sat across from him and tossed her pink backpack on the table. "So, what are you working on today?" She smiled, displaying perfect white teeth, and blinked her eyes. "Fancy meeting you here again, huh? Maybe we could get coffee after studying for a while. I've got a ton to do. What—"

Alex raised his hand to stop her monologue. "Sorry, Brandy, I'm behind on my research and don't have time for anything other than reading or writing."

Her mouth turned down like a three year-old being denied ice cream. "Oh, poo. I'd hoped we could get to know each other."

"I have a girlfriend." Alex was desperate to stop her.

"Are you engaged?"

"No."

She grinned, tilting her head so that her long blonde hair draped over her face, and pulled a book out of her bag. "No problem then."

Alex didn't like the way she said that but what could

he do? Moving to another table would be plain rude. He'd ignore her. He opened a book on the history of Texas education and began to read and type notes in his laptop.

Occasionally he'd glance up to notice Brandy's head buried over a book, her hair hiding her face. After four hours of having his butt planted in the chair and making pages of notes, he shut down the laptop. Brandy's head popped up.

"Oh, you're done studying?"

"Yep, time to head home."

"Have a good night then."

"Yeah, you, too." Alex headed toward the exit and felt her eyes boring into his back. One thing he didn't need was some little girl getting a crush on him. God, he was thirty-four, way too old for crushes—unless the crusher was someone like Maggie.

~~*

It was early evening when Brandy exited the library, Alex clearly in sight. He headed to the same parking lot where she'd parked her car. She was curious about him so she'd follow him and see where he lived. College Station wasn't all that big so he'd be easy to follow. After going down several rows in the lot, he climbed in a luxury SUV in the end spot. How did a college student drive such an expensive car? Must have rich parents, perfect—looks and money.

She ran to her own fancy sedan and jumped in just as he passed her row. She threw the car in gear and was able to get a couple cars behind him.

She'd never followed another car before, at least not

like this. It wasn't that hard although she nearly lost him when he sped through a light and she had to stop. Her heart nearly beat out of her chest while she waited for the light to turn green. But she caught him at the next light, turning onto Highway 6.

It was easy to keep his vehicle in sight on the well-lit street. She expected him to turn but he kept going and soon she saw a sign for Navasota, 23 miles. Obviously he didn't live in College Station. She had nothing better to do—her studies could wait—so she'd stay behind him until he stopped.

The traffic was light and she stayed a car or two back from his vehicle. That's what the cops did on TV so the perp wouldn't see them. It must have worked, as he didn't do anything weird.

He turned right in Navasota, taking a loop around the little town then turned right again. Now he was headed for Brenham. Is that where he lived? Why live in such a backwards, crappy town? Yuk. But she followed him anyway. She knew the way by heart as her grandparents lived there.

Once in Brenham, he made a few turns then pulled into the driveway of a large house. She drove by it slowly and stopped. Shit, it was a B&B called The Blue Barn Inn. Why would a good-looking guy like Alex live there? Hmm, she definitely needed to visit him again.

~~*

Alex cut off the engine and hastily exited the SUV. He ran around the side of the Inn to check out the street. All he could see were brake lights then the driver sped up and headed down the roadway. He rubbed the back of his neck. He'd had the strangest feeling driving home. He needed to relax more. Concentrating on the dissertation non-stop was getting to him. He shook his head and chuckled. Next he'd be seeing elves and fairies.

~~*

Maggie hated being behind, late, whatever. It was after seven and she had yet to get dinner going. Sunny had fed Tyler and left to put him down for the night. That'd give her time to get something prepared. Something quick meant something simple. A Cobb salad would be perfect. She put bacon in the microwave and sliced boiled eggs while it cooked.

"Maggie—"

She jumped and the knife in her hand rose in front of her. Geez, it was only Alex. She lowered her hand; embarrassed she'd gone into attack mode.

"Hey, did I miss dinner? Can I snag a doggy bag?" He stood just inside the door, with a lopsided smile and a sexy flannel shirt that screamed unbutton me.

Maggie shook her head to dislodge the image of his chest minus the shirt. "I'm just starting. You're welcome to eat with Sunny and I."

He hesitated, his brow in a momentary scrunch. "Yes, I'd like that. What can I do to help?"

Under normal circumstances Maggie would usher a guest out of the kitchen with a glass of wine and a plate of appetizers, but Alex was different. He'd crossed from guest to friend-mode over the weekend. She'd accept his offer to assist with dinner.

"First, I could use a glass of wine. Chardonnay is in the frig. Would you pour a glass for Sunny and I?"

"I can do that." He moved to the cabinet for wine glasses and then the refrigerator.

Sunny walked in and went to Maggie giving her a hug. She whispered in her ear, "Sorry for giving you a hard time earlier." She accepted a wine glass from Alex. "Bless you, I need some adult time. Tyler is finally asleep."

"All right," he said. "How adult are we getting here?"

Maggie looked up from slicing an avocado. "She means adult talk."

He handed her a wine glass wearing a sexy grin. "I know that."

She rolled her eyes. "Right. Sunny would you get some garlic breadsticks out of the freezer, please."

"You got it." She moved around Alex hovering in the middle of the kitchen. "Alex, get yourself a glass of scotch then sit at the table.

"Sunny," Maggie said, a bit louder than she intended. "Alex is our guest here. I'll get his scotch."

Alex raised his hands. "No need for that. I can help myself since I know where you keep the booze." He winked at Sunny.

Maggie held her breath for a moment so she wouldn't laugh. "Works for me. Dinner will be ready in just a few minutes."

Not quite ten minutes later they sat around the oak table with their salads and bread.

"Excellent dinner, as usual," Alex said. "Thanks for including me."

"It's part of our agreement," Maggie said, then

regretted her words. "What I mean is no problem."

"I have something to tell you guys," Sunny said. "I talked to Robert again today."

Maggie stopped eating, a fork near her mouth. "Robert? You mean Robert the ghost?"

"That's the one. He appeared while I was changing the sheets in the Lonestar Room."

"Interesting. What did he do?" Alex sipped his scotch.

"He floated in the corner, sort of swaying back and forth, like he was rocking a baby. Didn't say a word."

"Rocking a baby, that's weird." Maggie said.

Alex hitched up one side of his mouth. "I bet he was dancing, with his arms around his imaginary partner."

"Exactly." Sunny speared the air with a breadstick. "He thought he was dancing with the love of his life, Grace."

"Yeah, speaking of Grace. Alex, what have you discovered about her?" Maggie tilted her head and twirled a lock of hair with her finger. "I can't believe we forgot about your research."

Alex slapped his hand playfully against his forehead. "I completely forgot I started it."

"Guess your mom showing up with Roger was too much to handle, huh?" Maggie knew he was okay with it but she had to tease him anyway.

"No," he shook his head. "No, that had nothing to do with it. I just forgot."

"That's okay. What did you learn?" Sunny said.

He explained about the school annuals and that Grace wasn't in the one that would have been her senior year. He told them that her father, Thomas Edwards, was the founder of Brenham national Bank and had built the house and barn. The property had been the family home until Thomas and his wife Alice had both passed away. Grace was their only child so it was sold to the Todd's, Maggie and Sunny's grandparents, in the early 1950s who then converted it to a boarding house and later a bed and breakfast inn.

"But I didn't find out why Grace wasn't in the annual for what should have been her senior year," Alex admitted.

"It wasn't because her parents moved," Maggie said. "I bet it directly related to Robert's death. We need to research Robert as well and find out all we can about Grace."

"I'll work on it tonight. I'm sick of my dissertation anyway."

"Seriously?" Maggie looked surprised.

"Isn't it a big deal?" Sunny asked.

"To get a Ph.D., yes, it is important. But let's be honest, my research topic is kind of boring. At least compared to creating video games."

Maggie chuckled. "I can see that. The getting bored part, I mean. But isn't that what dissertation topics are all about?"

Alex raised his glass. "Touché."

~~*

After dinner, Alex returned to his room. He'd devote half-an-hour to online research on Grace. Back in the day, if she'd run away from home, it would have been a big deal for a small town like Brenham.

He started his search with the local newspaper, *The Brenham Herald*, which had been publishing a daily edition for over a century. Thank God for the Internet and archives that had been digitalized.

First he looked for the story on Robert's murder to know the starting point for stories about Grace. It would have been easier if Sunny or Maggie had asked Robert what year he'd been shot. But never mind, there wasn't anything he couldn't find online, anything legal that is.

After ten minutes, Alex had found Robert's obituary, which provided some background information he was sure Maggie and Sunny would like to hear. He died in 1922 at the age of twenty-two. Poor guy hardly had a chance to start living. He'd attended business school in Houston and then worked as a teller at Brenham National Bank.

Interesting, Robert had worked for Grace's father.

Next he searched the newspaper's archives for stories on Grace. There were plenty on her attending parties, participating in school activities, and being a debutant. There were no stories after March 1922, the month Robert died. She must have run away from home shortly after he died or she went into mourning and left Brenham later. Finding Grace was going to take some work.

The last article on Robert's death was in October of the same year. The police had been unable to find the killer or even a motive for the murder. So they gave up.

Alex thinned his lips and shook his head—that sucked. After another moment he had an idea and needed to talk to Maggie.

He called her cell phone.

"Alex, what's up?"

She knew who was calling so that meant she'd programmed him as a contact. Good.

"I need to talk with you about Robert and Grace. I have an idea."

"Sure, I'll meet you in the living room."

Two minutes later, Maggie walked in wearing a bathrobe. Alex looked at his watch; just then realizing it was after ten p.m. "Sorry, I didn't realize it was so late."

"No problem, I was reading." Maggie curled her feet under her on the sofa. "What did you want to tell me?"

"I don't have the full story on Grace yet, but I did discover something interesting."

"Really?" Maggie looked eager to hear his story. "Tell me."

"Arthur Edwards built this house and the barn and Grace was his daughter."

"That's right and he owned the local bank." She slapped the cushion with her hand. "I never put Grace Edwards together with the man who built this place. Geez, dumb."

"Easy mistake." He grinned at her, hoping to enlighten her mood. "Did you know that Robert Graham worked at the bank when he was killed?"

Maggie sat up straighter. "No, I didn't know that. Do you suppose his murder had anything to do with his job?"

"Don't know," Alex replied. "But I figure it relates to that or to Grace."

"Grace?"

"Yeah, maybe it was another man who loved her and was jealous of Robert."

"Or, maybe Robert discovered someone stealing from the bank and they killed him to keep him quiet."

"That could be true as well." Alex couldn't help but notice how Maggie was getting into the story. He loved the way emotions crossed her face as she talked. Her eyes brightened noticeably, and even with the illumination of a single lamp, he could see the glow of excitement on her pale skin. She looked even younger and so alive.

She snapped her fingers. "Alex! Earth to Alex."

"Sorry, what did you say?"

"Before you zoned out on me I asked what we should do with this new information."

"I think we should talk to the Brenham police."

"Oh." She grinned slowly and spoke after a few moments. "This would be considered a cold case, right?"

"Exactly—block of ice cold case. We should do it. You have a vested interest in getting Robert's murder solved as it relates to the Inn's history and its reputation."

"You're right. Do you have time to visit the police station tomorrow?"

"How about after lunch?"

"I can do that."

They agreed on a time then Maggie returned to her room and Alex did the same. He quickly performed his nightly ritual and climbed into bed, clicking the TV remote. He rarely went to sleep without hearing the late night news.

He tried to pay attention to the news, but thoughts of

Maggie made it impossible to concentrate on anything else. She had the prettiest blond hair and her green eyes reminded him of shamrocks. Which actually was kind of lame that he'd even think that.

Ah, the B&B manager who had captured his eye and his . . . his interest. Nothing would come of it though. He didn't have time for anything like that. He had to stay on his Ph.D. schedule, no excuses.

Yet she had him on edge—hyper-vigilant of her words and every move she made. He nodded to himself. Maggie was a woman any sane man would strive to hang on to.

Alex felt something brush across his arm. He shivered. It happened again and the feeling unnerved him. As he rubbed his forearms, he heard a low, hoarse voice in the distance: "Don't play with Maggie if your heart isn't true." What the hell?

He straightened up and looked around his room lit by the TV screen. He was definitely alone; at least, he thought he was.

Damn.

Chapter Nine

October 27, Tuesday

Alex held the door open so Maggie could enter the Brenham Police Department ahead of him. On the drive over, they'd agreed to ask for the police chief. They stopped at a high counter manned by a gray-haired officer.

"Hi, I'm Maggie Todd, manager of The Blue Barn Inn here in Brenham and—"

"Maggie Todd, holy smokes, I haven't seen you since you were just a young un' with your grandmother."

Maggie blinked, not recognizing the man at all. "You knew my grandmother?"

"I sure did. She was a good friend of my mother's."

"That sounds like her. She knew just about everyone in Brenham." Maggie pictured her grandmother for a moment then quickly focused on the reason for their visit to the police station. She gestured toward Alex. "This is my friend, Alex Brady, and we're here to see the police chief. It's official police business."

"Official business, huh?" The officer's gaze switched from Maggie to Alex and back to Maggie. "All right then. Let me check on the chief's availability. Y'all wait right here."

"Yes, sir." Alex said as the officer retreated down a

hallway to their left.

Maggie scoped out the station. It wasn't that big and the walls were an unattractive gray color with the requisite number of posters and official looking notices. All in all, it was a depressing space. She couldn't imagine working in it day after day without becoming severely depressed.

The officer returned. "The chief can see you for a few minutes." He frowned and wiggled a finger at them. "He's a busy man so bide your time. Now, come around the desk and follow me." He headed for the hallway once gain.

"Thank you." Alex rolled his eyes behind the man's back.

Maggie grinned and elbowed him in his side as they followed the officer. She mouthed, "be nice" to Alex.

The officer motioned for them to enter the office at the end of the hall. "Remember, Chief Morgan has only a few minutes for you."

Maggie nodded, walked past him to the desk and pushed out her hand, which the chief accepted. "Thanks for seeing us without an appointment. I'm Maggie Todd and this is Alex Brady."

"Nice to meet both of you. Have a seat." After they occupied the gray metal chairs in front of his desk, the chief spoke again. "What can I do for you? I assume this isn't a social call."

"No, it isn't," Alex said. He glanced at Maggie. "We were wondering how you work cold cases."

The chief's face registered surprise. "What kind of cold case?"

"Murder," Maggie said matter-of-factly.

"Murder, huh? That's a serious crime. We don't deal with much of that around here."

Maggie couldn't gauge the attitude of the chief. Was he being straight or humoring them? "The one we're interested in happened over ninety years ago."

"You're kidding." The chief leaned over his desk.

"No, we're not." Alex replied. "The murder occurred in 1922. My research indicates the crime was never solved . . . it sounds like the police just gave up."

"That's quite an accusation."

Maggie wiggled her hand from side to side. "No, no, we're not making an accusation. It's what the newspaper article said. I'm sure police work was a lot harder back then."

"Okay, I agree with that. Now what do you want from me?"

"Do you have any case files from that year?" Alex asked.

The chief rubbed a hand over his jaw. "Well, we might. Don't know for sure. There's a bunch of stuff in the basement. Could be there."

Maggie wondered if he was playing with them. But what would be the reason? It made no sense.

"Do you have an inventory of what's down there?" Alex asked.

The chief looked at Alex as though he had just grown a tail and waved it across the chief's desk. Maggie put a hand over her mouth to hide a smile.

"Chief, bottom line, we're wondering if the murder of Robert Graham can be re-opened," Alex stated. "Is it true that there is no statute of limitations on murder?"

"Yes, that's true. We don't deal with many cold cases around here, not many homicides either. Why are you so interested in this particular case? Who is this Robert Graham?"

Maggie looked at Alex, he raised his chin and half-smiled. She knew what to say. "This may sound strange to you yet it's the truth. The man who was killed, Robert Graham, never left the location . . . the barn where the murder took place. He's still there."

"He was buried in a barn?" Chief Morgan asked.

"No, you misunderstood me," Maggie said. "Robert has a grave somewhere but his spirit remains at the Barn."

"What do you mean his spirit remains? That sounds ridiculous." The chief leaned back in his chair, disbelief evident on his face.

"I know this is hard to believe but yes, Robert's spirit has remained at The Blue Barn Inn." Maggie decided to be totally open. "In fact, I've talked to him."

The chief bolted up straight. "You are freaking kidding me. Are we talking about a, a—"

"That's right," Alex interjected. "Robert Graham is a ghost."

The chief looked around the office and under the desk. "Is this a damn joke? Am I being punked?"

"No. Oh, no. Chief Morgan, we mean you no disrespect." Maggie had never considered he'd think their visit a joke. What the hell? "Let me explain. Alex is one hundred percent correct. The ghost of Robert Graham remains at my family's B&B. He's been there since his death."

The chief's face paled to a gray shade as he spoke. "Hard to believe. Didn't he have a funeral?"

"I'm sure he did," Maggie replied.

Alex shifted in his chair. "Chief Morgan, we're not here to play a joke on you. We're really interested in solving Robert's murder."

"Why? It happened a long time ago," Chief Morgan said. "Whoever killed him is dead."

"True," Alex said, running a hand through his hair. "What if the killer's family is still in Brenham? Don't they deserve to know?"

"Deserve, how? What difference does it make now? I can't charge a family if one of their own killed someone over ninety years ago."

Maggie looked at Alex and narrowed her eyes briefly then she focused on the chief. She'd made a decision. "Agreed. Nothing worthwhile can come from reopening this cold case. It's too bad his killer wasn't brought to justice."

"Are you sure about this?" Alex asked.

"Yes. I have an idea of how to make it right with Robert."

"Okay." Alex rose from his chair. "I guess we're done here." He shook hands with the chief. "It was nice to meet you."

"Same here." Chief Morgan gave a curt nod to each of them.

"Thanks again." Maggie exited the office with Alex behind her. Once in the hall she touched his arm. "Let's talk about this after dinner. I have an idea and I need time to think about it."

Alex nodded and they walked out of the police station. Maggie was on autopilot as they drove back to the Inn—debating the pros and cons of an outrageous idea.

~~*

Alex brought his dinner tray to the kitchen a few minutes after eight. He hoped Maggie would still be there and willing to discuss her idea related to Robert the Ghost. He chuckled to himself. A month ago he couldn't have imagined he'd be thinking about a ghost and a real ghost at that.

He'd never given serious thought to any one ghost in particular but that didn't mean he doubted their existence. He figured ghosts were in the same ballpark as demons and angels and miracles.

He'd truly become to believe in another sphere of life—didn't exactly know what to call it—when he was in high school. His best friend, Jake Dexter, had been involved in a car accident the spring semester of their junior year. He'd been headed home from a trip to the grocery store for his mother when a drunk driver had sideswiped him.

Naturally the car plowed into the driver's side and Jake had to be extracted by the fire department. He had a broken arm and leg, fractured ribs, and a severe blow to the head. He was placed in a coma for three weeks due to brain swelling. He didn't wake up for another four weeks. The doctors had said he might never wake up. It was a wait and see situation that was awful for Jake's family.

That's when Alex learned to pray and to believe in miracles.

The day before Jake woke up, Alex had visited him after school. He'd tell Jake about his day and what was going on with their favorite sports teams. During that visit a young woman came into the room, saying she was a hospital volunteer. She reminded Alex of Sleeping Beauty—long blond hair, blue eyes, and she wore a blue and white striped dress with a white bib apron over it. He'd never forget her voice. It was low and sweet and reminded him of cotton candy for some silly reason.

She smiled at Jake lying in the bed and spoke so quietly to him that Alex couldn't hear her words. She held his hand while she talked. Right before she left she brushed her hand over his brow and spoke at his ear. She then waved at Alex and seemed to float out of the room while the air glittered around her.

It was the weirdest thing Alex had ever seen. He ran after her and she'd disappeared. The duty nurse said volunteers weren't allowed to visit Jake.

The next day when Jake woke up, Alex knew for certain that the young girl had been an angel who had performed a miracle for Jake. Ever since that day, he'd believed in and accepted things that couldn't be explained by intellect, such as the ghost of Robert Graham living at Maggie's B&B.

Maggie was in the kitchen, taking cookies out of the oven. His mouth watered at the delicious aroma and once again, Alex thanked his luck for snagging a room at a B&B with such great food.

"Those look delicious."

"They are." Maggie threw a smile in his direction.

"I'd be happy to be your taste tester." He laid the dinner tray by the sink then accepted the bar cookie she offered.

He had the entire thing in his mouth in two bites. "Mmm, is that pecans or walnuts?"

"Pecans. It's a new shortbread recipe I was testing." Maggie handed him another cookie then closed a round container. "I thought they might be nice for the afternoon cookie tray."

Alex finished the second cookie. "You've got a winner. Do you have time to talk about your idea for Robert?"

"Of course, let's go to the living room to be more comfortable. Do you need anything to drink?"

"Thanks, I'm fine." Alex followed her and sat in one of the chairs. He waited for Maggie to get settled on the sofa then spoke. "What's the idea you mentioned at the police station?"

Her lips pressed together in a slight grimace then her face relaxed. "Yes, I do have an idea, and I've given it a lot of thought. I need your help though."

That revved his engine. "Of course, I'll do whatever you need."

"Glad to hear that."

Maggie eyes fluttered and Alex's libido responded in kind. Blood pumped through him, heating his gut.

"Alex, I think you're the best person to really figure out what happened to Grace Edwards once she ran away from home. Once we know that, we can talk to Robert."

"Talk to him about what?"

"I think we need to give him a choice. One, we figure out how to get him to pass to his grave, or two, we give him a role here at the Inn."

Alex chuckled. "How do we help a ghost pass to his grave?"

"No freaking clue . . . we'll Google it."

"Okay. I agree with that. What about his role at the Inn?"

"That's the fun part. I think we should convince him to stay here and be part of the . . . uh, the ambiance. We can advertise that the Inn is haunted and every once in a while he can show himself to a guest and keep the legend going."

"Why would he want to do that?"

Maggie twirled a long tendril of golden hair around one finger as her teeth scraped against her lower lip. Her innocent action seemed almost erotic. Alex shifted at the subtle tightening of his groin. Jesus, there was something about the way she looked right then that went straight through him. He'd never had that reaction to a woman, even his ex-fiancé. He rubbed a hand over his forehead, looked up as he suddenly realized Maggie was speaking to him.

"I'm sorry, did you say something? My mind wandered for a second, there."

Maggie frowned. "I said I think he'll do it if we give him information on Grace and her life after she left Brenham."

"Yeah, that might do it." Alex stood, turned away immediately to hide his body's reaction to her. The sooner he got out of this room, the better. "I'll continue with my research on Grace and you talk to Robert. Deal?"

She gazed at him from the sofa. The light from the lamp behind her glowed around her face—she was absolutely beautiful and looked like she belonged on those sexy magazine covers. Crap, he was losing it.

"That's a deal, Alex."

Chapter Ten

October 31, Saturday

"Sunny, come on, we need to do it now." Maggie yelled up the back stairs. Hopefully, all the guests were out for the day since it was almost one o'clock. The front bell trilled. "Geez, no one should be here until three," she muttered as she hurried to the door.

After opening the door she wondered how she looked as she wore an apron with the slogan "I cook For Wine" splayed across a grouping of grapes and wine bottles. Perfect.

A couple carrying duffle bags stood on the porch. No doubt this was the booking for the Mockingbird Room, two hours early.

"Good afternoon, welcome to The Blue Barn Inn."

The very handsome man spoke. "We're Zoe and Ansel Delaney, a bit early for our reservation."

Maggie quickly transitioned to host mode. "Not a problem at all. Come on in, and I'll show you to your room." She stepped back for the couple to walk into the foyer and snagged their room key from the basket on the foyer table.

"This is lovely," Zoe said as they walked up the stairs. "I love this wallpaper."

Maggie had heard that same comment a million

times and it made her smile every time. She'd helped her mother pick out all the wallpaper and paint colors on her Christmas vacation not quite two years ago, a few months before her father's heart attack.

Ansel stopped in the middle of the upstairs hallway. "You have an interesting energy in this house."

"Energy?" Maggie replied. "I'm not sure what you mean."

Zoe placed a hand on his arm. "Oh, he has a sensitivity to spirits and things."

"Really?" The mention of spirits unnerved Maggie. She opened the door to their room. "You'll find information about the Inn and Brenham in the book on the dresser. Breakfast is at 9:00 a.m. in the dining room. Since this is Halloween we're having a special wine and cheese social in the living room at five. I hope you can join us."

"Thanks," Ansel said. "I hope I'm not out of line in asking, but is this house haunted?"

Maggie took a step back as though a sand bag had hit her chest. How in the world could this man know that? Had Robert done something that had drawn this guest's attention? Should she tell the truth? Oh, what the hell, a form of the truth usually worked.

"My sister says that it is," Maggie replied.

"Really?" Ansel stopped in the middle of the room. "I'd be interested in talking with her."

Zoe threw an arm around his waist. "Hey, we're here on vacation, not to do research."

"Research for what?" Maggie asked.

"I'm writing a book on haunted buildings in Texas."

He shrugged. "It's a hobby, stress reliever."

"Sounds interesting." Maggie was on high alert. What did this man sense? The lights in the room flickered. Damn that Robert.

"Maybe I need to add this B&B to my list," Ansel commented.

"Sweetheart, please give it a rest. We're on vacation," Zoe declared with a playful punch to his arm.

Maggie walked to the bathroom with Zoe. "Whatever works, right? This is the bath. Let me know if you need extra towels. Also, we have a wide variety of DVD's in the living room in case you'd like to watch a movie."

"This is great," Zoe said. "Thanks for the invite to the social."

"My pleasure," Maggie said. "If you need anything or have a question, please call the number listed in the book. I live on site so I'll be around to help you." She handed over the room key then hurried down the stairs and straight to the kitchen.

"Thanks for starting without me. The Delaney's arrived a couple of hours early."

"No problem," Sunny said while pulling the slimy guts out of a pumpkin. Eight others were lined up for de-sliming. "I put Tyler down for his nap. He's not old enough for this. So, I'll clean and then you cut the face. You're much better at that than me. I've got one ready for you."

Maggie wrinkled her nose as Sunny dropped seeds and pumpkin innards on newspaper spread over the table. "I know, you're right about Tyler, next year. Okay, I'll carve." She picked up the carving knife to begin her masterpieces.

Almost an hour had passed before Sunny cleaned up the newspapers, found the candles for the jack-o-lanterns, and declared her part of the work completed.

"Good, I need to talk with you." Maggie picked up the last pumpkin to carve a face. She was out of ideas and repeated the first design.

"Tyler should have another hour to go on his nap, so talk."

"This relates to Robert and his presence here." She relayed the conversation with Alex and the curious question from their new guest.

"Wow, this guy could feel that we're haunted?"

"Exactly, how weird is that?"

"Not any weirder than me talking to a ghost in my bedroom." Sunny looked at the baby monitor on the counter. Tyler was still conked out.

"What do you think about dealing with Robert?" Maggie hoped her sister leaned toward capitalizing on a resident ghost.

"Sounds good to me. If we can tell him that Grace had a good life, I think he'll be more settled with his situation."

"You think he'd be willing to stay at the Inn?"

The refrigerator door open and closed. Drawers did the same, rattling their contents.

Maggie and Sunny looked at each other, frozen in place.

"Holy shit." Maggie gained her senses and stood, walked along the bank of cabinets. "Robert, are you here? Somewhere?"

Silence.

"Guess he's being shy." Sunny said as she placed a candle in each pumpkin. "Ya know, I'm getting used to Robert showing up every now and then."

Maggie returned to the table with her knife to finish carving the last pumpkin. "Yeah, but will he want to remain here?"

"Who knows? But it seems worth a try." Sunny smiled. "If I were him, I'd rather stay here around the living, rather than confined to a cemetery among the dead."

Maggie pointed her knife. "Yeah, there is that. Let's get the pumpkins on the porch. I'll test the sound system for the spooky music."

"Halloween is too much fun."

~~*

The half-moon illuminated the clear and seventy-degree sky, providing just the right amount of light for trick-or-treaters to scurry down sidewalks. But not quite enough light to fully eliminate the worry that a scary goblin might be behind a bush or a fence.

Maggie sat on the front porch with Alex, both in white rocking chairs placed in front of the door. A table between them held a black witch's cauldron filled with candy. A huge spider's web with plastic spiders stretched over the entire back wall of the porch. Flashlights on the floor behind their chairs provided an eerie glow.

The candy bucket was almost empty and Maggie was pleased with the number of children who had stopped by. A candle-lit pumpkin on each step had provided just the right look for the kids to walk up the steps to the porch. They were so cute in their costumes. Super heroes and Disney princesses were very popular this year.

Maggie pulled a basket from under the table.

"What's that?" Alex asked then watched Maggie pull out a bottle of wine and two glasses. "Ah, I like your idea of treats."

"I figure we might as well finish this off. It was left over from the happy hour." Maggie poured the wine and handed a glass to Alex. "Enjoy."

"Thanks."

A car stopped in front of the Inn, two people emerged and skipped to the porch. Both were dressed in a witch costume, although the taller one looked like a teenager. They walked up the steps and shouted, "trick-or-treat" in unison.

"You guys are out late," Maggie said as she placed candy into each plastic pumpkin they held toward her.

The taller witch took off her hat and shook out long blonde hair. She looked provocatively at Alex. "Hello, there. Taking a break from studying?"

"Looks like you are, too." Alex remained stoic, his face a mask of indifference.

"Sure, taking my little cousin out for some treats." She smiled widely while taking the hand of the little girl. "Have you gotten a treat yet?"

Alex sat up straighter. "I'm way past tricking or treating."

She winked at him. "That's too bad. I'm sure I know a trick or two that you'd find a real treat." She turned and led her cousin down the steps. Her car roared down the street.

Maggie looked at Alex with her mouth open. "Who the hell was that?"

"Jesus, that girl is crazy weird." He slugged down half his wine. He must have noticed the question still on Maggie's face. "I met her at A&M's library. She asked me out for a drink but I turned her down."

"Little young for you," Maggie teased, thinking she totally understood the girl's attraction to Alex. He was a very good-looking man.

"Definitely young. Weird that she'd show up here though. I figured her for living near campus."

"It looks to me that you have an admirer." Maggie fluttered her eyelashes at him. "Don't lead her along if you're not interested." She burst out laughing.

He shook his head. "Hey, not funny. That girl gives me a serious case of bad vibes."

"I'm sure she's nervous around a hunky older man."

"You think I'm hunky?"

"Never mind." Maggie had to keep her thoughts about Alex in check. No matter how hard she tried she couldn't stop thinking about him. "Let's change the subject. What's your plan for getting the goods on Grace Edwards?"

"To be honest, I've called a friend of mine to do the real digging. He does it for a living."

"Don't tell me you hired a detective?"

"He's a private investigator."

"A PI?" Maggie was truly surprised he'd hire a professional. This was one more check on the "good guy" list for Alex. "That's fantastic. How soon will we know anything?"

"Hard to tell. I hope to have a preliminary report in a couple of weeks. We don't have a lot to start with so it may be impossible in the end to learn what happened to Grace."

Panic ripped through Maggie. How could the Inn afford the cost of a professional investigator? "Wait—I'm not sure this is such a good idea."

"Why not?"

"The Inn is on a tight budget—"

"There's no cost involved. My buddy is writing a book on locating missing people and he wants to include Grace's case as an example."

"Shouldn't we get someone's permission for that? Like her family."

"Do any of the Edwards family descendants live in Brenham?"

"Not that I've heard of."

After another thirty minutes, they called it a night, blew out the candles, and removed the spider web from the porch. Maggie carried the basket and cauldron while Alex locked the door.

"Thanks for keeping me company." Maggie wished the evening didn't have to end, but she had no good excuse to keep Alex from going to his room.

"Will I see you in the morning? I'll need a good run to clear my head."

"Maybe." Maggie gave him a quick nod and headed for the kitchen. She didn't want to think about Alex right then. If she did, she'd eventually admit to herself she was one hundred percent attracted to him. Once that happened, it might make her think twice about returning to Los Angeles. She would NOT let a man get in the way of her plans.

She left the basket and candy on the kitchen table then walked through the office to her bedroom. Once she took a quick shower and donned a sleep shirt, she went to the office to check reservations for the next day.

Good, no check-ins. Three rooms were staying until Monday and then a middle school mini-choir from Houston would stay until Friday. Although this was good for the bottom line, it meant a ton of work for her and Sunny as the Inn would be fully booked. Plus in her experience, middle school kids were noisy and disorganized. Hopefully sometime during the week, she'd be able to catch up on the bookkeeping and all the other paperwork that seemed to multiply overnight.

She noticed a large envelope under a catalog and pulled it out. She'd forgotten about it last week and pulled out a sheaf of papers with the name Adams & Smith, PC on the top one, a letter addressed to her.

"What is this?" She quickly read through the letter and had her answer. Her parents had prepared their wills, which created an irrevocable trust, and she was the trustee.

She read the second page of bullet points and her stomach thudded to the floor. Damn. The trust included a provision that The Blue Barn Inn could not be sold—never, ever. It had to stay in the Todd family. If neither Maggie nor Sunny wanted it, they had to agree on that. Then it would go to her father's sister's son, George, an investment banker in San Francisco who didn't give a damn about Brenham or the Inn or Texas.

She clutched the papers against her chest and sat on her bed. She read them through again then stared at the ceiling.

Her parents were going to be really pissed when they found out she'd taken out a bank loan to renovate the Inn so she could sell it. Maggie's stomach rolled and she felt dizzy.

Perhaps she had taken her role as manger a bit too far by starting a major renovation without their approval, or at least their knowledge. Her eyes gazed at the papers again and her heart nearly stopped. She'd made a huge mistake.

Yep, they will be royally pissed when they find out. She had to tell them . . . now, not when the renovation was completed.

She crawled under the bed covers and turned out the bedside lamp. Moonlight filtered through the sheers and cast a shadow on the carpet.

Now she had no choice but to call her parents. Oh yeah, she was in major trouble.

Chapter Eleven

November 2, Monday

Maggie had spent all day Sunday cooking and working on the books for the Inn. She'd put off thinking about her parents' will and their eventual reaction to the bank loan until the start of the workweek. Once the breakfast dishes were finished on Monday morning, she called her parents in Florida.

And, wouldn't you know it, there was no answer. She left a message for them to call as soon as they returned home. She decided to check the Inn's email and took care of several online reservations for Thanksgiving. After one more room they'd be full. She hadn't expected that.

She then checked her personal email, as she hadn't looked at it for at least two weeks. There were ninety-two messages. Near the top of the list was one from her mother. She clicked on the link and read the message.

She rolled the chair back from the desk and took a deep breath. Her parents had decided to take a driving vacation in their new RV to try out the navigation system. They didn't know where they were headed but they'd be gone at least two weeks.

Great . . . just great.

Panic set in—they would kill her. Not because of the bank loan but because she hadn't told them straight off. She jumped from the chair and paced to the bedroom window, turned and marched through the kitchen to the dining room. Retracing her steps she performed the same loop several times, her mind on overdrive.

Damn, damn, damn! Why had she been so headstrong in planning the renovations and getting the bank loan without consulting with either of them? Oh man, they were definitely going to kill her when they found out. She stopped in the kitchen with a terrible thought—worse than killing her, they might disown her.

She needed to talk with Sunny and found her cleaning a room upstairs.

"Sorry to bother you. We need to talk."

"Sure." Sunny tossed the final pillow on the bed and gathered soiled sheets and towels in a laundry bag. "What's up?"

"I need to talk with you about Mom and Dad."

"Uh-oh. Let me finish this room and I'll meet you in the kitchen. I'll need coffee."

"One fresh pot coming up."

Twenty minutes later Sunny walked in. "Okay, we'll have some time to talk."

Maggie poured two mugs and set a plate of sugar cookies on the table.

"Cookies, huh?" Sunny teased. "This must be serious."

Maggie sat in the chair across from her sister and admitted to herself she had no clue where to begin, but she really needed Sunny's advice.

"I've screwed up, big time," Maggie blurted. "Mom and Dad will kill me when they hear about the bank loan and the renovation."

"I already told you that. Why are you just now making sense?" Sunny scowled at her big sister and braced her arms over her chest. "Tell me, what happened?"

"Oh, don't sound so superior," Maggie said, a sick feeling rolling through her stomach. She rubbed her face with both hands then looked at Sunny. "This is bad."

Sunny's fist pounded the table. "Damn it, just tell me. What happened?"

Maggie worked at clearing her head. She was acting like a silly, over-dramatic teenager. "I received a letter from Mom and Dad's attorney. It included their wills."

Sunny rolled her eyes. "What's so terrible about that? Old folks draft wills all the time."

She had to make Sunny understand. Maggie worked to keep her voice normal. "The problem is that in their wills you and I inherit the Inn. It can never be sold. If neither of us wants it then it goes to Cousin George."

"George! That skirt chaser? No way can we let that happen."

"Sunny, that's a terrible thing to say."

She pouted for a moment. "You're right. He's a woman chaser. But that's beside the point. Based on the wills, I don't think Mom and Dad will agree with your motivation for the bank loan or your plan to sell the Inn. Especially since you want to get rid of the Inn so you can go back to Los Angeles."

Maggie swallowed hard, nausea threatening.

"You're right. I don't know what I was thinking to get the loan without consulting them."

Sunny frowned. "Sure you do."

Maggie stared at her sister. "What do you mean by that?"

"I mean that you didn't want to come to Brenham in the first place. I think you used the Inn as an excuse to come here after your boyfriend broke up with you. It helped you save face with all your friends in LA."

"How can you say that?"

"Easy. All you talk about is going back to LA, but I think if you really felt that way, you'd have gone already. Why the hell can't you admit you like Brenham? This place is great and I hope Jason, Tyler, and I can make a home here."

Maggie snorted. "Looks like you have a job then, taking care of the Inn."

"Whatever. What about Mom and Dad and the bank loan and the renovation? They'll be angry with me for not stopping you so I'm in this as deep as you are. We need to come up with a plan, together."

"They'll be even angrier if they think I involved you in one of my schemes."

"Forget that. We'll say it was both our idea because we both plan to stay in Brenham and we need as much business as possible to support us. Using The Barn as an event spot is one way to ensure that."

Maggie rested her elbows on the table and held her head in her hands. She needed to think. To think about why she'd been so hardheaded. To think about the best way to tell her parents that she had screwed up so big that she couldn't see a reason for them to forgive her.

She had to tell the truth and not involve her sister. Sunny had warned her she was making a mistake. She didn't deserve to have any part of the blame heaped on her for the mess Maggie had created. She'd apologize to her parents for being a bonehead and that should leave Sunny's good daughter reputation untarnished.

Maggie raised her head and placed a hand over Sunny's and squeezed. "You are the best sister a girl could have. I hope you know that. But this is my situation, not yours. I'll tell Mom and Dad the truth, once I hear from them."

Sunny rose and wrapped her arms around her sister and kissed her cheek. "You are the world's best big sister. Thanks, and I love you."

Maggie hugged her back. "Thanks, sweetie. Love you, too."

Sunny stood straight and pulled the baby monitor out of her pocket. "Tyler is awake and it's nearly noon. Let's go out for lunch."

"I like that idea. Holler when you're ready."

~~*

Alex drove home to Brenham from College Station breathing a huge sigh of relief. He'd been at the library since six a.m. and that girl, Brandy, had once again shown up and asked him out for a drink, at eleven in the morning no less. He tried to explain that he had a girlfriend and then let her assume it was the girl on the porch at Halloween.

When he'd declined an offer for lunch, she'd thrown herself into a shameless Lolita act of seduction that had made him blush. He'd decided if she couldn't stop herself, he'd stop it for her. With enough material to get into serious writing mode, he packed up his stuff and headed out, leaving her cursing to herself at the table.

By the time he crossed Brenham city limits, his hunger pangs were out of control. Since he'd eaten only coffee and a donut for breakfast, he pulled up to the Farmer's Market for a to-go lunch.

Greg, a work-study student from the high school, was at the take-out counter. "Hey, how are you?"

"Just fine, Mr. Alex. What can I get for you?"

"Club sandwich on wheat and fries," he rattled off. "And a large iced tea."

"Got it, give me a few minutes."

Alex nodded and stepped back, glancing to his left at the tables filled with the weekday lunch crowd. Maggie and Sunny were over by the far wall with Tyler in a high chair.

He ambled over to their table. It would be rude not to.

"Hey, ladies, how's it going?" He ruffled Tyler's hair.

"Good," Sunny said. "We're taking a break. How about you?"

"I've been at the library since dawn. Fun times."

"But all the work is worth getting a Ph.D. Right?" Maggie said.

"Right," he said, rubbing a hand over the stubble on his jaw. "That girl from Saturday night showed up again. She is definitely weird."

"Maybe she has a crush on you," Maggie said.

Alex shook his head. "I don't know. She's pushy and crude. I'm done with my research for a while so I doubt I'll see her again."

"Sounds like good riddance to me," Sunny added.

"Got that right." He noticed Greg waving at him. "Looks like my take-out is ready. I'll see y'all later."

He paid for his lunch and headed for the Inn. Maggie sure did look nice in that pink sweater. Definitely accentuated her breasts. Of course, she had a lot more going for her besides looks—brains, dedication, and a good sense of humor. The only thing he couldn't figure out was her desire to return to California, which made it clear to him that pursuing a relationship with her was a waste of time.

~~*

Sunny spooned applesauce into her son's mouth. "Guess what, Tyler? Alex likes Auntie Maggie. Just think, he could be your Uncle Alex one day. What do you think, huh? Would you like an Uncle Alex?"

"Don't be ridiculous. We're just friends." Maggie speared a tomato in her salad.

"Ah-ha, so you're more than inn manager and customer."

"What are you getting at? We've become friends the past few weeks. So what? Big deal."

"Nothing, not getting at anything. But the two of you make a very nice couple."

"Sunny, you've inhaled too many cleaning fluids. There is nothing going on between Alex and me. I'll never get involved with one of our guests."

"Why not? Is there a rulebook that says you can't?"

"Why are you even talking about this?"

"Why are you raising your voice?" Sunny countered.

"I am not."

"Are too."

"Am not."

Sunny began laughing. "Forget it. But if you do decide to stay in Brenham, you might think about dating. You know, get some action."

"The only action I want is in the kitchen. And I haven't said I'm staying here. First, I need to figure out what to do with the Inn and not totally tick off Mom and Dad."

"You're not alone with that."

"Thanks, sis. We'll come up with something."

Driving back to the Inn, Maggie couldn't get Sunny's words about Alex out of her mind. Would they make a nice couple? Was she couple material? Was Alex? When he'd mentioned his ex-fiancée, he seemed to be grateful she was out of his life. Maybe he wasn't a commitment type of guy, or maybe the ex hadn't been the right woman. Her thoughts went round and round. In frustration, she pounded the steering wheel.

"What's wrong?" Sunny said, pulling Maggie out of her thoughts.

Damn, that wasn't good, she'd been driving on autopilot. "Nothing is wrong. My hand had a cramp."

She pulled into the driveway and parked in the back. The parking area was full of trucks from Jim's crew. She hadn't talked to him since Friday morning. "I'm going to check on the renovation."

"Okay, I'll do more laundry," Sunny said with just

the right amount of grimace.

Maggie helped her get Tyler out of his car seat and kissed his head. "You be a big boy for your mama and help her with the laundry."

"Ha ha," Sunny quipped. "It's nap time."

Maggie grinned and placed a loud kiss on her sister's cheek. "I won't be more than ten minutes and then I'll help you."

She swung through the back door of the Barn, marveling at the progress Jim and his crew had made. She found him in the main room, looking at the bar. "Wow, you are making fantastic progress."

"Thanks, a couple of my team came off another job early so we've had extra hands."

"That's great. Have you had any problems? Anything I need to know? Anything I can help with?"

"No, Maggie." He gave her a crooked smile. "We're good so far. No need for you to worry. Everything is on schedule. I'll need you to double check the paint in a few days."

"Sounds good."

Maggie turned away to take a quick tour of the remodeling. She started with the kitchen and marveled at the progress. The bottom cabinets were in and the space for the center worktable was outlined on the floor. She felt like jumping up and down. The space will be perfect for preparing meals.

Next she poked her head in the hallway to the restrooms/changing section. She smelled something sweet. Hmm, what was that? She looked in the women's room, nothing much had been done to it other than demolition. Next she swung toward the men's room and the smell became stronger, gardenias maybe.

She flipped on the light and pulled back. "Robert, what are you doing?" He spread over the floor in the form of a fog or a mist with his head in a corner.

His head popped up. "I'm relaxing and staying out of the way. Those workers don't need to see me."

"Why don't you go to the attic?"

"I do when it's too noisy down here." The fog moved back into the form of a human. "I like this room, helps me concentrate."

"Helps you, huh?" Certain he was teasing her, she decided to go for it. "What do you concentrate on?"

"Shakespeare."

"What?"

"I keep thinking about that eternal question, 'to be or not to be.' Get's me pondering life."

She chuckled. "I bet it does. Nice seeing you, Robert, I need to get back to the Inn."

"Good night, good night. Parting is such sweet sorrow, that I shall say good night till it be morrow." He winked at her.

Shaking her head at Robert's silliness in quoting *Romeo and Juliet*, she returned to the Inn, pleased with the remodeling progress.

She found Sunny loading the washer with sheets. "Guess who I just saw?"

Sunny twisted around to look at her. "Santa Claus?"

"No, Robert. He was hiding in the bathroom at the Barn."

"Doing what?"

"Nothing really, just hanging around, staying out of the way of the crew."

"That's a good thing," Sunny said drolly. "We don't want one of Jim's workers to run into our resident ghost."

Maggie laughed. "Right you are. Do you need help with the laundry?"

"Nope, got it handled. Don't you need to work on paying bills? You were complaining about it last night."

"You're right." Maggie sighed; she hated doing the books and hadn't quite finished yesterday. It was so tedious and boring. She'd rather be in the kitchen creating and testing recipes. Food was so much more interesting than writing checks for bills and balancing the bank account.

She plopped in the chair at her desk and sighed again. How much longer would she be doing the Inn's books? Her parents might decide to boot her out and hire a real manger—an innkeeper who wouldn't drown the Inn in debt behind the owner's back.

She wouldn't know that until one or the other returned her call. It probably wouldn't be for a couple of days, assuming they check their messages. Since retiring, returning calls didn't seem to land high on their list of priorities.

Her jaw clenched, she opened the bookkeeping program on the computer. She set her mind to boring but necessary work mode and opened the file folder of invoices that needed to be paid.

Two hours later, Maggie stretched her arms to the ceiling, relieved that she was nearly done. She caught movement out of the corner of her eye and jumped in her chair.

Alex strode into the office.

Her hand flew to her chest. "Geez, don't sneak up on me like that."

"Seriously, are you having the vapors? I knocked on the door."

"Vapors? Where'd that come from?"

"Sorry, I've been reading a reality-based historical novel."

"I've been doing office work. What can I do for you?"

He leaned against the doorframe. "I heard you mention the other day that you needed to refresh your stock of spices."

"That's true, I need to drive to Houston one day soon."

"How about this Saturday?"

"Why? Are you driving down yourself?"

He nodded. "I need to meet my college advisor so I have a meeting at one o'clock on Saturday afternoon. I thought you could drive in with me and do your shopping while I'm meeting with Professor Bradford."

"Hmm, that might work."

"I also need to check on my townhouse. We could stay the night and have a nice dinner at whatever restaurant you choose."

"What time would we leave and then return?" She might be able to make this work.

"Mid-morning on Saturday and whenever on Sunday. I'm open so that'd be up to you."

Maggie nodded; thinking a night away would do her some good. "A little round-trip to Houston is sounding just fine right now. I'll check the weekend reservations and with Sunny and then let you know in the morning."

"Sure." Alex fidgeted in place for a moment, as though he wanted to say something. Maybe he thought better of it, because he turned suddenly to leave. "I better get back to my reading."

Maggie leaned back in her chair, craning her neck to watch him walk away from her. Her stomach somersaulted at the sight of worn blue jeans molded perfectly to his firm butt. Nice. Damn if the man didn't look good coming and going.

Once he disappeared from her view, she sat up reluctantly and shook her head. Alex was a combination of personality and looks all rolled up into one perfect package. His ex-fiancé must have been a flaming idiot.

Chapter Twelve

November 7, Saturday

Maggie swung onto the Scott Street exit off I-45 South. She had ten minutes before the designated time to pick up Alex after the meeting with his advisor. She was early due to light traffic on the Houston freeway and found a prime parking spot on the University of Houston campus.

She used the few minutes of waiting to plan a new recipe—chicken, blue cheese, and walnuts. Her personal creation based on a Cobb salad. At Alex's approach, she backed out of the parking space and pulled alongside the curb.

He greeted her with a wave as she exited the vehicle to let him drive.

"How did it go?" She climbed in the passenger seat and buckled up while Alex did the same.

He looked at her with a million-watt smile. "It went exceptionally well, as a matter of fact. Professor Bradford was happy with my progress so I should complete my dissertation per my master schedule."

"Good for you." Maggie meant it, but it did bring up an issue for her. "I suppose when you're done you'll be leaving the Inn and Brenham."

He glanced at her, his face blank. "Yes, that's the

plan. I'll need to go wherever I can find an open position—if I want to teach."

"Of course, I hadn't really considered what came after the Ph.D." She could've kicked herself. She sounded stupid and clueless. Of course a university teaching job was the goal after earning a doctorate degree. She didn't want to think about Alex leaving Brenham so she stared out the window. Stowing that thought at the back of her mind, she zipped her lips shut with an invisible key.

~~*

Alex sensed a change in Maggie. She'd shifted toward the window in her seat and hadn't said a word in ten minutes. He had no idea what he'd said to upset her. His instincts told him to leave her alone and not press. No problem, acting normal was a virtue.

He drove in the late afternoon traffic to his condo in the University Park section of Houston. It was two blocks from Houston Cullen University and four blocks from one of the best selection of restaurants outside of the downtown area. He exited the Southwest Freeway to Dunlavy and turned left. He drove the two blocks to his condo and pulled in the parking garage, pressing the control for the gate.

"Here we are." Alex swung into his parking spot on the first floor of the garage. "We'll have some down time before we head out for dinner."

"Sounds good."

Alex grabbed their overnight bags and within five minutes, they'd taken the elevator to the top floor of the building, exiting to the foyer.

"Why are their only two doors on this floor?" Maggie asked.

Alex looked at her, initially surprised by her question. "There are only two units, the penthouses are the largest units in the building." He punched in a code on the keypad lock and pushed on the door. "Come on in. I hope it's not a mess."

~~*

Maggie followed Alex into his condo. After five steps she stopped and her mouth fell open. Oh. My. God. This condo was to die for. While she gawked, Alex turned on lights and opened floor to ceiling curtains all from a control panel on a wall.

"Wow, nice condo." Maggie walked further into the loft-like space. "Actually, this is fantastic."

"Thanks. Make yourself at home." Alex walked to the kitchen on the left side and opened up a couple of cabinets then moved to the windows. "Looks like the ex left without creating a decorating problem for me."

"Your decorating looks great to me." She noted the soft beige of the walls, and the over-stuffed sofa and matching club chairs and ottomans, all covered in the same becoming brown-gold tweed fabric. She had to wonder if any of it was his choice, or perhaps a decorator's. Although it lacked the typical leather and glass bachelor motif, a huge flat screen television dominated one wall.

"Follow me. I have one guest room that should work for you."

She followed him down a hallway to the right and passed a set of wide double doors to the guest room. The door was open and light streamed into the room. A king sized bed covered in a floral comforter dominated the room. The colors of soft yellow and cream played against the dark wood floor to create a soothing mood.

"This is a beautiful room." Maggie turned back to Alex.

"Thanks, my mom likes it, too. There's a bathroom through that open door. Let me know if you need anything." He walked out the door then his head popped back. "I'll meet you in the kitchen in an hour."

"Sounds good." Maggie placed her suitcase on the bed and unzipped it. She shook out a red sweater with a vee neckline enhanced with black beads and a pair of fancy black jeans. Ones that hugged her butt and made her thighs look slim. Red ballet flats and a black cardigan completed her dinner outfit. It should work, unless Alex suggested a swanky restaurant for dinner.

She hung the clothes in the closet and went to the bathroom for a refreshing shower. She stopped just inside to look at the walk-in shower. A wide glass door led to stone lined walls, a bench, and multiple raindrop showerheads. It felt like being in a spa.

After enjoying a mini-spa treatment followed by sufficient time spent primping, Maggie declared herself ready for dinner. She ignored the rustle of butterflies in her stomach. This wasn't a date, merely a mutual need to eat. She fluffed her hair one more time and gave her reflection the once over. "Not a date, not a date," she muttered softly to herself.

She found Alex standing behind the kitchen island with a wine bottle in his hand. The stainless appliances, along with the cherry cabinets and golden granite counter tops created a sense of luxury. She loved it.

"I adore your kitchen." She walked around the island, in total awe of the restaurant quality stove—complete with grill. "This is to die for." She ran her hands appreciatively over the top of the burners.

"No, it's just a stove." He poured two glasses of wine. "I hope pinot noir is okay. Just had an urge for it."

"Mm, sounds good." Maggie accepted a glass and tasted the wine. "It's delicious, thanks." She moved to the other side of the island and settled on one of the stools. "Honestly, this is a fabulous kitchen."

"My mom helped me design it. I've had a couple of dinner parties but the ex didn't cook, so it's not seen a lot of action."

"I'd love to cook here."

"What would you prepare, say for dinner?"

"Let me think." She tapped a finger against her lips. "I think a dish with shrimp and pasta and asparagus. Probably a lemon and olive oil sauce, green salad, and garlic bread."

"What about dessert?"

"I'd be too full."

"Okay, make a list of what you need and I'll order it in."

"Seriously, you get groceries delivered?"

"Once in a while, there's a large store a couple blocks away. Would you prefer cooking in my kitchen or going out to dinner? Your choice."

Maggie didn't have to think longer than two seconds. "Cook, of course."

Alex fist pumped. "Yes, I hoped you'd say that." He opened a drawer and pulled out a note pad and a pen. "Make your list and I'll call it in."

An hour later the food had been delivered and Maggie watched Alex unpack the bags. She noticed several things not on the list. "Is that ice cream?"

"Uh-huh, figured we might need a dessert after all." He pulled another package from a bag.

"And cookies, I think you might be right." Maggie sipped her wine while Alex put away the groceries. She took a few minutes to investigate the condo. The place really was fabulous—exceptionally roomy with superb lighting. She carried her wine glass to the windows, gasping as she realized there was a terrace. "Mind if I go outside?"

"Great idea. Let me unlock the door for you."

Once outside, Maggie walked to the edge of the terrace and gazed at the park across the street. It was beautiful, filled with majestic oak trees to provide plenty of shade. Flowerbeds lined both edges of the sidewalk and a path bordered by a white picket fence wound into the trees.

Alex approached silently, the woodsy scent of his cologne alerting her to his presence. Without a doubt, she'd think of him every time she caught a whiff of that particular scent. "You have a beautiful view."

He joined her at the railing. "It's especially nice at night when the trees are all lit up."

"I'm surprised to see it in the heart of Houston."

"There was a huge uproar about building a green space rather than renovating the block into more retail space."

Maggie finished her wine and glanced at Alex. "I'm glad green won out for a change."

"Me, too. I went to the city council meeting and it was brutal. Those in favor of the retail developmental called the park supporters tree-huggers. No arrests were made but it came close."

"I guess Brenham is tame to you after the excitement of Houston." Maggie's gaze lingered on the lovely park.

"I could say the same for you. You moved back from Los Angeles. That place is a lot crazier than Houston."

She raised her empty glass. "True. Are you hungry? How about an appetizer to get started?"

"I like that idea." Alex grabbed her hand and led her into the condo. "Do you mind if I check the college football scores?"

"Not at all." Maggie walked to the refrigerator. "Let me know if you see the Longhorn's score. They played Oklahoma State today."

"Will do."

While Alex concentrated on the television, Maggie pulled together toasted crostini, along with olives and feta. Light appetizers that went well with Alex's choice of wine. She pulled the crostini from the broiler just as Alex walked around the island counter.

"Your team won today and so did Stanford." He high-fived her and grinned. "I guess we have something to celebrate tonight."

"Looks like it." She arranged the appetizers on the counter. "I'd like another glass of wine."

Alex refilled their glasses. "Sorry, my host skills aren't usually so lax."

"No problem. I'm guessing the actual use of your kitchen appliances has you out of sorts."

He tapped his glass to hers. "Touché."

Maggie stood on one side of the island with Alex on the opposite side. Finally, their gazes found each other.

"So, here we are, alone, in the big city." Alex took a bite of the crostini and smiled. "This is good. Damn, you should be the chef of some fancy restaurant downtown."

"Thanks for the compliment but I'm not that kind of cook."

"Says who?"

"Says me. I'm not into highbrow dishes. I like easy to prepare, everyday recipes. Sure I believe in presentation but that's as fancy as I get."

"Whatever you call it, I think you're fantastic."

Maggie knew she was blushing at Alex's kind words. "I do love to cook. Sunny thinks I should stay in Brenham and start a catering business. I'm actually thinking about her idea."

"That means you wouldn't return to LA."

"That's right. I think small town living might be growing on me."

"We're alike in that. I had intended to apply for a teaching job in Boston but now I'm considering applying to schools in small towns. Actually, A&M will be at the top of my list."

"Really? You said in the car you'd be leaving Brenham." Maggie was totally surprised by this tidbit of information. She had assumed Alex would be heading out of Texas. "That's good news. Our dinner tonight can be a celebration of sorts—me possibly staying in Brenham and you, close to it."

"Excellent idea." Alex smiled and ate a couple of olives. "These are good. You have the best ideas for food. I'd marry you just for your cooking." He popped another crostini in his mouth and chewed.

Maggie couldn't believe he'd said what he said. Apparently he didn't realize what had come from his lips as he stuffed more food in his mouth. The man liked to eat when he set his mind to it. Which made her think of Michael, her ex-LA-boyfriend. He ate like a finicky little girl and picked over most of her cooking, preferring wheat germ and protein shakes.

"Thanks for that. Dinner won't take long to prepare so I was wondering if you'd like to show me around the park before I start."

He stood. "I like that idea. Did you bring a jacket? It's cooler now."

She shook her head and he walked down the hall and returned with a yellow hoodie. "This should work. My mom left it here."

Five minutes later they were heading out the front entrance of the condo complex. They ran across the street rather than going to the street light.

"Now we're jaywalkers." Alex took Maggie's hand in his.

The physical contact surprised her but she didn't pull away. In fact, she couldn't help but notice how perfectly her hand fit in his. She nudged him gently. "I hope we're not headed toward a life of crime." He grinned at her, his cheek creasing in a way that made her want to kiss it.

"Me, too. There's something I want to show you."

He led her down a brick path that curved left then right and headed into the middle of the park. After a couple of minutes they came to a round open area with a flagstone pathway that circled a large round fountain. Water splashed from four urns embedded into a central cylinder. Lights at the bottom of the fountain colored each stream of water. It reminded Maggie of Bernini's Fountain of Four Rivers in Rome. She'd read a book about Bernini in a college art class.

"Oh . . ." she breathed, almost reverently. "This is gorgeous. It's like finding a little piece of paradise in the middle of this urban park."

"I know. Most people have no clue about this. It's called Lover's Landing. I think the design committee leaned toward the romantic side."

Maggie pulled in front of him to look at the water in the fountain's base. She wasn't all that surprised to see coins on the bottom. Alex joined her. "How cool, people are making wishes. Isn't that popular at that fountain in Rome?"

"Yes, it's the Trevi Fountain. The coins help with the park's up keep."

"Let's throw one and make a wish. Do you have any change? I walked out minus my purse."

Alex handed her a quarter. "At the Trevi you throw the coin over your left shoulder with your back to the fountain."

"I can do that." Maggie turned around and stood close to Alex who had done the same. What to wish for?

His cologne wafted over to her and she became even more keenly aware of his presence. He smelled every bit as delicious as he looked and she couldn't help but think about how much she liked this man. Truth be told, she probably did more than like him, but she wouldn't think about that right then. She would, however, make a wish—that she and Alex could become more than friends, lovers in fact.

"Do you have your coin in the proper position?" Alex glanced at her. "Looking good. On the count of three—one, two, three."

Maggie threw the coin over her shoulder. She laughed and spun on her heels, giving Alex's bicep a playful punch. "That was fun. Are you ready to become a chef's assistant?"

He slung an arm around her shoulder and squeezed. "I believe I'm up to that challenge. As long as you don't go all food-Nazi crazy on me." They headed back to the condo hand-in-hand.

~~*

Alex's gaze stayed on Maggie as she assembled the shrimp and pasta. Her cheeks flushed becomingly as she concentrated on tossing the dish just right. Meanwhile, he focused on her—studied her during the entire process of meal preparation. Her joy of cooking outshined anything he'd ever seen before—but nothing matched his delight at watching her do what she loved in *his* kitchen. Her sister was right on the money in suggesting she start a catering business in Brenham. Yeah, that might fit perfectly with his plans. Hell, it did fit just right. Now, he had to convince Maggie they had a future together.

She placed the pasta dish on the counter and clapped her hands. "Dinner is ready." She added the salad and the garlic bread. "I hope you're hungry. This recipe makes a lot of pasta."

"You don't have to worry about that." He rose and patted his stomach. "I've grown quite attached to your cooking." He pulled another bottle of wine from the under counter cellar. "This is a crisp white. I've been told it goes well with seafood."

While Alex uncorked then poured the wine, Maggie settled at the counter. He soon joined her and raised his glass.

"This seems like the right time to make a toast. I've had a great day and I hope you have as well. Here's to good times and better friends." He tapped his glass to hers and noticed her shy smile. Perhaps she would be amenable to his plan for something more.

"I agree. No worries or thoughts of responsibilities until tomorrow."

He sent her a lop-sided grin. "Party time."

~~*

Maggie sat cross-legged on Alex's sofa with a bowl of chocolate mint ice cream and a plate of peanut butter cookies on the table. Alex reclined next to her, his legs crossed at the ankle rested on the table. They had agreed on a movie from Alex's rather extensive collection. She had no idea he was such a movie buff.

"I've always liked *Pretty Woman*," she commented as the film began. "It's one of those movies you can see a hundred times."

Alex glanced at her and rolled his eyes. "Your movie

is first then we're watching *Fast and Furious*."

"I know." She smiled and slid the spoon in her mouth, enjoying the combination of flavors.

Alex threw an arm around her shoulder and squeezed. "Thatta girl, you're a real trooper."

She nodded and scooted closer to Alex. "That's what my granddad used to say when I'd rake leaves for him even though I hated it."

He kissed the side of her head. "I'd walk through fire for my grandfather so I understand your dedication."

"Yep, we're a couple of softies." The DVD finally came to the movie. She wiggled her butt into the back of the sofa, getting situated just right next to Alex. "Here we go, Richard Gere at his finest."

~~*

"Julia Roberts isn't bad either." With Maggie so close, Alex had to work at keeping his desire under control. The last thing he needed was to jump her on his own couch. Talk about the ultimate dumb ass thing to do.

Instead, he concentrated on the movie. When it came to the scene where Vivian climbed on the piano at the hotel, he nearly lost it and imagined coaxing Maggie down on the cushions. Instead, he pulled her close to plant a gentle kiss to her head. He'd planned to end it at that, but he found himself nuzzling his way to her ear.

She leaned into him and after a moment turned her face to his. He took that as an invitation and brought his mouth to hers. Tentative at first, he tasted her, nipping softly, until she pressed closer. Relieved at her response, he deepened the kiss and felt the sweet push of her tongue toward his.

Need. Raw need coursed through his veins. Maggie had bewitched him.

His arms encircled her. He held her as though she were a delicate flower until she nibbled on his lower lip. Any pretense of innocent fooling around evaporated in an instant.

"You do know what you're doing to me," he growled.

"Uh-huh," she replied against his lips. "Sure do."

That was all he needed. He rolled off the sofa and stood, staring at Maggie—flushed, beckoning him with her swollen lips and dazed expression. He lifted her from the couch in one fluid motion, tucked her snugly in his arms, and walked with purpose to his bedroom. Richard Gere? By the time he was finished she wouldn't remember the man's name.

Time to put all those piano lessons to good use.

Chapter Thirteen

November 8, Sunday

Sunny's head snapped up. The sound of breaking glass or something clattering on the driveway had her jumping out of the chair she'd fallen asleep in while reading. She looked out the window and saw something or someone slowly moving across the driveway. Crap. She glanced at Tyler, sleeping soundly, and hurried out the door of their bedroom.

Once on the first floor, she grabbed a flashlight from the utility room and eased out the back door. She moved slowly toward the Barn, slashing the beam of light from right to left in front of her. Nothing moved around her, leaves were scattered over her path to the Barn. It was as though she'd walked into a vacuum of space.

She stopped a few feet from the front door to listen. Had she imagined that sound in her bedroom? She stepped slowly to the right. A couple of feet ahead, a trashcan was on its side, the lid still intact.

Ah, that must have been the noise she heard— probably a stray dog trying to serve up a free meal. After breathing a sigh of relief, she gave the Barn a five-second cursory glance and turned back to the Inn.

She hadn't moved five steps before another sound

clattered behind her. She whirled around, fear spiking every breath. The Barn looked the same, nothing out of the ordinary. She let out of slow breath. Must be a cat following that dog and making more noise.

All was well—until the front door of the Barn banged in the breeze. She froze. That door should be locked.

Go forward or head back to the Inn and wake up her tired father as her parents had arrived out of the blue on Saturday afternoon. No, she was old enough to handle this without involving them. She'd give the Barn a quick look and then go to bed.

She walked slowly toward the door, her shoes crunching the leaves on the concrete. The flashlight kept her from tripping over her feet. Stopping a foot from the Barn's front door, she swung the flashlight's beam over the door and stopped at the doorknob. Oh, no . . . crap.

Unlike the heroine who goes down the dark basement stairs after hearing a noise, Sunny knew it was not wise to enter a building with a broken lock. Damn, now she would have to wake up her parents. She turned her head slightly and held her breath, straining to hear any noise on the other side of the door. The only noise was the rustle of the leaves.

She let out the breath, feeling a bit silly, and turned around to head back to the Inn. Before taking a step, a swooshing racket came from the Barn and someone plowed into the back of her, knocking Sunny to the ground. The side of her head hit the concrete and her eyes slowly closed.

"Miss Sunny, wake up. Please . . . please wake up.

Miss Sunny!"

She rolled over to her back. She had no idea how long she'd been laying there but guessed it wasn't long— not much more than a minute or two. She was a little groggy and her head hurt when she rubbed it with her fingers. After slowly opening her eyes, she brought her fingers in front of her eyes. No blood— that was good. She mostly had the wind knocked out of her.

"How do you feel?"

Shit! Robert stood over her and stared at her with an intensity that surprised her. She closed her eyes and waved a hand at him. This was a first. She needed to get back to the Inn.

"Can you talk?"

Her eyes cracked open and she sat up gingerly, her head pounding with the movement. "Yes, I'm okay. What happened?"

"A young man came inside and began to swing at things with a big hammer. Then he sat in the middle of the big room on the floor and smoked a cigarette. That's when I approached him."

"Didn't that scare him off?"

"No, I asked him his name and he wouldn't tell me. He laughed at me and kept saying talking to a ghost was uh . . . freaking cool. Whatever that means. I told him he needed to leave and he laughed more."

"Sounds like he was high."

"I don't know what that means but I sensed you were outside and came to look for you. Then all of a sudden he came running through the foyer and out the door and ran right into you. Last I saw of him, he ran around the side of the Inn."

"Did he say why he broke in?" Robert shook his head.

Sunny began to shiver. She could feel the cold concrete though her jeans. After rolling to her knees, she stood slowly, just a bit wobbly. Then she heard an explosion followed by glass breaking. Through the open door, she saw flames and turned to Robert.

"Make yourself scarce, I'm calling 9-1-1." She hurried as fast as she could to the backdoor of the Inn and met her father coming down the step.

"What happened?" He wrapped his arms around her. "Are you okay?"

She nodded as sirens wailed in the distance. "Oh man, Maggie is gonna be upset."

~~*

After sweet wake-up sex and a shower with Alex, Maggie strolled to the guest bedroom to get dressed. She was in a daze, a light-headed and heart-thumping daze from spending the entire night in Alex's bed.

As she entered the bedroom, her cell phone rang. It was in her purse on the bed. She quickly pulled it out.

"Maggie, where have you been? I've been trying to reach you for hours."

"I'm in Houston with Alex. You know that. What's got you in such a tizzy?"

"Tizzy? You think I'm in a tizzy. Hell no, I'm in full blown panic mode."

"Oo-kay, what's going on?"

"If you'd bothered to answer your phone or read a damn text message you'd know. There was a fire last night at the Barn after Mom and Dad arrived for a visit. They're—"

"A fire . . . at the Barn? Mom and Dad are there? Holy shit. I'm on my way home." Maggie threw the phone back in her purse and pulled on jeans, a cotton top, and her running shoes. She packed her duffel bag and rushed to the kitchen.

Alex smiled when he saw her. "What would you like for breakfast?"

"No time. We need to get back to Brenham. There was a fire at the Barn and my parents have arrived."

"What?"

"Can we leave now?"

"Pour coffee while I get my bag? Travel mugs in the cabinet next to the refrigerator."

She opened the cabinet door as he hurried to get his things.

Ten minutes later they were on the road headed toward Brenham.

Maggie considered calling Sunny but decided against it. She didn't need any added stress during the hour and a half they'd be on the road. How bad was the fire and how did it start? What was the condition of the remodeling? Why had her parents arrived without warning and at such a lousy time?

Alex must have sensed her distress as he reached out for her hand and placed it on his thigh holding it tight. "Everything will be okay."

~~*

An RV with Florida plates was parked next to the dumpster. Maggie jumped out of Alex's SUV the second he pulled behind the Inn. Her mother walked out of the front door of the Barn at the same time.

"Mom, why didn't you tell us you were coming to visit?"

Trudy Todd, a fit, petite sixty-five year-old with silver hair and bright blue eyes, spread her arms and hugged her oldest daughter. "It's good to see you." She pulled back and gazed at Maggie. "Why didn't you tell us you were taking out a bank loan and remodeling the Barn?"

Maggie's stomach did a loop-de-loop. She knew she'd have to face her parents eventually, but not reaching them by phone had given her a false sense that it would be in the future, i.e., not so soon and not under these conditions. But right then, the damage from the fire took priority.

"Can we talk about that later? Right now I want to see the fire damage. I didn't see any fire trucks so it couldn't have been that bad."

"They left about thirty minutes ago. The arson investigator will be back though."

"Arson?" Alex stood next to Maggie and offered his hand to Trudy. "I'm Alex Brady. I have a room at the Inn."

Trudy looked from Alex to Maggie and then back. She shook his hand. "Nice to meet you. I gather Maggie was with you in Houston."

"Yes ma'am, we both had errands there and decided to drive down together."

"I see. Maggie, I know you're itching to look inside. I'll go find your father."

Maggie nodded then headed toward the front door with Alex close behind. Her nerves were in turmoil and she clenched her fists before walking into the Barn. Alex grabbed her hand at their first glance of the main room a few steps inside the door. Her breath hitched and she stood motionless, glaring at the sopped mess in the middle of the room.

"What in the world happened?" She couldn't believe her eyes.

A hand touched her shoulder and she swiveled her head around.

"Quite the sight, huh sis?" Sunny slid an arm around her sister's waist. She leaned her head against Maggie's shoulder. "It looks terrible but it could have been so much worse."

"What happened?" Alex walked further into the room still holding Maggie's hand and pulled her along with him.

Sunny explained she left the Inn to investigate a noise. "The bad guy broke in through the front door," Sunny explained. "We need to get a solid door by the way. We need to add a dead bolt lock, too."

Maggie wanted to stamp her foot like a child. How could she be so stupid to not secure the Barn properly during the remodeling? It screamed she was way over her head with this project.

"Then what happened?" Alex asked.

Sunny told them about Robert's involvement and talking to the teenager.

"What about the fire?" Frustration rolled off of Maggie like drops of sweat.

"The guy set it and plowed into me as he ran out the door. Dad heard the explosion and immediately called 9-1-1."

"Did I hear my name?" Bill Todd had come up behind them.

Maggie reached out to hug her father and was grateful for his presence even though she knew she'd have to face his disapproval.

"It's good to see you, Dad."

"You, too. I am surprised about all this remodeling you contracted without talking to us."

Trudy placed a hand on his arm. "Now, Bill, we can talk about that later. Right now, we need to clean up this mess."

"I'd like Jim Evans to look things over before we do any repairs." Maggie pushed hair tendrils behind her ears.

Alex spoke to Maggie. "I'll go to my room so you can talk with your family."

Maggie nodded without really hearing his words then realized she hadn't introduced Alex to her father. "Dad, this is Alex Brady, he's a boarder here and a good friend."

The two men shook hands and Alex left.

Her father's eyes narrowed. "A boarder is a good friend of the Inn's manager? Did you go to school with him?"

"No, I met him here when he rented a room." Maggie didn't want to discuss her relationship with Alex with her father. She hardly knew how to define it.

"Bill, let's not grill Maggie about Alex right now,"

her mother said, saving the moment. "What are we doing about this damned fire?"

~~*

"Talk about a crappy day." Maggie sat on Alex's bed holding a glass of cabernet and feeling sorry for herself. "If my parents knew I was in your room they'd kill me, that's assuming there'll be anything left of me to kill after the loan and fire fiasco."

"I'm glad you're here." Sitting in the chair pulled up to the bed he grabbed her free hand and rhythmically stroked his thumb over the top. "Tell me what happened after I left."

She blew out a slow breath. "First my dad yelled at me for taking out the bank loan and starting the remodeling project without his approval." She held up her hand. "Yeah, I know, I had it coming but it still sucked."

He squeezed her hand and topped off her wine glass from the bottle she'd brought. "Guess I can't blame your dad but I'm sorry about the fire."

"Me, too. After he stopped yelling he called our insurance agent who came over immediately. He then called the fire chief who came over with a police detective. Insurance will cover most of the damage."

"That's good news. Do the police have any leads on the teenager?"

"Hell no. Sunny never saw him and we can't tell anyone that Robert talked to him. Maybe the kid did it because he doesn't like my family, the Inn, or maybe it was a stupid teenage prank."

"I don't know. That seems a little over the top for a

prank."

"The police detective said the same thing." Maggie couldn't believe she was calmly discussing what a detective said about a fire at the Barn. The fact that she was the one talking about said discussion, and in the room of a guest at the Inn no less, seemed even more far-fetched. Granted Alex was now a special guest, but still, it was weird as hell.

"Maybe it was personal."

"I know who could have hired the kid to start the fire," she said.

"Yeah?"

"Yeah . . . the Adams family."

"The Adams family, wasn't that a TV show?" Alex's eyes crinkled with laughter. He stopped short at her glare. "Sorry. Didn't I meet some lady named Adams and her son when we went out to dinner with my mom and Roger?"

She nodded. "You met Mildred and Hank. Herbert Adams is the grandfather of Mildred's husband. Remember, he's the guy who murdered Robert."

"You're right. She was nasty toward you."

"Exactly," she said, waving her finger at him. "Maybe they learned we went to the police about Robert's murder."

"That makes sense." He leaned over the bed, kissed her nose, and settled back in the chair. "You are so cute. Do you suppose Mildred knows what the grandfather did?"

She warmed at his "cute" remark, slid a stray strand of hair behind her ear. "I don't know all that much about the family. My parents might know something." Maggie sucked in a deep breath at the obvious. "If I ask either of them about Herbert or Mildred, I'll have to tell them why I'm asking and—"

"And that involves admitting to one or both of them that you and Sunny have actually talked to the resident ghost."

Maggie scooted her butt to the edge of the bed and placed her legs between Alex's knees. She leaned into him and kissed his chest at the opening of his shirt. "Bingo."

He wrapped her in his arms and pulled her off the bed onto his lap. "I say we have a powwow with your folks tomorrow and tell them the whole story."

She pulled back to gaze at his face. "I need to tell Sunny. You want to be involved?"

"Yep, I'm part of this story, too, doing all that Internet research and all." He buried his face against her neck and began nibbling. "We can figure out a plan to approach them after breakfast. Right now I have other things on my mind." He nibbled his way along her jawline to her lips and kissed her thoroughly.

She leaned into him and rested her head on his shoulder. "I'm so glad you're here."

"Me, too." He found her lips again and the kiss quickly deepened. The slow burn of passion ignited, had them moving to the bed. He whispered against her hair. "Please tell me you have some free time."

"Mm, how much time do you need?"

"Only the rest of the night." He began to unfasten her denim shirt. "I get lonely in this bed by myself."

She reached for the button on his jeans. "Lucky for you and me, I have no appointments for the next ten hours."

"Hmm . . . perfect."

Chapter Fourteen

November 9, Monday

Maggie pulled Sunny into the pantry as soon as her sister stepped in the kitchen Monday morning. Their parents were out front with Tyler looking at the flowerbeds.

"I need to talk with you."

Sunny stepped back, frowned. "You don't have to manhandle me. What's up?"

"Sorry." Maggie quickly smoothed her hands over Sunny's shoulders. "I need your help. Alex and I think we know who started the fire."

"Really? That's awfully fast." Sunny crossed her arms over her chest. "How did you two come up with your suspect?"

"We were talking last night in Alex's room and I think it's someone in the Adams family."

Sunny lifted a hand to stop her. "First of all, I do *not* want to know that you were in Alex's room. Second, I need coffee before we have this conversation." Despite the harshness of her words, Sunny's smile betrayed her joy at hearing about Maggie's trip to Alex's room. She exited the pantry and poured a cup of java before turning to Maggie. One hip leaning against the kitchen counter, she addressed her sister. "Now, tell me how you came up with someone in the Adams family starting the fire."

"What?" Bill Todd headed for the coffee pot. "The Adams family has been in Brenham for close to a hundred years."

Sunny handed him a mug and looked at Maggie while he stirred in cream and sugar.

Maggie swallowed her nervousness. "Where's Mom?"

"She took Tyler to wash his hands."

"Right," Maggie said and reminded herself she needed to finish preparing the morning's meal. Guests would be arriving in the dining room in less than thirty minutes. "Dad, I need to get breakfast served but after everyone has eaten, Sunny and I need to talk with you. It's important."

"Is this about the fire?" Bill asked.

Maggie nodded. "And there's something else we need to discuss. I hate to put it off, but right now I need to fry some hash browns."

Bill nodded. "Fair Enough."

Two hours later, Maggie sat at the kitchen table with her parents waiting for Sunny who had left to put Tyler down for his morning nap. All of the Inn's guests had departed after breakfast as severe thunderstorms threatened. Alex rapped on the doorframe and zeroed in on Maggie. "Still want me here?"

"Absolutely." Maggie rose and sat next to her mother. "Please join us. You're part of this now."

"Really, Maggie?" Her father's brows had drawn into a single thick line. "I thought this was a family discussion."

"The subject matter includes Alex. Please give us a chance to explain."

"All right, but you'll need to prove to me why an Inn guest is involved in Inn business," Bill said. "I don't like it . . . I don't like it one bit."

"Give them a chance." Trudy patted his hand. "You'll see, it'll be okay."

Sunny rushed into the kitchen and sat next to Alex. "What did I miss?"

"Nothing," Trudy said. "Now that everyone is here, let's get this show on the road. What's going on?"

Maggie glanced at Alex and sucked in a breath. "I'll start since it was my idea to renovate the Barn. The truth is, well . . . I, Alex and I think Mildred Adams might be responsible for the fire."

"I hope you have proof for making such an accusation." Bill looked first at his daughter then at Alex and sipped from a coffee mug. "You do have some sort of evidence, right?"

"Not exactly," Maggie replied.

Trudy leaned forward in her chair. "What does that mean?"

Sunny rolled her eyes, leaned forward, and spread her hands on the table. "Let's cut to the chase. I need to get to Wal-Mart while Tyler's sleeping. Y'all know about the ghost here, right?"

Bill nodded and Trudy shrugged.

"Good. Maggie and I have both talked to him and he told us who killed him. It was Herbert Adams, Mildred's husband's grandfather. Alex and Maggie think Mildred started the fire in retaliation for them going to the police about Robert's cold case. There, now you know the basics. I'll leave y'all to take care of the details." She nodded at Maggie. "I need to buy diapers." Sunny rushed out of the kitchen.

Bill stared at the ceiling and Trudy opened her mouth then closed it.

Damn. This wasn't proceeding according to plan. Maggie's gaze alternated from one parent to the other, finally landing on Alex. His calm face in the sea of turmoil gave her courage to continue. "I can explain all of this."

"Just say what you need to say, sweetheart," Trudy said. "Your father and I are curious about the ghost."

"Sunny saw him first, in her bedroom. He mistook her for his girlfriend, Grace, and spoke to her. Then I saw him in the yard by the Barn and we talked. He told me about this murder. It was really sad and . . . plain stupid. It seems to me the Adams family has a defect of some kind."

Her father sent her a disapproving frown. "No need to trash the family. Mildred's mother was a good friend to your grandmother for many years."

Alex leaned over the table. "Do you suppose the family knows about Herbert and Robert?"

Crossed arms and an eye roll accompanied Bill's low harrumph. "They're a close knit bunch. Who knows if they share family secrets? Good business people though."

Trudy tapped one nail thoughtfully on her chin. "I think they do."

Bill turned to his wife, the curve of his mouth

hinting at his willingness to humor her. "Okay, miss know-it-all, they do what?"

She slapped his arm playfully. "Stop being contrary. I think Mildred does know about the murder and the ghost as well."

"Good," Maggie said. "This adds more support for our theory."

"Not so fast." Bill held up both hands life a traffic cop. "Trudy, why do you believe this?"

"Well . . . I'm not proud of this." Her lips thinned into a line then she blew out a loud breath. "I heard Grandma Todd and Mildred talking in the kitchen one day. I was going in to start some cookies and stopped when I heard them talking. I honestly don't know what made me lurk outside the door. Maybe it was that their voices were so low and then I got curious."

"Mom, really . . . lurking?" Maggie giggled as she spoke.

"It just happened."

"We're all hanging on the edge of our seats here, Trudy." Bill said, hiding a smile behind his hand. "What did you hear?"

"Drink your coffee, sweetheart. You're testy today." Bill nodded and Trudy continued. "They were talking about Grandfather Adams, Herbert, and the man who was killed here, Robert Graham. Apparently Herbert and Robert liked the same girl who was the daughter of the man who built this house."

"That's Grace Edwards," Alex interjected. "She was eighteen when Robert was killed."

"Tell me again who killed Robert," Bill said.

"Herbert Adams," Maggie and Alex said in unison.

"And you know that because Robert, as a ghost, told Maggie?" Bill asked. "Could be true, I suppose. I know Herbert was never convicted of a crime. I remember seeing him around town when I was a kid."

Maggie took the opportunity to run with the story. "We think Mildred might have started the fire to warn us about talking with the police and stirring up trouble for her family. Makes sense, don't you think?"

"Didn't Sunny say you'd already gone to the police?" Bill asked.

"Yes, Alex and I already did that," Maggie said. "We're speculating that the fire is Mildred's warning not to go further into investigating Robert's murder."

"Are you going further?" Trudy rose and approached the coffee pot.

Alex laid his hand on Maggie's. "No, we're not. We've already discussed this with Chief Morgan and concluded there's nothing to be gained by investigating a cold case."

"But Mildred wouldn't know that," Maggie added.

Bill cocked his head, gave his daughter a sidelong glance. "You know, Mildred has hated the chief ever since he turned down her invitation for the Sadie Hawkins dance in eighth grade."

"Seriously, over a Sadie Hawkins dance? That's kind of hard to imagine." Maggie smothered a giggle.

"Anyway, that's our current theory on who might have started the fire." Alex concluded. "Or it might be nothing more than a random act of violence. Are there any gangs here?"

"Yes. Unfortunately it doesn't hit only the big city." Bill raised his cup as Trudy refreshed his coffee then sat down. "We've had issues for many years. You think this might have been some sort of gang event?"

Alex shrugged. "It's another theory."

"Fair enough. I have a question for you two." Bill wagged a finger between Maggie and Alex. "Either of you or Sunny tick off anyone the last couple of weeks?"

"Hmm . . ." Trudy tapped a finger against her chin. "Maybe it's someone you'd never think of, like an old boyfriend you jilted, or someone you cut off in traffic and he's out for wicked revenge."

Maggie stood. "Both of you are totally off base. We've made no one mad or—"

"Maggie, wait," Alex said, motioning for her to sit down again. "They may be onto something. What about that girl Brandy, the one who came here on Halloween?"

"What about her, other than she was way too old to be trick or treating?" Maggie replied with a quick grin for Alex.

Bill leaned forward. "Who is this Brandy person?"

"She's a student I met at the A&M library," Alex replied. "I—"

"A&M?" Bill frowned. "Aren't you a little old to be an undergraduate?"

"Dad, really, Alex is working on his Ph.D. and he has a degree from Stanford." Maggie wanted to crawl under the table. Her father could be so rude sometimes.

Bill slid his gaze to Alex, half-grinned. "Okay. So what's the story with this girl?"

"I don't know how I caught her attention in the

library," Alex explained. "She asked me out several times and I think she might have followed me home once, not sure about that. And then she shows up here on Halloween night. I figure she assumed Maggie was my girlfriend after I told her I had one."

Maggie winked at him. "Yeah, that ticked her off all right. Honestly, I think we need to admit we don't have a clue who started the fire."

"Perhaps we should table the discussion for now." Trudy rose and tapped Bill on the shoulder. "Come on big guy. We need to go into town and see what's up."

"Mom, what does that mean?" Maggie watched her mother carry mugs to the sink. "Don't try to play detective about this."

"Wouldn't think of it," Trudy said over her shoulder as she pushed Bill out the door into the dining room.

Maggie rose and began putting the mugs in the dishwasher. Within seconds she felt Alex's hands on her hips and his mouth on the back of her neck. She giggled. "Be careful. They might come back."

He turned her around and kissed her mouth firmly. "I'm heading out so we won't be tempted to get into trouble."

"Actually, that sounds like fun." Maggie wrapped her arms around his neck and planted kisses along his jawline.

He untangled her arms from his neck and stepped back. "I'll hold you to that. I'm going to the library to see if Brandy is around."

"Don't you think she's a silly flake?"

"Yeah, but I want to ask her what she was doing

Saturday night. If I can find her." He kissed her quickly and wiggled his eyebrows. "I'll see you later for some of that trouble." After patting her butt he strolled out of the kitchen.

Maggie watched him walk away from her and shook her head, amazed at the difference one week had made in her life. She liked it.

Once the kitchen was clean, she started for her office to check the reservations for the week. Before she'd taken three steps, the main doorbell buzzed. She reversed direction toward the foyer. She pulled back the sheer curtain an inch and looked out the side window. Her heart sank. "What the hell?"

Maggie paced in front of the door, shaking her hands in front of her waist. "Damn it, I don't need this right now." The bell rang again.

She took a deep soothing breath, relaxed her hands, and opened the door.

"Hello Michael. You're a long way from Los Angeles." Why the hell was her ex-boyfriend standing on her front porch and grinning like a three-legged wolf winning a dance contest?

"Babe, it's good to see you." He wrapped his arms around her and hugged her tight. Then he stepped back and kissed her hard on the lips. "I'm here to take you back to the City of Angels—right where you belong."

Maggie pressed back into the foyer. "How did you find me?"

He followed her, dragging a rolling suitcase. "Easy, Google. Now, are you gonna be a good little hostess and find your long-lost boyfriend a room? Or should I simply stay with you?" He pulled her into his arms and nuzzled her neck. She shoved him away from her.

"Maggie?" Sunny walked down the hallway, returned from the store. "Who the hell is this?"

Maggie pulled further away from Michael and pushed his arm off her shoulder. What the hell was wrong with her? Like always, Michael was getting the best of her and he hadn't been there five minutes.

Moving closer to her sister, she pointed to him. "This is Michael Shaw, an old friend from LA. Remember, I told you about him."

Sunny stuck out her hand. "Nice to meet you. I'm Sunny, Maggie's sister."

Michael licked his lips then took her hand and brought it to his mouth. "So very nice to meet you."

Sunny tugged her hand from his, frowning. "Yeah, whatever. Why are you here?"

"To take your sister back to LA, of course."

Sunny's eyes widened and she shuddered.

Maggie rubbed her back. "Michael is staying just for the night. Is the Lavender Room ready?"

Sunny nodded, her mouth set in a crooked line. "I think I hear Tyler." She turned and hurried down the hall.

"Who's Tyler?" Michael asked.

"Her son," Maggie replied. "Now Michael, you stay right here while I get the room key."

"Sure, doll, can't wait to see the room." He winked at her and leaned against the wall, arms over his chest.

Maggie felt his eyes drilling into her back. Naturally, she wore a pair of old and tight blue jeans. Damn him. It's just like him to show up now—just in time to complicate an already complicated situation. She pulled the room key from the slot and headed back to the foyer.

She found Michael looking at the bulletin board. "I have your key so follow me up the stairs."

He turned to her, grinning. "Show me the way." He pulled his suitcase behind him—thump, thump, thump. "You've been working out, Maggie-Girl?"

"Shut up, Michael." She hated him using that nickname and she hated him being in Brenham. Thankfully, his room was close to the stairs. She opened the door and walked in. He strode past her and tossed his suitcase on the bed. He performed a slow twirl, examining the space.

"Not the Beverly Wilshire, but it'll work." He rubbed his hands together. "So what's our agenda for today?"

"No clue about your agenda, but mine isn't any of your business." His only reaction was a slight narrowing of his eyes. She placed the key on top of the Inn binder on the nightstand. "There's plenty of information about local restaurants and shops in the binder. We serve breakfast every morning at nine a.m. sharp. There are plenty of current DVD's in the living room in case you'd like to watch a movie." She moved to the doorway. "Any questions?"

"Yeah. Why are you acting this way?"

"What way?"

"Like you have a stick up your butt." He moved to her and put his hands on her arms. "Sure you don't have time for a little getting re-acquainted action?" He leaned closer to her and she backed away. "Damn it. Why do you keep moving away from me?"

"Michael, I don't know what you thought would happen by coming to Brenham, but I'm not returning to LA."

He scrunched his face. "Of course, you are. You're a big city girl. You'll shrivel up and die in this burg. In fact, you'll—"

"I really have to go now. We can talk about this later." She closed the door in his face and hurried to the Barn to talk to Jim. All thoughts of Michael vanished as she formulated a plan to get the renovation back on track after the fire.

~~*

Alex had been sitting at his usual table in the A&M library for over two hours without spotting Brandy. He was about to call it a day when he saw her walking between the tables to his right. He turned a page of the book in front of him and jotted a note on the yellow legal pad next to it.

She quietly sat across from him and placed her backpack on the table. As it came into his line of vision he lifted his gaze and smiled at her.

"Hey, Brandy," he whispered. "Is it raining out there yet?"

She returned the gaze, the subtle lift of a single eyebrow the only indication she'd heard him. She reciprocated with a slow, seductive smile. "Hello, Alex. Yes, it's raining like crazy. I'm surprised you're here. Didn't you finish your research?"

"Mostly, I'm just checking on a couple of things. How have you been?"

"Good. Can't wait for the Thanksgiving break." She pulled a textbook and a bright pink binder from her backpack. "Studying gets so boring."

"You don't like being a student?"

"Not really, but my daddy will disinherit me if I don't get a degree with at least a 'C' grade point average, so here I am."

"Hmm." He wondered how to steer the conversation to the past weekend. "I admit, not everyone is cut out to attend college but I admire you for making your father happy."

"You do? Really?"

"Sure I do. Of course you can't study all the time. What do you do for fun?"

"The usual—bars and clubs." She grinned and leaned over the table. "In fact, this last weekend my roommate and I went to Houston. I met the coolest guy Saturday night."

"You were in Houston on Saturday night?"

"Uh-huh, we left the club after midnight and then drank coffee for hours at a pancake place. I really like this guy."

"Good for you." Alex mentally crossed her name off the list of potential arson suspects. He closed the book and tossed it and the pad in his messenger bag. "I need to get going. Happy studying."

"Wait. I need to say I'm sorry."

"For what?"

She shifted in the hard library chair. "I kinda had a crush on you and sorta stalked you."

Alex sighed. The truth was out. "No problem,

Brandy. I was once your age."

She blinked. "Okay, thanks. Be careful driving in the rain."

Alex ran from the library entrance to his vehicle and was drenched by the time he threw himself in the front seat. Damn, he should've stayed at the Inn. He backed out and slowly made his way out of the parking lot, splashing parked cars as he drove. The rain was worse on the highway and he gripped the steering wheel. The slow-going traffic had him settling in for a long drive home.

The constant drumming of the rain on the windshield and the slap, slap of the wipers had Alex's nerves on edge. He didn't mind driving in snow, but heavy rain irritated him. Rather than being on a lousy road packed with traffic he could have been in a cozy living room with a beautiful woman and a glass of wine. He again wished he hadn't left the Inn.

Five miles outside of Brenham, the traffic slowed almost to a stop then sped up again. The double-cab truck in front of him quickly switched to the left lane. Twenty yards ahead, a car was jack-knifed across traffic lane and the shoulder, directly in front of Alex. He slammed on the brakes and his vehicle hydroplaned. Attempting to steer into the skid he overcompensated and the SUV slid toward the shoulder, clipped a motionless dump truck with enough momentum that the SUV left the roadside and rolled over twice moving down an embankment. It landed upright in a rain-swollen ditch.

The vehicle finally stilled, its four tires settling deep in the mud. The air bag had deployed, slamming into his chest. Alex blinked several times to get his bearings, and for some reason, found it a struggle to keep his eyes open. Within a few short moments, he lost that battle.

~~*

"Geez, Maggie, I didn't think we'd ever get rid of Michael." Sunny wiped down the kitchen table after dinner. "No offense, but what the hell did you ever see in that slime ball?"

"I have no idea. I look at him now—and there's nothing." Maggie sighed heavily. "Obviously, I've come to my senses."

"Obviously." Sunny took a couple of small glasses from the cabinet and retrieved a bottle of cream liquor from the refrigerator. "Let's sit for a bit. I need some adult talk after Tyler's meltdown at dinner."

"I think that's what convinced Michael to turn in early, so yay Tyler."

Sunny laughed. "I should have expected it since he didn't have much of an afternoon nap." She poured the liquor and sat at the table. "I'm really happy you're staying in Brenham. I hope I can convince Jason to stay here once his tour is over. This is a great place to raise Tyler."

"Hold on, I haven't decided one-hundred percent. I'm still weighing my options."

"What about Alex?"

"What about him?"

"Won't he have an impact on your decision?" Sunny watched Maggie over the rim of her glass.

"We're friends and—"

"Friends with benefits, right?"

"Sunny! As I was saying, we're good friends. I don't know anything more than that." Maggie *would not* think further than that about her relationship with Alex. She had this fear of over-analyzing the situation to the point of sabotaging it—just as she'd done with Michael. "I have a feeling it won't be easy to convince Michael I'm not returning to LA."

"Hmm . . . how about you turn it around? Try to persuade him to stay in Brenham. That might turn him off real quick. Give him a tour of all the hot spots like the Farmer's Market and the fair grounds." Sunny grinned and rolled her eyes. "Take him to dinner at The Longhorn and introduce him to some of the locals. That should get him to hightail it back to California in no time."

"Little sister, you're a genius. We'll go to lunch tomorrow and then do a grand tour of the town."

"Good. Now tell me what Jim said about the remodel of the Barn. Will it be ready for Emma's wedding?"

"That's the plan. Although, I was a little unnerved by Jim's response to the fire. He seemed to take it personally."

"That's weird."

"Exactly what I thought," Maggie said, sipping her drink. "Guess he's a truly responsible contractor."

"The main thing is that he gets past the damage and gets back on schedule."

Maggie nodded and checked her watch. "Right, let the police figure out the identity of that teenager. It's almost nine o'clock and I need to do some paperwork.

Mom and Dad will be back from their bridge game by ten."

"Why did they go? They should've stayed home with us."

"I know," Maggie said. "Betty Gerry did a good job of laying a guilt trip on them. Said they haven't been back to Brenham in so long, yada, yada."

"I remember her from when we were kids. Where's Alex?"

"Still at the library I guess."

"He sure is dedicated. Anything I can do to help with the paperwork?" Sunny gathered the empty glasses and put them in the dishwasher.

"No, go on to bed or better yet, have a long, leisurely soak in the tub."

"Great idea. See you in the morning." Sunny skipped out of the kitchen.

Maggie was so damned lucky to have Sunny to share the responsibility of the Inn. They made a good team. After settling at the office desk, she pulled out her notes on marketing the renovated Barn. She pulled out a large pad of paper and colored pencils. She worked close to two hours designing the Barn's new page on the Inn's website along with new print material. Michael had told her more than once she was nuts and wasting her time designing with paper and pencil when there were so many software programs out there for creating print material.

It didn't matter to her what he said. She'd design her own way and that was that. She rose and stretched her arms over her head. The wall clock showed it was after eleven. "Crap, it's late, I'll be dragging in the morning if I don't get some sleep." She walked to her bedroom and exchanged her clothes for her softest flannel nightgown before climbing into bed.

After one last mental review of the brochures, she finally closed her eyes. Within seconds, the Inn's business line rang. It never rang at night so it took her by surprise.

"Maggie, this is Emma Walters. I'm on duty at the hospital."

Maggie's first thought zoomed to her parents. "What's wrong, Emma?"

"Isn't Alex Brady one of your boarders?"

"Yes . . . yes he is. Is there a problem?"

"He was in a car accident a few hours ago and was brought here. I—"

"Is he okay?"

"I can't tell you that." Emma's voice lowered to a whisper. "The only reason I called you is because my mom told me that you and Alex were friends and I know he doesn't have family here."

"That's correct. I'm on my way." Maggie jumped off the bed. "What room is he in?"

"Just ask at the nurse's station, third floor north."

"Okay, will do. And, thanks for calling, Emma. I owe you one."

She pulled on jeans and a tee shirt and headed out of her bedroom. The cold floor caused her to stop and look at her feet . . . shoes, shoes would be good. She pulled short boots out of the closet and a hoodie sweater. Once fully dressed, she hurried to the kitchen and left a note for Sunny and her parents in case she wasn't back in a couple of hours. She went back to her bedroom for her purse and keys.

Once on the road to the hospital, Maggie took a deep, shaky breath. She said a silent prayer that Alex would be okay. The thought of losing him had her thinking how very much she wanted him in her life, permanently. Frankly, either of those situations scared the hell out of her.

Chapter Fifteen

November 10, Tuesday

Maggie stepped out of the hospital elevator on the third floor and studied the sign before her. North was to the right. She hurried down the quiet hallway past patient rooms on either side. The subdued lighting was a silent reminder that it was the middle of the night. She reached the nurse's station and it was empty. Emma must be with a patient.

She'd find Alex's room herself and began to look at patient names above the room numbers affixed beside each door. She started with the room across from her, no Alex Brady. The slap-slap of footsteps sounded behind her. She turned and the hallway was empty. That was weird. She moved quickly to the next-door and focused on the small whiteboard with a patient's name.

"Maggie?"

She twitched, took a breath, and turned.

A young woman with blond hair and bright blue eyes, wearing pink surgical scrubs, stood two feet away. She stuck out her hand. "Hi, remember me, I'm Emma Walters."

Maggie fisted her hands, getting her bearings. "Emma, of course, sorry I didn't recognize you from when you visited the Barn. You look so different with your hair up and in your work clothes."

"No problem. This is my professional look." She shifted a clipboard in her arms. "Follow me. I'll take you to Mr. Brady's room."

Maggie nodded and walked behind Emma to a room at the opposite end. "Is there anything I should know about his condition?"

"Since you're not family, I really can't tell you that. But Alex has regained consciousness. When the doctor comes a bit later for rounds you can talk with her about Alex's situation since he'll be awake." Emma opened the door and motioned Maggie into the room. "If anyone asks, just say you're his sister. But I didn't tell you that. I'll be back in a bit to check on him."

"Thank you so much," Maggie wrapped one arm around Emma and squeezed. "I'll keep good watch over him."

"I'm sure he'll be glad to see you. I put a blanket on the chair in case you get cold." Emma nodded then quickly left the room.

Maggie tiptoed to the chair next to the bed and deposited her purse. Alex didn't stir. She stepped closer and studied his deathly still features. The white blanket was pulled halfway up his chest and both his hands rested on top of it. There seemed to be a long lump along the left side, maybe a fracture of some sort. His shoulders were draped in a standard hospital gown and judging by the steady rise and fall of his chest, he appeared to be resting peacefully.

She turned her attention to his face, taking in every

feature, including the broad bruise on his forehead that couldn't diminish his handsomeness. His paleness had her wondering if he was in worse shape than Emma had led her to believe. Then again, the young woman had assured her he had already regained consciousness. Fearful of waking him, she kept her hands to herself and settled in the chair.

Even though Alex wasn't in critical condition, dread gripped Maggie's heart like a vise. They'd just acted on their attraction to each other, consummated their feelings with two wonderful nights of lovemaking. She had the distinct feeling it wouldn't be enough. She wanted— needed more from him than just a physical relationship. Maggie clasped her hands together and prayed. "Please, Lord, let Alex be okay and heal as he should."

After watching him for several long minutes, she shivered in the coolness of the room and drew the blanket over her. She closed her eyes, intending to rest them while she waited. She soon dozed off.

~~*

Eyes still closed, Alex concentrated on the soft rustle of noises around him—all hinting at him being in the hospital. The occasional beep of a cardiac monitor, muffled voices outside his room, and the thermostat controlled heat kicking on and off—each and every one a comfort, because they proved he was still alive.

His head somewhat clouded from a dull ache, he forced himself to remember previous events. The drive back to Brenham, pounding the brakes of his SUV to avoid—well, he wasn't sure what he was trying to avoid—and last, waking up in the ER with someone in pale green scrubs calling his name.

Pain flashed in his memory. His head and torso had hurt like hell, and his eyes had continued to water and burn like fire as he struggled to open them. He remembered bits and pieces of a conversation—someone telling him he'd been in a car accident and he was at the Brenham hospital. At first he couldn't remember why he wasn't in Houston, but he'd eventually been able to tell them he'd been residing at the B&B to write his dissertation. He'd kept his eyes open long enough for someone to look at them with a penlight before passing out again.

The pain had subsided for the most part. He raised his right arm and noted the IV, ah, pain killer meds. No wonder he felt better. He turned slightly and noticed a figure huddled in a chair next to the bed. He leaned slightly over the bedrail for a better view.

"Maggie?" he whispered. He swallowed and licked his lips. Reality dawned. She came to the hospital for him. He fell back on the pillows and his heart filled with . . . with something that he'd never experienced before.

Maggie had come to the hospital. He couldn't put into words what this simple act meant to him.

He counted the tiles in the ceiling as he considered every emotion rolling through him—gratitude, happiness, excitement, a sense of serenity, and last on the list, a confidence that he was in the right place with the right person. Yep, they all danced around the one big emotion—love. He was in love with Maggie. Without a doubt, without a smidgeon of uncertainty, Alex Brady was in love with Maggie Todd.

Before he had a chance to roll with his admission, a nurse walked in the door pushing the blood pressure machine.

"Mr. Brady, good morning. I'm Emma, your night nurse." She retrieved the hand control and raised the head portion of the bed until he was in a semi-upright position.

"Hi," he croaked, his throat dry as cotton. "What time is it?"

"Almost six-thirty. The doctor will be here soon." She wrapped the blood pressure cuff around his arm and pushed a button on the machine.

Alex watched Maggie wake as the nurse spoke. She stretched her arms and arched her back, then must have realized where she was. She bolted forward in the chair and noticed Alex watching her.

"Hey, how's our patient?" Maggie rose, rubbed a hand across her face, and stepped closer to the bed.

"The patient is fine and it looks like you both got some much needed rest." Emma removed the cuff and held a skin thermometer against Alex's forehead.

Maggie nodded then picked up Alex's left hand. "How do you feel?"

"I've been better. Did you hear what happened?" Alex squeezed her fingers, grateful for her touch.

"Only that you were in a car accident."

"In the ER they told me I slid off the road, turned over a couple of times, and ended up in a ditch."

"I need to get more ice." Emma retrieved an ice bag off Alex's chest from under the blanket. "I'll be right back."

Once Emma left, Maggie bent over and kissed Alex gently on his mouth. "I'm so thankful you weren't hurt any worse."

"Me, too," Alex said and sighed. "At least I don't have any broken bones."

Maggie's eyes widened and she gasped. "Crap, I haven't called your mother. I need to—"

"No." Alex interrupted her, a fierce look on his face. "Please, do not call my mother. This is no big deal and she'll get upset, drop what she's doing, and come here. I don't want her to worry."

"But, Alex, she'd want to know."

"Yeah, well, this situation is more of a need to know. I'll tell her at Thanksgiving." No way would he upset his mom with news of his accident. She deserved to concentrate on her own life with Roger and not worry about her son's stupid car wreck.

Maggie scrunched her lips for a moment then smiled. "Whatever you say."

The nurse returned with another woman who must be the doctor, based on the white coat she wore.

"I'm Doctor Mora. How are you feeling this morning?" The woman smiled so pleasantly at Alex that he was instantly put at ease.

"Not too bad. Although my head is hurting and my chest feels weird."

"I'm sure you don't remember everything from yesterday. You have a concussion and bruised ribs. You're a lucky man considering your accident."

He watched Maggie's face pale at the doctor's words. "Yeah, I agree. When will I be released?"

The doctor nodded at Emma who placed the ice bag on the left side of Alex's chest. "I want to keep you one more night. It's a precaution to make sure there are no lingering effects from the concussion. Plus, it will help to give your ribs a rest."

Alex's initial response was to complain but then he remembered he could be in much worse shape. Another night in the hospital was no big deal. "No problem. I'd rather not take a chance."

"Good," the doctor replied. "We'll keep icing your ribs for a few more hours and continue with the pain medication. Let us know if anything feels strange or the pain escalates. Okay?"

"Will do, thanks."

"I'll be by to see you later today." The doctor turned and answered a cell phone as she left the room.

"The doctor ordered regular meals so you can eat what you want." Emma handed him a menu for the day. "Just call in your breakfast order using the number at the bottom."

"Sounds like room service," Maggie said.

"Uh-huh," Emma said with a laugh. "But it's still hospital food. There's a cafeteria on the first floor if you want anything, Maggie. I can bring you coffee though."

"That would be fantastic," she replied.

Emma nodded and left.

Maggie bent over and kissed Alex again. "Thank God you're all right. Let's call in your breakfast."

Within minutes Maggie had placed the breakfast order and returned to his side.

His heart full with gratitude, Alex couldn't keep his

gaze from the woman he loved. It had been a long time since he'd had such hope for the future—a future that included Maggie. He reached his left hand to her and she grabbed it and squeezed. He closed his eyes and sighed. He truly was home.

~~*

Once Alex had finished his breakfast, he could hardy keep his eyes open. Maggie took that as her cue to leave so she gave him a kiss and headed home. Other than Michael, the Inn had one guest this week, a gentleman who had business with a couple of retirement facilities. Sunny or Trudy had no doubt handled breakfast. She'd have to make it up to them since preparing the meals for the Inn was her responsibility.

She walked in through the back door close to nine-thirty and found everyone in the kitchen, unfortunately that included Michael.

"Hey guys, I'm back."

Michael leapt out of his chair and wrapped his arms around her. "Babe, I've been so worried. You shouldn't be driving around in the middle of the night."

She stepped back, pulling herself from his arms. "I'm a big girl. Don't worry about me." She looked at her mother. "Any breakfast left?"

"There's a plate in the microwave," Trudy said.

She turned and Michael blocked her. She rolled her eyes and walked around him to retrieve her breakfast.

"How's Alex?" Sunny said as she unstrapped Tyler from his booster chair.

"Pretty good, considering he rolled his SUV and has a concussion and bruised ribs."

"Oh my goodness, that sounds serious." Trudy rose and stood behind Bill, placing her hands on his shoulders. "Is there anything we can do to help? Take him cookies or stay with him?"

"Thanks, Mom, but that's not necessary." Maggie sat at the table with her breakfast plate. "He'll be released tomorrow and needs to rest today. I'll check on him later this afternoon."

Michael stood off to the side with one hip leaned against a counter. "Good, whatever. Since I'm here, Maggie, I expect you to spend the day with me."

She turned her head to Sunny and winked. "I was thinking the same thing." Maggie rose and walked to Michael, putting her hand on his arm. "I think it's time for the grand tour of Brenham. I know you're going to love it."

"Uh, sure, I like that idea."

"Go get a jacket. It's chilly still. I'll meet you at the back door in ten minutes."

Michael hurried out of the kitchen while Maggie's parents looked at her like she'd grown horns. She waited a beat until he was up the stairs.

"I know how you feel about Michael. Believe me, he and I are over, once he accepts it. Sunny came up with a plan to get him to leave. I'll convince him how wonderful it is living in Brenham and that he should move here."

Bill nodded and smiled. "Reverse psychology, good idea."

~~*

As she drove to Adams Nursery, one of Brenham's hot spots, she considered calling June to let her know about Alex's accident. She still felt that June should know. But on the other hand, it really wasn't her business to get between Alex and his mother. She compromised with herself—as long as Alex was released tomorrow, she wouldn't call June. Fair enough.

"Where is it that we're going?" Michael looked out the window of the SUV, a bored expression on his face. "All the streets look alike, old trees and old buildings."

"I know, isn't it fabulous?" Maggie gushed. "We have great history here. We're the county seat for Washington County, the birthplace of Texas. It was one of the earliest settlements in the state. In fact—"

"I don't need to know the history."

"Sure you do. If you're going to live here, it helps to learn the background."

"Live here?" Michael's voice was a squeak.

"Uh-huh. I figure you'd rather live here than LA. There's so much to do and hardly any traffic, well, compared to LA."

"Where did you get that idea?"

Maggie reached toward him with her hand and squeezed his thigh. "Oh, babe, I know you'll love it here."

She watched him out of the corner of her eye. Michael didn't look happy. In fact, he looked confused and grumpy. Good. They drove in silence for another five minutes, until Maggie pulled into a parking lot.

"Why are we stopping here?" Michael looked like he'd swallowed a rat.

"Come on," Maggie chirped as she sailed out of the car. "This is Adams Nursery. It's a very old and prominent family business in Brenham. I thought it might help you get a lay of the land, business-wise that is." She opened the front door and smiled to herself as he entered in front of her. If her plan succeeded, he'd be heading due west first thing the next morning.

For at least an hour, Maggie provided the ten-cent tour of her favorite flowers and plants. Michael said few words as she gave him little opportunity with her non-stop monologue. They'd gone through half the nursery and arrived back in the main entrance area.

"What do you think?" Maggie beamed as she hugged Michael's arm. "Isn't it just wonderful?"

He shrugged. "It's okay I guess. I'm not much into green stuff."

"Really?" She looked at him with her hands on her hips. "I thought you loved to garden. Aren't you the one with pots of herbs on the terrace?"

"My cleaning lady does that. She says the pots make me look good."

"I see." Maggie debated about pushing it further then heard her name called and turned around. Hank Adams walked toward her. She hadn't seen him since the dinner at the Longhorn. He stopped in front of her, smiling. That put her on full alert.

Hank glanced at Michael and his eyes narrowed for a second. He quickly refocused on Maggie, and she introduced Michael to him. Neither man seemed terribly impressed with the other.

"I want to apologize to you," Hank said. "My

mother was out of line the way she talked to you that night at dinner. She gets her nose out of joint sometimes about our family history and for some reason it was one of those days."

Maggie's breath hitched and she braced herself next to Michael. "You're aware of your Grandfather Herbert and Robert Graham?"

"He told me a couple of days before he died. He wasn't proud of what he did, but he wasn't strong enough to go to the police either."

"Hmm." Maggie relaxed but had no clue how to respond. This conversation was a first. "But your mom's okay about it, right?"

"Yeah, fine." Hank waved at someone calling to him standing at the other end of the long hall dividing the nursery in half. "I have a question for you about the fire at your place."

"You heard about that?"

He grinned. "I know everything that goes on in this town. Anyway, do you suppose it might have been related to gang activity?"

"We've considered that but don't know anything for certain." Maggie glanced at Michael as he rolled his eyes. "Why do you ask?" She wouldn't share what Robert had told Sunny.

"The same night as your fire, we had some graffiti painted on the side of our building. Somebody dumped the contents of trashcans over a new garden area we hadn't finished yet. They left quite a mess."

Maggie's pulse hiccupped and raced along. "Really? I wonder if the police have connected the fire and your graffiti."

He shrugged. "I haven't talked to them yet. I just heard about the fire yesterday. That got me to thinking and here you are."

"I guess I could talk to the detective who came by," Maggie suggested.

Hank's name was yelled again. He absently patted her arm. "Think about it and let me know what you decide. We should talk to the police together."

"Okay, sounds good."

"I'll see you later." Hank nodded at Michael then jogged to the other end of the hall.

"Really, Maggie, that guy runs a prominent business?" Michael raised his chin and smirked. "Looks to me like he needs to go to school and learn about managing a business. This place is a dump."

She stiffened at his words—the conceited ass—but she managed to ignore them. "Let's continue our tour. Come on, it's lunch time." She grabbed his arm and led him to the parking lot. "I'm taking you to the best hamburger place west of the Mississippi."

Little was said on the drive to the Farmer's Market. She hoped the "best hamburger place in Brenham" would be the final nail in the proverbial coffin for Michael. Surely his big city arrogance would mock the restaurant and convince him he couldn't survive in a small Texas town.

She watched his face as she diagonally parked in front of the diner. His nose wrinkled and his lips thinned. Good, not liking it already.

Maggie dropped her keys in her purse and stepped

out of the car.

"Here we are, one of our very best dining establishments."

"Seriously?" The sneer on his face showed absolute disdain.

Maggie hurried Michael in the front door and scanned the tables looking for Fran. They made eye contact and Fran walked to a booth along the far wall.

"Come on," Maggie said cheerfully. She'd get through this lunch if it killed her. "Our booth is to the left." Michael followed her as she threaded through the tables in the center. He walked with his arms to his sides and dead center of the aisle to avoid touching anything.

"Good to see you, Maggie." Fran placed two worn menus on the tabletop. "I don't know your friend here."

"This is Michael Shaw, he's from Los Angeles." Maggie slid in across from him and smiled sweetly. "He decided to finally visit our little burg."

Fran raised her eyebrows and grinned. "Isn't that nice, welcome to Brenham. I'm sure you'll love it here. Beats the hell out of the big city. Now y'all look over the menus and I'll be back in a jiffy." She winked before she turned and walked to the kitchen.

Michael rolled his eyes and picked up the menu. He studied it for a good five minutes, scowling as he examined it from top to bottom.

Maggie sat quietly, waving a couple of times at people she knew. She wondered what was going through his mind—was he rethinking their relationship or crafting creative ways to get her back to LA? Didn't matter, she'd made up her mind.

They both ended up ordering cheeseburgers and fries. Michael acknowledged that the burger was good but he didn't much like the surroundings. Maggie surmised this through several negative and nasty comments including "Anyone here graduate from high school?" and "This place hasn't been updated since World War II." She congratulated herself on her plan. The more Michael hated Brenham, the easier it would be to get him out of her life.

Once he'd paid the check, Michael smiled and seized Maggie's hand lying on the table. "So, babe, what's next on the agenda? Does this town have any sharp boutiques? Let's get you a new outfit. You're looking a tad on the dreary side."

She once again resented his words. Dreary? He thought she looked dreary. Damn him. "How sweet of you to think of my wardrobe . . . but no, no boutiques here. We drive to Houston for the fancy stores." No need to mention Trina's Treats, a to-die-for store with the cutest trendy clothes.

He sighed, heavily. "Really, why do you live here?" He moved his right arm in a sweeping motion. "This place is tacky and the people, well, they aren't the sort of people we know in LA. Don't you miss all the action and the fun in California?"

"Would you like dessert?" Deflection in any situation counted as a character strength in Maggie's world. "Let me take you to the world's best ice cream. Come on, let's go."

An hour later, after Michael had sampled close to half a dozen flavors of Blue Bell ice cream at their factory store, he was finally happy.

"Man, that's good ice cream," he said. They were once again on the road. "Where to next? Didn't you say you were going to visit that guy in the hospital? Let's get that out of the way so we have the rest of the afternoon and evening to ourselves."

Maggie checked the digital clock on the dashboard, almost three-thirty. A visit to Alex at the hospital might well be the final nail in the "Operation Michael" coffin. Surely, he'd be convinced to go back to California once he met the competition. Honestly, she couldn't understand why he was being so hard headed about their relationship. She'd never have moved back to Brenham if he hadn't broken up with her in the first place. She shook her head, once again wondering what she'd ever seen in this dumb ass.

"Sure, let's drop by the hospital and you can meet Alex."

~~*

Alex was officially bored. He'd had a morning nap, a so-so lunch, and an afternoon nap. And now, he'd flipped on the television but couldn't find a program to keep his attention. He just wanted to go home, back to Maggie and The Blue Barn Inn. Although the nurse had taken away the ice bag, he continued to receive meds through the IV. He wanted to pull it out and—

"Alex, fantastic, you're awake," A smiling Maggie came into the room with some guy tailing behind her.

"Doing better." He was glad to see her but took an immediate dislike to the guy with her—too smooth and smarmy for his taste. My God, even his jeans had a crease down the center of the legs. No card-carrying man worth his salt sent his jeans to the dry cleaners.

She stopped at the foot of the bed. "How are you feeling?" The guy stood too damned close to her and stared at Alex wearing a smirk on his face.

"I'm fine. Who's your friend?" Alex had the distinct feeling this visit could only go downhill. Who the hell was this jerk?

"Sorry, this is Michael Shaw. He's a friend from LA."

Alex scratched his head. "Don't remember you mentioning a friend visiting."

"I came to surprise my girlfriend," Michael said as he placed his arm around Maggie's waist and pulled her against him. "I'm here to take her back to California, where she belongs." He placed a loud kiss on her temple. "You're one of her boarders at the B&B?"

This asshole was her boyfriend? Alex fought to control his emotions. He wanted to plant his fist on the guy's too pretty face. He watched her snuggle against him. She liked this guy? She could have him. Alex was done.

"I am for now, but I'll be leaving soon. I've got things to do." Alex ignored the surprise on Maggie's face. He'd known for years he was a lousy judge of women and he'd once again proved it. She'd been playing with him until her LA boyfriend swooshed in to lay his claim and convince her he couldn't live without her. No problem, Alex could deal with that.

Maggie shrugged off Michael and stepped to the bed. "Are you still being discharged tomorrow?"

"Not sure," Alex replied. "Depends on what the doc says in the morning. Anyway, thanks for coming by, nice to meet you Michael." He wanted to be alone so bad he damn near yelled.

"I want to drive you home," Maggie stated.

"Whatever." Alex's comeback was harsher than he intended. "Thanks for visiting."

Maggie frowned before giving him a small wave and then pulling Michael through the door.

Alex closed his eyes and swore to himself. Without a doubt he had the absolute worst luck of any man on the planet when it came to understanding women. Here he thought they were climbing the first steps toward a future together and poof, it evaporates with the arrival of her boyfriend.

Damn it. He would not go through this again. As soon as he could get his vehicle situation straightened out he'd head to Houston and his condo. He could finish his dissertation there.

At least he had a home.

Chapter Sixteen

November 11, Wednesday

Maggie hurried to clean up after breakfast, anticipating a phone call from Alex. She wanted to be ready to taxi him back to the Inn as soon as he called. And thankfully, Michael had gone to his room to finish a work project. He'd been putting it off since his arrival, and now it was crunch time. She hoped to convince him to leave the next day.

While she waited for Alex's call, she'd test a new recipe for sugar cookies. The dough needed to chill before she rolled it out so she started to gather her ingredients on the long center island.

"What are you doing?" Trudy asked as she entered the kitchen. "Your father is helping Jim, so I have some free time."

"Does that mean you guys aren't going to yell at me anymore about the bank loan and the renovation?"

Trudy stopped alongside Maggie and rubbed a hand over her back. "Yes, the yelling is over. I think you've learned your lesson, like a good daughter should."

"Thanks, Mom. I really am sorry I didn't talk to you guys first . . . but renovating the Barn is a smart business move."

"That it is, sweet pea." Trudy pointed to the items on the counter. "What are you making here?"

"Trying out a new sugar cookie recipe. The last one was too dry."

"Sounds like fun. I'll help."

"Cool. There's an apron in the pantry."

Trudy retrieved the apron and tied it around her waist. "Where's Sunny? Maybe she'd like to join us."

"No way. She's doing her monthly cleaning schedule since we're almost empty. I never interrupt her once she's started." Maggie dropped cubes of butter in the mixer bowl.

"Why not?"

"Mom, don't you know how overly organized daughter number two is now? Plus she'd rather dust than make cookies." Maggie spread her hands in a "go figure" motion.

Trudy shook her head. "I remember her room always being a mess when she lived at home. Let me see your recipe."

"Motherhood has whipped her into shape." Maggie handed the card to her mom and cracked eggs into the stand mixer's bowl. A single flip of the switch started the blending process.

"I think the recipe needs another cup of sugar and double the vanilla," Trudy said.

"Okay." Maggie looked at the digital clock on the microwave—10:57. Why hadn't she heard from Alex? Maybe he was waiting for the doctor to discharge him. She'd heard that could sometimes take hours. Oh well, she'd be patient. And she'd have freshly baked cookies for him when he returned home.

~~*

The sky slipped toward dusk by the time Alex finally got to the Inn. The doctor didn't give the discharge order until early afternoon and then he had to wait for the discharge nurse to get all the papers together along with a pain killer prescription. He'd refused his last dose since he'd be driving. He could tough it out.

He'd called Fran Walters before lunch and she'd agreed to drive him from the hospital to a rental car agency. When she arrived she'd already retrieved his messenger bag from his SUV towed to a wrecker lot somewhere. He'd deal with the vehicle once he got back to Houston. She was a real sweetheart and didn't ask one question as to why she was helping him rather than Maggie. Although she did give him a strange look which he had expected.

Once he had the rental car he stopped by a drugstore to fill the pain killer prescription and then a fast food drive-in for a burger and fries. His plan was to slip in the back door of the Inn. He could hide out in his room without anyone knowing he'd returned. Seemed like a good plan.

Until it wasn't. The minute he stepped inside the back door holding his burger bag and prescription, Maggie came down the hall from the living room. She must have been looking out the front window.

"Alex, my God, where have you been?" She threw her arms around him. "It's so good to see you."

The warmth of her arms nearly undid his resolve. He could easily have caved so he stepped back from her and untangled her arms. "Sorry, my ribs are still sore."

"Oh, I'm sorry. Why didn't you call me? I've been waiting to pick you up. How do you feel? How did you get here?" She stroked her hand over his forehead. "Are you hungry?"

He raised the bag of fast food. "I'm good. A friend took me to get a rental car. I'm leaving early in the morning and have some stuff to do. I'll see you later."

"What? You're leaving? Where are you going?"

"I'm going back to Houston to finish my work." He moved to the door of his room and turned the key in the lock. "My prepayment should take care of everything on my bill."

Maggie's eyes were wide and he could tell she was close to tears. What a joke.

"Why are you leaving? I thought we were—"

"I'll be heading out early." He walked into the room and turned to her. "I'll leave my key on the desk. Have a great life with your boyfriend."

"But wait, Michael and I aren't—"

He shut the door in her face.

And felt like a jerk doing it.

He did not want to think about the combined look of surprise and despair as the door closed.

After eating his dinner, he swallowed a painkiller. He relaxed a bit before taking stock of his belongings. Packing shouldn't be a big problem. He hadn't accumulated much since he'd been in Brenham, paper mostly. He could stuff everything into the two suitcases he'd brought with him. Tyler's book and fire truck stayed on the closet shelf.

He placed clothes for tomorrow and his toiletry kit on the desk chair then packed everything else. He finished in less than thirty minutes and settled on the bed, flipping on the TV for some news—anything to keep his mind off Maggie.

He debated about calling his mother to let her know he was fine after a car accident and that he was returning to Houston. She'd fuss at him for not telling her earlier about the accident and disagree with him for leaving Brenham.

He blew a heavy breath. How had his life gotten so damned complicated?

He pulled his cell phone from his pocket and touched his mother's contact. If he were fortunate, she'd be busy or asleep or had lost her phone.

This was not his lucky week.

"Alex, sweetie, how are you?"

"Good. How are you?"

"You're stalling, what's going on?" June continued to amaze Alex. She had an innate sensor that detected stress and comforting needed like no one else. No wonder Roger wanted to marry her.

"I wanted to give you an update on what's going on with me."

"Oh?"

"I'm moving back to the condo tomorrow."

"Why? Surely you're not done with all your school writing."

"Um . . . no, I'm not done writing but I think I'll work better in Houston."

"Better in Houston, huh? Does this have to do with

Maggie? I thought you two were getting to be friends, good friends."

"Yeah, we're friends I guess, but she has a boyfriend."

"Oh. I didn't know that. Working at home is probably for the best then. Let me know when you're home. You can have lunch with Roger and me. We've been trying out new recipes a couple of times a week. Tomorrow is sweet and sour pork."

"I'd like that. I'll call you once I'm at the condo. Good night, Mom."

Alex decided not to tell her about the accident. What purpose would it serve? He was fine with no lingering after effects other than sore ribs and a bit of a headache. The pills took care of that. He figured after tonight he'd hold off on another pill until he reached his condo.

He stripped down to his boxers and flopped on the bed. He wasn't really tired and needed to wait an hour before another pill. He flipped though the channels looking for ESPN. Sports always took his mind off his problems.

But wait, he didn't have any problems. He was leaving them in his rearview window when he drove out of Brenham in the morning. He set his phone for a five a.m. alarm. He'd be long gone before Maggie woke up to run.

The last thing he needed was to talk with her again. Or see her again. Or think about how he felt about her.

Right, no problems at all.

~~*

Although she was in shock, Maggie managed to get

through dinner with her family and Michael without anyone being the wiser, except for Sunny, of course. She came back downstairs as soon as she put Tyler down for the night. Michael had returned to his room to finish his work project and Bill and Trudy had decided to visit a neighbor.

"What's going on?" Sunny went to the wine cellar and pulled out a bottle of red. "I figure we might need this since Alex wasn't at dinner." She opened the bottle and grabbed two glasses from a cabinet.

Maggie plopped in a chair at the kitchen table. "Everything is so screwed up." She bowed her head and tears welled in her eyes. Brushing them away with the back of her hand, she sucked in a deep breath. "Alex is leaving tomorrow, going back to Houston."

"Why? I can't believe he finished his dissertation already. Surely he—"

"He thinks Michael is my boyfriend."

Sunny sat and poured the wine. She handed a glass to her sister. "Now, why would he think that?"

"At the hospital yesterday, Michael may have called me his girlfriend." Maggie spoke quietly, knowing full well what Sunny would say.

"You didn't correct him in front of Alex," Sunny said matter-of-factly. "That was a rotten thing to do. Geez, sis, the poor guy had just been in a car accident and you take Michael with you to the hospital. Why in the world did you do that?"

Maggie raised her hands to stop further questions. "I know, I know. I should never have taken Michael with me and I should have corrected him about the 'girlfriend' comment. I'm a big jerk."

"For once, I agree with you." Sunny grinned then drank her wine. "Tell me exactly what Alex said to you."

Maggie gulped her wine then repeated the conversation at the hospital and the one in the hallway. "I have screwed up to the nth degree."

"True. But why didn't Alex want to talk with you? Seems to me he would have wanted to hear you confirm what Michael said."

Maggie poured more wine in her glass. She chewed on the corner of her mouth while she thought about Sunny's question. Why didn't Alex confront her about "being Michael's girlfriend" rather than accept it and brush her off? He didn't give her a chance to explain. "He didn't ask me for any explanation, just accepted what Michael said."

"Did I hear my name?" Michael walked into the kitchen wearing a tee shirt and pajama bottoms, totally decent but strange for him all the same. Usually he dressed like a male model.

"Do you need something?" Maggie said with much more politeness than Michael deserved.

"I'd love to have a glass of wine with you." He winked then stationed himself across from Maggie. Sunny rose to get another glass and poured him some wine.

Maggie wanted to scream. She'd had it with this man. "Michael, you need to leave. You need to go back to California."

He casually sipped his wine and smiled slowly. "Babe, I thought you wanted me to live in Brenham. I've been thinking about that and it makes sense."

"No, it doesn't." Panic coursed through Maggie. What had she done?

"It does. I've worked all day on this stupid project and still have another couple of hours before it's finished. Who wants to work that hard? I bet there's a need for marketing experts here." He looked at Maggie, licking his lips. "I bet we could start our own company. You know, deal with the hicks and the farmers. Are there ranchers here, too? Whatever, we—"

"No," Maggie yelled, nearly jumping out of her chair. She willed herself to remain calm. "Michael, we are not starting a business together. I'm not your girlfriend. You do not want to live here. LA is your style. Go home."

He reached out and patted her hand like it was a dog's head. "Aw, babe, you're just tired. We can talk in the morning." He rose, drained the glass Sunny had provided, walked around the table, and kissed the top of Maggie's head. "Good night. Maybe we should go house hunting tomorrow."

Michael walked out of the kitchen while Maggie made a stabbing motion with her hand.

"That man doesn't listen." Sunny shook her head. "He simply won't take a 'no' from you."

"It's so unlike him. He usually doesn't like any kind of confrontation."

"Hmm . . ." Sunny tapped a finger against her chin. "What can we do to persuade him to leave?"

"How about I kick his ass out the front door first thing in the morning?"

"You can try." Sunny sighed. "This is just so weird. Men don't act like this. Maybe he's playing a game of some sort."

"Like if I say 'yes' then he'll dump me again?"

"Maybe," Sunny said. "But that's sick in so many ways."

"I know." Maggie started to laugh. "Maybe I should try that, too. We could do an experiment."

Sunny started laughing as well. "Or we could have Robert scare the crap out of him."

"Why do you say that?"

"I saw him today when I was cleaning. He smiled and watched me clean. Didn't say a word though."

Maggie drained her glass then rose and placed it in the sink. "Unfortunately we don't have a resident ghost who performs on command. I'll figure something out to coax Michael back to California."

Sunny put her glass in the sink then hugged her sister. "I have faith in you. Michael won't know what hit him."

"Uh-huh." Maggie squeezed her shoulder. "Good night."

Sunny hugged her and walked toward the back stairs.

Maggie went through the dining room to the hallway. She had a half-baked idea to try to talk with Alex before he left. She stopped at the door of his room and raised her hand. But she didn't knock. She turned and walked through the Inn to her bedroom.

While changing into pajamas, she reasoned with herself that it was late and he was probably asleep. That's why she didn't knock. She slid under the bedcovers and turned on her side.

Yeah, it was nearly midnight and too late to talk with Alex. That explanation for not knocking on his door made complete sense, while unfortunately, the truth did not.

One light still burned on the second floor of the Inn late Wednesday night, actually Thursday morning. Michael had worked his fingers to the bone punching the keys on his keyboard. God, he hated doing all this busy work. He was more of a Public Relations guy, wining and dining clients rather than actually working for them.

But, whatever, PR Manager would be his next job title if he worked things right back in LA. He made one last change on the proposal project, wrote a decent message to his boss, and clicked the Send button on his email account. He rose from the desk chair and stretched his arms to the ceiling. Damn, his back was full of knots. He turned around and jumped a foot off the floor, his heart pounding like he'd run five miles full out.

Backing up toward the door, he stumbled over his shoes. What should he do? The . . . the thing on his bed moved. It slid to the foot of the bed and waved its arms around in front of its body, not that there was a body. It seemed like a man, maybe, but it was transparent without its sides being clearly defined. The body shape was clear then became distorted, then slowly swirled around an axis of some sort. Then it was clearly a man's shape.

He stared at it so hard his eyeballs hurt and he finally remembered to breathe.

"Wha . . . what do you want?" Did this thing even talk? It slithered off the bed and floated toward Michael. *OMG, it was a ghost.* He staggered backwards and his back hit the door. The thing stopped moving, just stood still, not more than three feet from him. "Why are you here?"

The ghost stood, floated actually, in front of him. He had to get away from it. Sneaking his arm behind his back, he searched for the doorknob.

Michael had a problem, the door opened into the room, not out into the hall. He'd have to be quick to get out of the room. His hand found the knob.

The thing floated closer and now resembled a human. A hole appeared where a human mouth would be located. Smoke or fog spewed from the hole and flowed over him.

Michael stiffened instantly. He was frozen in place at the stupid Inn.

The apparition raised an arm toward the window of the room. "Leave this house. You are not wanted here." The words were clear but gravelly sounding.

"Wh, what did you say?" The fog became very cold on Michael's skin.

The ghost moved closer to him. "Leave this house or you will die." It moved right through Michael, through the door, and was gone, disappearing before his eyes.

Immediately, the cold lessened and his brain began to function again. Damn straight he'd leave this house. Maggie had no appeal to him any longer. She really was a small town girl—boring as a stick.

He checked his watch, almost three a.m., the perfect

time to get out of this crazy house and on the road. He quickly packed his suitcase and stuffed his laptop into his computer briefcase. He scribbled a note for Maggie to leave on the kitchen table: "Sorry to leave w/out saying bye . . . you're right, this town sucks."

He left the note and rolled his bag to the backdoor and to his car. Within ten minutes he turned onto Highway 290 heading toward Houston.

Hot damn, California! I'm coming home, baby.

Chapter Seventeen

November 12, Thursday

The temperature dropped considerably over night, just two weeks before Thanksgiving. Maggie finished cleaning the kitchen after breakfast and hugged her arms around her chest. Maybe she should start a fire in the living room. She felt chilled to her bones.

But the weather hadn't put ice around her heart, Alex had when he'd left earlier that morning. She'd had a hard time sleeping and woke earlier than normal for her usual run. As she stretched on the porch, she'd watched his rental car creep down the driveway then turn into the street. It drove slowly by the front of the house then sped up and turned a corner.

Surely Alex saw her plain as day on the porch. He didn't even honk. She'd stomped her foot in frustration and went back inside. Screw running; she'd needed coffee, lots of coffee.

And now, over four hours later, her mood hadn't improved. Although the one bright spot in her morning was Michael leaving, skulking away in the middle of the night. At least he had left her a note. She had no clue why he'd left as he did, but it made her happy that he was headed back to California and out of her hair for good.

Maggie glanced around the empty kitchen. Why not start a fire and think about preparing the Inn for the holidays. Surely her ability to think straight would return once she focused on a goal rather than her broken heart.

She hurried out the back door to gather a load of wood from the box. Upon returning, she met her mother at the living room entrance.

"Building a fire, sweetheart?"

Maggie nodded and unloaded the wood in the large basket to the side of the fireplace. "Thought I might as well inaugurate the cold weather with a fire."

"That sounds like a fine idea to me." Trudy smiled and patted her arm. "I'll make hot chocolate and we can talk."

As she knelt and added kindling to the grate, Maggie muttered, "Tired of talking, nothing helps." She added a couple of logs and pulled a long match from the box on top of the mantle. Striking it on the brick hearth, she used the flame to light the kindling in several places. The wood was dry so it didn't take long before the logs caught fire.

Maggie gathered her notebook and pen and sat cross-legged on the comfy sofa in front of the fireplace. Regardless of her heartache at Alex leaving, her sense of belonging in Brenham and at the Inn nearly had her weeping. Finally, her life had a path, one she'd do her best to follow even if she'd be traveling alone.

She watched the fire gain momentum as the flames expanded around the sides of the logs, crackling and popping. She'd loved watching a fire since she'd been a little girl. Its warmth had always made her feel secure and well, loved. Yep, she'd always known the security of her parents' love.

She hadn't thought about that in a long time.

Trudy came back carrying two mugs and handed one to Maggie. "Here you go." She settled in a club chair to the side of the fireplace. "Where's Sunny this morning?"

"She took Tyler to a children's hour at the library. Not sure he's old enough to enjoy it but she's trying."

"Maybe he should attend one of those mother's-day-out programs." Trudy smiled as she spoke. Maggie had always admired her mother's easy smile. She habitually found the good and positive in any situation.

"She's talked about one at the First Methodist Church. I guess it depends on whether she's still here next fall."

"Right . . . depends on Jason's enlistment. Being an Army wife can't be easy for family planning."

"No kidding," Maggie said licking her lips. Her mom made the world's best hot chocolate. "I've been thinking about them. Do you suppose I could convince Sunny and Jason to settle here in Brenham? I know that's selfish on my part."

"I like the idea too, but it's up to them. Sunny could continue to work here but what about Jason? I can't imagine there would be enough work to keep him occupied or even interested."

"Maybe he'd want to go to college. Sunny said he graduated high school with a high GPA."

Trudy was silent for several moments, her gaze locked on the fireplace. She sipped her drink then looked at Maggie. "Times like this make me sorry we moved to Florida. If only—"

"Mom, no, don't be sorry. You did what was best for Dad and his health. That's what's important."

"I know you're right."

"Plus, you guys have made friends down there and seem awfully busy." Maggie would love for her parents to live in Brenham but she wouldn't push it. They were happy in sunny Florida and that's what was important. "We all need to visit for holidays, either here or there."

"That reminds me. We're leaving first thing on Saturday morning. We booked a Caribbean cruise over Thanksgiving and need to be back in time to get ready."

"Really? I'd hoped you stay until then."

"Not this time, sweetie." Trudy rose and picked up Maggie's empty mug. "We'll be back for Christmas though. You can count on it. I'll be right back." She left with the dirty cups.

Maggie opened her notebook and wrote "Thanksgiving Dinner Menu" at the top of the page. She chewed on the pen's clicker while she considered her options. Turkey was the traditional mainstay that all the side dishes rotated around. Did she want a traditional meal or to go in the opposite direction, say enchiladas? Or be really edgy and not cook at all. That of course wasn't an option as they had guests booked over the holiday.

Trudy returned carrying a small book.

"Where's Dad? I haven't seen him since breakfast."

"He took the RV over to Arthur Sims' car place. Get it checked out for the trip back to Florida and do guy stuff." Trudy sat on the sofa next to Maggie. "I have something for you."

"What is it?"

"I found this at the secondhand bookstore yesterday and thought of you and Alex." Trudy smiled knowingly. "I realize things have changed with him leaving but this book might give you something to think about. It contains famous love letters written through the years. Some of them are simply heart wrenching."

Teary eyed, Maggie accepted the book from her mother. "Thank you." She rubbed her eyes and faced Trudy. "I really screwed up with Alex."

"I do think you made a mistake in taking Michael to the hospital and—"

"It was worse than a mistake, it was . . . a huge error."

"As I was saying," Trudy said, raising an eyebrow. "I also think Alex is at fault for not giving you a chance to explain that Michael was being a jerk with his insinuation. Heavens, both men left on the same day."

"That was strange, wasn't it?"

"Maybe it was a simple coincidence. What are your plans concerning Alex?"

"Plans?" Maggie hadn't thought any further than wallowing in her heartache.

"Of course, plans. You're not going to let Alex get away with this, are you?"

"Honestly, Mom, I've been so upset I can't think straight."

"You need to talk with him. At least write him a letter. But, give it a few days. Give him time to think about the wisdom of moving back to Houston." Trudy nodded at the book. "Read some of those letters. You never know, they might give you inspiration."

Maggie leaned over and gave Trudy a one-armed hug. "You are one smart mama."

The backdoor slammed and footsteps sounded moving down the hallway.

"Hey, where is everyone?" Sunny called out.

"We're in the living room," Trudy yelled.

Within seconds, Tyler ran around the corner and went directly to Trudy. "Gammy, Gammy." He held his arms out to her and she lifted him onto her lap.

"Hey big guy, did you have fun at the library?" Trudy kissed the top of his head.

"He was actually pretty good, listened for over five minutes before he got antsy." Sunny lifted a tote bag. "We got some books after that. Let me get that coat off of him."

"Would you girls like to go to lunch?" Trudy combed Tyler's soft curls with her fingers.

Sunny looked over her shoulder. "Sure, as long as we go now. Tyler won't make it more than an hour before needing a nap."

"Sounds good to me. Meet y'all at the back door in sixty seconds." Maggie headed to her bedroom for her jacket. Lunch with her mom, sister, and nephew— exactly what she needed to boost her spirits.

~~*

Alex stopped for coffee and a sausage-biscuit at a drive-thru a few minutes from his condo and still made it back before eight a.m. He hated returning to Houston but what else could he have done? Michael, the asshole, had made it perfectly clear that Maggie was taken.

He dropped his luggage in the condo's foyer and kicked a suitcase on his way to the terrace. He took his coffee and biscuit with him, hoping the cold air might cool his anger.

He sat on a chair and sipped the strong, hot coffee, letting it warm his throat. He inhaled the biscuit and eventually finished the coffee. That would tide him over until lunch with his mom and Roger.

Damn.

He gave his mother a hard time on a regular basis because he loved her. But she was too smart not to see through the "Maggie has a boyfriend" explanation. Even though she was the best mom in the world, she wouldn't hesitate to question his story if she had doubts.

He rose and glanced toward the park across the street, remembering the joy in Maggie's face when he'd taken her there. He pushed the memory aside and grabbed his phone. He may as well call his mom now. He'd put off calling her long enough.

Three hours later and still feeling like crap, Alex had managed to unpack his suitcases. He stood in front of the bathroom sink and splashed cold water on his face. Studying himself in the mirror, he easily noticed the shadows under his eyes and lines around his mouth that had appeared overnight. *Jesus Brady, get your shit together.*

Determined to get the lunch over with so he could pout in private, he marched back to the kitchen, gathered his cell phone and shrugged on a jacket. June would be waiting for him. He paused suddenly as a new thought struck him. This would be his first time in her new home—the one she now shared with Roger.

Unbelievable.

He released a low groan, wondering if this day could possibly get any worse.

Thirteen minutes later, he parked his rental car in front of Roger's one-story Mediterranean style house. Although he'd given Roger his blessing on their engagement, Alex still felt weird being at their home for the first time, especially since they weren't yet married. He walked up the flagstone path to the front door and shook his head as he pushed the doorbell. Damn, was he old fashioned, or what?

The arched dark oak door opened immediately. June stepped forward and threw her arms around her son. Alex hugged her back.

"Hey, Mom, good to see you."

June pulled back and searched her son's eyes. "Are you okay?"

He smiled. "Yes, of course. Where's Roger?"

A knowing look crossed June's face then she tucked her arm in his. "He's in the kitchen finalizing our lunch. Promise me you won't be too honest if the food tastes terrible."

"You can count on me to be discreet." He pressed his lips together to keep from laughing. Leave it to his mom to take the edge off a lousy mood.

June escorted him to the back of the house on shiny oak floors. They entered a huge combination kitchen and family room. The dark furniture contrasted sharply against the walls painted in a light yellow color.

"Alex, it's good to see you." Roger came around the island counter and offered his hand. "Welcome back to Houston."

"Thanks." Alex shook his hand and lifted his nose to the air. "Appreciate the lunch invitation. Something smells really good by the way."

"Hope you like Chinese." Roger moved to the stove and stirred a wide pan. He turned around and brandished his hand over the stove. "On today's menu we have sweet and sour pork and stir-fried rice. June, I think we're ready."

"We're informal here." She grinned and motioned for Alex to sit at the counter where placemats were already set. "How about a beer? We have a new brand we're trying."

"Sounds good, it's five o'clock somewhere." Alex chuckled at his escalating comfort level in Roger's, now June's, home. His earlier anxiety about their living arrangement evaporated faster than spit on the Fourth of July.

Roger dished the food into wide blue bowls and June served the beer. They both joined Alex at the counter with June seated in the middle.

"I changed the pork recipe just a tad," Roger said. "I added broccoli to make it healthier. Hope you like it."

Alex added a good portion of both the pork and the rice to his plate and tasted the pork. At least the man could cook. He mentally sighed, so far so good.

"This is good. Kudos to the chef."

Roger beamed at him. "Thank you, Alex. June and I

are trying the cuisines of different countries."

Alex wiped his mouth with a napkin. "Seems like a great idea since you like to cook."

June giggled. "We have an ulterior motive. It's our method of deciding where to go on our honeymoon."

"Really?" Alex looked up, totally surprised. What a cool idea. Maggie would love it. Damn. "Have you narrowed down any locations?"

Roger put his hand over June's. "I think we've decided to visit France and Italy."

"Excellent choices. Mom, I know you'll love the cuisine of both countries."

Alex left three hours later. He'd had a great time with them, first discussing places to visit on their honeymoon and moving on to NFL football with Roger, a huge Texans fan. Alex had an up close and personal opportunity to see them as a couple and he liked what he saw. Go Mom.

His earlier reservations about June and Roger marrying had evaporated. He actually welcomed having Roger as a stepfather and told him so. That brought on tears from June and a hug from Roger. He felt good. Having Roger as a member of this newly formed family felt right, perfect in fact. They made plans to get together with Roger's sons the next week.

He couldn't help but think about Maggie as he drove back to the condo. She would appreciate their idea of cooking different cuisines to determine a vacation spot. It had the right amount of fun to appeal to her. He loved her for that.

Alex nearly plowed into a truck in front of him. Had

he just admitted to himself that he loved Maggie? Beads of sweat suddenly appeared on his forehead. He wiped them off with the back of his hand, finally seeing the truth of the matter.

He pounded on the steering wheel with one fist. Damn if this wasn't the absolute worst time to be in love—the real kind of love—the kind that blasted his guts and sent him into emotional overload.

He released a low growl at the futility of the situation. Loving Maggie now, or at any other time, was nothing but a waste of his emotions. She already had a boyfriend.

He calmed himself by thinking about the table of contents of his dissertation as he parked in the garage and rode the back elevator to his condo floor. After pulling a beer out of the refrigerator, he once again settled in a lounge chair on the terrace.

Even with sunshine and a clear sky, the temperature had dropped a good thirty degrees and he was chilly without a jacket. He looked at the street below, his thoughts centered on Maggie, and how things had become so screwed up so quickly. He didn't even know when the boyfriend had arrived in Brenham.

Had Maggie asked him to come? Or, had he traveled from California on a whim?

When he'd said his good-byes after lunch, his mother had cautioned him about accepting things as they appeared on the surface. She'd counseled him to think again about not giving up on Maggie and jumping to conclusions.

Alex squinted his eyes at the sun. Yeah, he'd think

about it—in a couple of days after his anger at Maggie and the situation had exhausted itself.

~~*

"Hey Jim, how's everything going?" Maggie had trekked through the back door of the Barn to find Jim. For the past week she'd been derelict in keeping track of the renovation's progress, and she intended to correct that now.

He pulled a filter mask off his face. He'd been spraying insulation on the walls of the main dining room. "Nice to see you. Lots to do, but we're making progress."

She glanced around the space and didn't see any evidence of the fire. "Looks like you've finished the cleanup." She motioned for Jim to follow her toward the foyer by the main door where they could talk in private. "Please be honest with me, do we have a chance in hell of finishing according to our original schedule?"

"We're working our butts off to get back on schedule. I should know for sure by the end of next week."

Maggie nodded. "Fair enough." She'd keep her fingers crossed for the super human intervention they'd need to get back to her original timeline. "I trust you. I know this can't be easy."

"Thanks, Miss Maggie, I appreciate that."

They walked back into the banquet area. Hammering from the bathroom suite area to the left accentuated just how hard Jim and his crew were working. "It's so weird that we're in this situation. I still can't imagine who started the fire." No way could she share that Robert had talked to the kid who started the fire.

"Ya know, sometimes the most unexpected person is responsible." Jim nodded at her and stepped away. "I need to get back to work."

What a strange thing to say. What did it mean? Maggie watched him retrieve the hose, realign his facemask, and begin to spray the insulation once again. She shook her head and retreated to the back door of the Inn—too many unanswered questions.

The house was silent so she made a beeline for her bedroom and the book of letters her mother had given to her.

After getting comfortable on the bed, propped against a slew of pillows, she finally opened the book and turned to the table of contents. Letters from various famous people were listed while the second half of the book was a how-to on writing your own love letter.

Maggie laid the book on her lap and considered writing a letter to Alex. It didn't need to be a full on love letter . . . but it could be a letter that explained how sorry she was for the screw up with Michael. She closed her eyes and imagined the words she might use . . . I screwed up, I'm sorry, please forgive me.

Her eyes zipped open. Damn, she sucked at writing anything other than advertising copy or a grocery list and definitely needed help with the words of love. She opened the book to the first passage with words from Elizabeth Barrett Browning:

You have touched me more profoundly than I thought even you could have touched me - my heart was full when you came here today.

Henceforward I am yours for everything.

Her body sagged in the bed. Good grief, she was doomed. How in the world could she ever express her feelings for Alex so eloquently? Well, she couldn't and she wasn't expected to. She thumbed through a few more pages and landed on words from Victor Hugo:

My adorable and adored, I have been asking myself every moment if such happiness is not a dream.
It seems to me that what I feel is not of earth.
I cannot yet comprehend this cloudless heaven.
My whole soul is yours.

Yep, she was definitely doomed. Her twelfth grade English class had not prepared her for mimicking these wonderful writers. Hmm, she'd try one more passage and flipped the pages to Johann Wolfgang von Goethe:

I can't help loving you more than is good for me; I shall feel all the happier when I see you again.
I am always conscious of my nearness to you, your presence never leaves me.
Adieu, you whom I love a thousand times.

That was it. She couldn't compete with the prose of great writers and would need to figure out the right words by herself. She scanned the first page of the how-to section and noted four topics related to your significant other: identify his number one physical attribute, pinpoint your primary emotion that comes to mind when thinking of him, name a trait or habit of his you love, and name a favorite activity he loves that you enjoy.

That was enough reading. She went to her desk for a pad of paper and a pen and sat in the yellow chair in the corner. She tucked the book beside her leg and poised the pen over the paper. This she could do.

Five minutes later with not one word on paper, she rose and paced her room. Maybe she was making this too hard, putting too much pressure on getting the exact right words. What she wanted to say rested in her heart. How to put that into words?

She decided to keep it simple and returned to the chair. Picking up the paper and pen, Maggie jotted down the four topics and then the first thing that came to her mind in response to each one. Hmm, this was better and gave her something to think about. She circled words from each of the topics: blue eyes, comfort, dedicated, and drinking wine.

Closing her eyes, she pictured Alex the first time he'd appeared in her kitchen. He was such a gentleman and didn't laugh when he caught her rubbing her butt after hitting the floor. She'd been intrigued right from the beginning. Hmm . . . maybe that would be a place to start. She began to write the words from her heart on paper.

Chapter Eighteen

November 14, Saturday

Mid-morning Maggie hurried out the back door of the Inn carrying a small Styrofoam cooler. She handed it to her mother as she exited the RV.

"What's this?" Trudy said.

"I made you lunch. I figured it would be better than stopping for fast food."

"Aw, thanks, sweetie. We'll stop under a nice tree and have a picnic." Trudy accepted the cooler as Bill came around the back corner of the RV. "Look, we have lunch."

"Great idea," Bill said while hugging Maggie. "I think we're ready to get on the road. Everything is ship shape."

Sunny carried Tyler down the back steps. "Wait."

Bill went to her and took Tyler into his arms. "We wouldn't leave without saying good-bye to our favorite grandson."

"He's your only grandson," Sunny commented.

Bill hugged Tyler. "Exactly, and we love him so much."

Trudy pulled Maggie to the front of the RV. "I want you to know that you're doing a terrific job managing the

Inn." She placed two hands on Maggie's shoulders. "Remodeling the Barn was a fabulous idea, and your father and I think it will be a huge success." Trudy hugged her oldest daughter and stepped back. "We're both thrilled you've decided to stay in Brenham."

"Thanks Mom, that means a lot." Having her parents' blessing of her plans for the Barn was a huge relief. Tendrils of excitement for the future swirled through her.

"I have one piece of advice concerning Alex. Give him time to figure out his own head but don't wait too long. Go to Houston. Go after him. You'll know when the time is right."

Maggie blinked back tears. "You're always so dead-on with your wisdom."

"Part of the mom-thing. You'll do it yourself one day."

"Come on, we need to get on the road," Bill called to his wife.

After a round of hugs and kisses, Bill and Trudy boarded the RV and drove along the driveway on the side of the Inn. Maggie, Sunny, and Tyler followed the vehicle and waved until it hit the street and turned right. The horn honked and they waved harder. Within seconds it was out of sight, on its way to Florida.

Maggie threw her arm over Sunny's shoulder. "I guess it's just you and me."

"Uh-huh, you and me."

They walked through the backdoor and headed to the kitchen. Maggie had a plan for the day with a task she'd been delaying. Today was the day.

Sunny opened the cookie jar. "What are you doing today?"

Maggie put on an apron and started to gather her ingredients. She came out of the pantry and faced her sister. "I'm doing something I've put off far too long."

"And what is that?" Sunny gave Tyler an oatmeal cookie with a cup of milk. Then took a bite of her own cookie.

"I plan to conquer the production of flaky pie crust."

Sunny coughed, nearly choking. "The production of pie crust?"

"That's right. I'll make it until I get it right using Grandma Todd's recipe."

Sunny rolled her eyes while grinning wickedly. "Whatever floats your boat. Tyler and I are going to look at Christmas catalogs and decide on the toys he likes best."

"Right, like he'll pick out his own toys."

"It's the mother-son bonding that counts." Sunny poured a cup of coffee from the carafe and grabbed Tyler's milk cup along with another cookie. "We'll be in the living room in case you need assistance."

"All right, y'all have fun dreaming about Christmas morning. I'll be right here," she murmured. "Attempting to make the perfect crust."

Maggie had purchased fruit, coconut, nuts, and chocolate for her pies. Baking would occupy her day and hopefully keep her mind off of Alex. She didn't know if there was a right time to contact him, but she did know it wasn't today, or even next week. She needed time as well, time to translate the words of her heart into an adult conversation with Alex.

So today was "perfect the pie crust" day with six different pies. She'd probably gain five pounds by looking at them when they were all finished. And then with the tasting, another five pounds. She chuckled at herself. Thank God she was a runner since she enjoyed her own cooking so darn much.

"My mother made pies."

Maggie slowly raised her head from chopping squares of chocolate. She hadn't heard Robert enter the kitchen. Right, ghosts didn't make noise when they moved, did they? He stood in the doorway leading to the dining room. The outline of his body was distinct.

"How are you, Robert? Thanks for helping my sister the night of the fire."

"You're welcome." He moved a step closer to the island counter. "What kind of pie are you making?"

"This is a chocolate pie." She itched to ask him about the teenager that started the fire and knew she needed to go slow. Last thing she wanted was an irritated spirit.

"I don't know what that is. My mother made apple pie and cherry pie and once in a while rhubarb. Apple pie was my favorite. I used to help her pick the apples."

"Did you live on a farm when you were a young boy?"

He nodded. "I hated it, too much hard work. That's why I went to business school when I graduated high school."

She added the chocolate to sugar and flour in a saucepan. "Then you started working for the bank?"

"I met Grace the first day of work—my lucky day." His voice broke and he backed through the door into the dining room. "I don't want to think about my Grace." He evaporated into the air.

"Damn," Maggie muttered. "Didn't mean to upset him." She sighed. She had a lot to learn about properly dealing with ghosts. She placed the saucepan on a burner and began to slowly add milk. Within five minutes she had the pie filling and poured it into a baked crust.

Right after she put the chocolate cream pie in the refrigerator, the business line rang. She went to the office to answer it.

"Maggie, is that you? This is June Brady."

"Hi June, how are you?" Her heart contracted with an immediate sense of dread. Had something happened to Alex?

"I'm just fine." June sounded calm and, well, motherly. Maggie felt close to her simply by hearing her voice. "I'm calling to make a reservation over Christmas. I hope you're not booked."

"Let me look at my system." Maggie sat down and clicked on the reservation system icon on the desktop.

"I'm also calling to book a wedding at the Barn."

Maggie's stomach plummeted to middle earth . . . a wedding? "That sounds great. Let's start with the dates."

"Roger and I would like a room, the same one we had in October if possible, from December 22 through December 28. Will that work?"

They'd be here during the Christmas holiday. Maggie's breathing quickened. Would Alex be with them? She checked the system and the Lavender Room was open.

"The room is open. I'll put you down. Should I use the same information as your last reservation?"

"Oh, that's wonderful. Yes, same info." June's voice bubbled with joy. "And, I'd like to book a wedding at the Barn for December 27th."

"That date is open and the names of the bride and groom?" Maggie crossed her fingers, hoping Alex wasn't the groom.

"I'm surprised you need to ask that," June said. "Don't you remember Roger and I became engaged in Brenham?"

Maggie rubbed a hand over her forehead. How could she forget that? "Sorry. I didn't think it would happen this quickly. What time of day were you thinking about?"

"It's a Sunday so we were thinking the ceremony at noon with a wonderful lunch afterwards."

"We can do that. We'll need to go—"

"And, Maggie, I just remembered. We'll need three additional rooms for Roger's two married children and Alex, of course. They won't want to miss the ceremony. Alex is back in Houston, you know. Silly kid."

"Christmas isn't our busy time. Let me check." She ignored the Alex comment and once again checked the reservation system. Of course she had three additional rooms available. "No problem, June."

"Good, put them under my name and credit card for starting the day after Christmas. We'll sort it all out once we get there. Can you send me the options you provide for the wedding lunch? Oh, and we need to talk about the ceremony and flowers I suppose . . ."

June trailed off and Maggie jumped in. "If you'll give me your email address I'll send you the brochures for a wedding at the Barn. We'll talk again after you've looked them over."

"That sounds perfect. I know it will be a wedding to remember. Now, I'm officially excited."

"Good," Maggie said with a chuckle. "Excited brides are the best brides."

"And Maggie, don't worry about Alex. Things will work out the way they should. Just give him time."

"My mom said the same thing."

"Will she be there at Christmas?"

"Yes, ma'am." Maggie knew both mothers would get along famously.

They ended the call and Maggie rocked in her chair, wondering if the marketing brochures were complete enough to send to June. Damn. She had a feeling they weren't. Definitely a job for tomorrow.

She booked the reservations and left the office to find Sunny folding towels in the utility room.

"Guess what? We have another wedding booked for the Barn."

"That's super. Who and when?" Sunny stacked the neatly folded towels in a laundry basket.

"The bride is Alex's mother, June, and—"

"And that guy, Roger," Sunny interrupted. "I liked them, nice people. When's the wedding?"

"Two days after Christmas. June just booked rooms for the whole family. What in the world will they do here?"

"If they all live in Houston maybe it's a chance to

get out of the traffic and enjoy a slower pace." Sunny opened the dryer and pulled out colored sheets. "If I remember correctly, you showed June and Roger a good time when they were here before Halloween. June probably figures that's normal for the Inn."

Maggie's brain twirled for a second, then bingo, a great idea for Inn traditions took hold. She leaned over and hugged Sunny. "You are a freaking genius. I need to finish my pies. I've got marketing work to do."

"What? What did I say?"

Maggie was already in the kitchen measuring pecans. She would master flaky pie crust if it killed her. For the first time in days she felt hopeful. She had a fantastic marketing idea for The Blue Barn Inn and she'd had a very nice conversation with Alex's mother.

Nothing major, but she'd take it.

Chapter Nineteen

November 20, Friday

Whew, the past week had been crazy busy and passed in a blur of activity. Maggie cleared the breakfast dishes then sat at the kitchen with her notebook open, ready to prepare the grocery list. With Thanksgiving less than a week away and all of the Inn's rooms booked, she had a ton of shopping to do. This would be her first major holiday as the Inn's manager and she intended to make it a spectacular one for her guests.

Before she entered one item on the grocery list, she reflected on the past few days. She'd managed not to dwell on Alex, at least no more than a minute or two every hour. She'd sent June the Barn's new brochures and consulted constantly with her on the wedding arrangements. At one point, Maggie had nearly buckled and asked June to intervene—to talk some sense into her son. But she didn't. Ultimately, good sense and patience prevailed, and she'd kept her mouth shut.

She'd also spent some fun time with Sunny picking out new floors, fixtures, and furniture for the Barn. Jim had directed her to wholesalers he dealt with and they'd been amazed at the vast array of products. Fortunately, Maggie had known exactly what she wanted for the space; otherwise her head would have been spinning like a top with too many options.

With each new decision, she became more excited about the Barn's prospects, along with her and Sunny's futures. Her sister's seed of an idea about Maggie starting a catering business had taken root, and Maggie now wanted to take it to the next level. A catering endeavor would intertwine the Inn and the Barn—providing delicious meals for both. She'd be open to other clients as well, if anyone would want her.

Rolling her eyes at the negative thought, she spread her Thanksgiving dinner recipes on the table and began the grocery list. She had an appointment with Emma after lunch to go over wedding details. Hopefully her suggestions for flowers and the food would appeal to the bride. If not, well, Maggie would adjust to make her first wedding client happy.

~~*

Emma Walters sighed and pushed her lips together, twin dimples appearing. "This will be the world's best wedding. Maggie, I love all your ideas."

"I agree," Fran said. She'd accompanied her daughter to this first meeting on the nitty-gritty details for the ceremony and dinner. "I do think a buffet is the best choice, gives everyone more flexibility."

Although she maintained a cool, in-control exterior to Emma and Fran, inside Maggie was clapping her hands and jumping up and down like a two year-old with her first red balloon. Mother and bride liked her ideas. This was huge. She'd never before arranged a wedding ceremony and reception, and her clients liked her plans!

"After Thanksgiving we can do a tasting for the appetizers and entrees to make sure you're happy with them." Maggie loved the idea of arranging a tasting. "You'll use Jamie's Cake Emporium for the wedding cake?"

"It's already ordered." Emma glanced at her mother for a moment. Maggie wondered what the look meant. "I have a favor to ask you . . . about the groom's cake."

"Isn't Jamie doing that?"

Emma shook her head. "Dustin isn't much of a cake guy, he likes pies more."

"Oh." Maggie thought that was weird.

"What Emma is asking is whether you could make his favorite pies for the reception in place of a groom's cake." Fran smiled at her daughter. "We were thinking of it as a dessert along with the wedding cake."

"I'd be happy to." Maggie realized immediately this would be a textbook way to advertise her pies for the catering business. And she'd just perfected pie crust. "What pies does he like?"

"His favorites are apple and pecan." Emma grinned like a beautiful bride on her wedding day. "I know this is a lot of extra work but it would mean so much to Dustin. Actually, it's a surprise for him."

"I'm not one to get in the way of a bride surprising her groom. Of course, I'll do it." Maggie couldn't think straight as to how this would impact her prep schedule but she'd make it work, with Sunny's help of course.

"Thank you." Emma excused herself to use the restroom.

"Maggie, I'm glad I have a chance to speak with you

in private." Fran gazed at her with a serious glint in her eyes.

"Another wedding surprise?"

"No, it's about Alex."

"Alex?" Maggie could barely squeak his name.

"I got to know him as he came into the diner for lunch a couple of times a week. He's a great guy."

"I agree." Maggie mentally repeated to herself "I will not cry, I will not cry."

"Well, I wanted you to know that I met him at the hospital after he was discharged and drove him to the rental car agency."

"You did that?"

"Uh-huh, he seemed really upset. I thought it was weird he didn't call you but I kept my mouth shut, didn't want to make it worse for him. I just wanted you to know."

Maggie was relieved Alex had the good sense to call Fran who had apparently helped him without asking a single question. "Thanks, Fran. He moved out of the Inn."

"Really?" Fran tilted her head, obviously surprised. "I thought he was staying here until that paper was written."

"Right after the accident he returned to Houston."

"That explains why I haven't seen him lately, but it surprises me. He seemed so happy, talked about you a lot."

Maggie opened her mouth—closed it without saying a word.

Fran lifted one hand. "Say no more. Sometimes men

can't see what's plain as day in front of their face." She leaned forward and patted Maggie's hand. "Don't you fret. Give him some time then go see what's scratching his knickers. Believe me, he'll be happy to see you."

"Okay, but what—" Maggie didn't finish her sentence as Emma rushed into the room, waving her hands.

"I have a fantastic idea how we can decorate the pies to tie in with the wedding cake."

Fran and Maggie looked at each other and smiled spontaneously. Doesn't everyone love a happy bride?

~~*

Maggie jotted notes from her meeting with Emma and Fran in her event notebook then traipsed out the back door to check on the Barn. She expected Jim to give her the latest update on the remodeling schedule. She met him in the middle of the parking lot.

"Miss Maggie, I was coming to find you. We need to talk." Jim frowned and dusted off his jeans with his hands.

Even though she predicted good news from him, his serious attitude added a layer of concern. If the Barn weren't finished on time there'd be no Emma/Dustin wedding. "Let's go to the kitchen for a cup of coffee."

He took his boots off at the door, set them on a step, and followed her to the kitchen. She motioned for him to sit at the oak table while she poured two mugs of coffee and set a plate of chocolate chip cookies within arm reach.

Maggie sat across from him, wrapping her hands around her mug in an attempt to anchor herself for bad news. "You said you'd know today whether we'll be able to maintain the original schedule. So . . . will we?" She raised her shoulders and scrunched her face in an attempt to ward off bad news.

"The schedule?" He looked at her with a blank face. "I told you on Wednesday that we were back on schedule."

"Huh?"

"Didn't I?" He rubbed a thick hand over his short hair. "Maybe I didn't. Sorry, things have been crazy lately. But, yeah, we're back on schedule. We'll have no problem meeting our original completion date."

Maggie's heart galloped around the table—whew, back on schedule. She sighed in relief. "What did you want to talk about then?"

He took a deep breath, his chest visibly rising and falling under his blue work shirt. "I'm sure embarrassed to have to tell you this. It's horrible." He stopped talking and rubbed his jaw. Whatever he had to say was obviously hard for him.

"Take your time. There's plenty of coffee."

"Ah hell, Maggie . . . my nephew, Danny Brown, started the fire." His voice broke with the last couple of words and his face had turned pale.

"What?" She scooted back in her chair for fear of falling off. "Your nephew . . . started the fire? Why?" Incredible. His nephew was the teenager Robert scared off.

"One of those damned gang initiation things—something about proving your manhood by committing a big crime." The pain was evident across Jim's face.

She reached out to him then drew back her hand. "I'm so sorry."

"He's my wife's younger sister's only son. No father around and the fool got into gangs after dropping out of high school. I've tried to intervene as best I could but . . . you know how it goes with teenagers these days."

"What happens now that we know?"

Jim looked down then raised his head. "I took him to the police station this morning—told them what he did. He's in jail."

"Jail? That sounds terrible. We need to fix this." Maggie rose. "Let's go to the police station right now."

"Maggie, please, no. He needs to learn a lesson from this."

She sat slowly, her face hot. "You're absolutely right. What's next?"

"It's up to the authorities. He did wrong and needs to pay for his actions." Jim pushed his mug to the side. "I'll let you know what happens. I figure your insurance agent will be notified by the police."

"Of course, I hadn't considered any impact on our insurance."

Jim rose. "Thanks for the coffee. I'm sorry this happened. If you want to cancel our contract—"

"No, no canceling. I appreciate you being so honest with me." She tapped a finger against her lower lip. "In fact, I have an idea. I'd like to help your nephew. Why doesn't he work for you on this project? You can keep an eye on him and maybe he'll learn the value of having a job rather joining a gang."

"Are you sure?" After she nodded he stood and stuck

out his hand. "I'll talk to the police and hope he gets probation. Miss Maggie, it's an honor to work for you." He walked to the kitchen door and turned back to her, a small grin on his face. "Gotta get back to work." Within seconds, she heard the back door closing.

Maggie stayed at the table thinking about Jim's poor misguided nephew. Hank Adams was right. The fire did have something to do with gangs, which seemed ridiculous for an all-American town like Brenham. She shook her head. What was wrong with young people nowadays?

Hopefully she and Jim could help Danny. What would Alex think of her idea?

Ah, Alex, she hadn't thought about him for a good hour. If only he were still in Brenham, staying at the Inn, and finishing his dissertation. Damn. Why had everything gotten so screwed up? It would be awesome to talk with him about Jim and his nephew.

She stood quickly, conviction running through her blood as she formulated a plan. Now she had two items on her "Get back with Alex" to-do list: write her love letter to him and then determine the absolute perfect time to execute the plan and head to Houston.

Chapter Twenty

November 23, Monday

A few minutes after midnight, Sunny plopped in the chair by the living room fireplace and opened her laptop. She clicked on a desktop icon, logged in, and put on her headset so she could hear and talk to her husband. The webcam on the computer took care of the video. It was only a minute before she viewed Jason's handsome face on the computer's screen.

"Hey, babe, how are you?"

"Hanging in there," Jason replied. He looked tired but made the effort to smile. "Things are okay here. How about there? How's Tyler?"

"Tyler is just fine. He sends a big kiss to you." She kissed her fingertips and blew a kiss to him through cyber space. "His new favorite food is spaghetti and meatballs."

"Just like his old man."

"That's right, babe, except half of your food doesn't end up on the floor or on your face."

Jason's laugh sounded forced to Sunny. Didn't matter. She was happy he still had a sense of humor after so many months in Afghanistan.

"True. There's nothing new here," Jason said. "What

going on there? Are y'all ready for Thanksgiving?"

"Oh, yeah, Maggie has been going nuts over the menu. We should have a full house of guests. Hopefully, next year we'll be together. Right?"

"You know I can't answer that." Jason blew out a breath. "A lot can happen between now and February when my tour is up."

"I know. But let me ask you a question." Jason nodded and Sunny continued. "When you're done with the Army, would you consider moving here, to Brenham?"

"What's got you asking that?"

"I'm pretty sure Maggie has given up on her idea to move back to LA."

"Why'd she change her mind?"

"Brenham has grown on her and she's thinking about opening a catering business. Anyway, that relates to my question. How about if *we* run the Inn?"

"Huh?" Jason moved back from the camera for a moment then leaned toward it. He looked worn-out to Sunny's critical eye. "You know I want to enroll in college when I get out."

"And that's why this is perfect for us. We can live here and you can go to A&M." Sunny wagged a finger at the computer screen. "See? I'll run the Inn and you go to school."

"And Maggie will do the catering?"

"If I can convince her to hook up with Alex and start that catering business."

"What? Why would she hook up with this Alex guy?"

"Because she blew off Michael, the dumb boyfriend from LA, and they had sex."

"Ooh, too much information." Jason chuckled. "You really think she likes him?"

"Well, duh, for Maggie sex equals major like. Help me come up with a plan to convince her to go after him."

"Go after him?"

"Alex got the wrong idea, thinking that Maggie still likes Michael, and he went back to Houston. It was such a lame move on his part."

Jason shook his head. "Hold on. Why did Alex think Maggie still has the hots for this Michael character?"

"Honestly, Jason, do you read my emails?"

"Of course I do." He glanced briefly to his side and raised a hand to his computer monitor. "Gotta go. Sorry I need to cut it short. Kisses to Tyler. Love you." The screen went blank.

Sunny logged off then shut down her laptop. She wrapped her arms around her chest. God, she missed her husband. Three more months and his current tour would be over. She prayed he wouldn't reenlist.

She'd come up with a plan to get Alex and Maggie together by herself. In the back of her mind, she had the notion that if Maggie and Alex got settled, then she and Jason would get settled as well. Sure it made no normal sense, but that's the way her mind worked.

"Your mind works fine."

Sunny froze. She recognized that gravelly voice.

"Don't be afraid." Across the room, Robert moved or floated into her line of sight.

She squeezed her eyes tight and counted to ten,

mouthing the words. She opened her eyes. Damn. She wasn't imagining a ghost. He still hung in the space between the floor and the ceiling ten feet or so in front of her.

"You do know I'm not Grace, right?"

"Yes. I can see the difference now. You're much older than Grace."

"What?" Sunny patted her face. Surely she didn't have wrinkles at twenty-three. She'd ask Maggie later. But more importantly, could this ghost read minds? "How did you know what I was thinking?"

"It's a skill I've learned to perfect over the years."

"How?" As in how in the freaking world could a dead man learn a new skill?

"I'm not certain, to tell you the truth."

"Oo-kay," she said slowly. "Are you here for a reason? I didn't know you roamed the whole house."

He moved backward, toward the corner bookcase. "I do not roam."

"Yeah? What do you call it then?" For some reason, Sunny's hesitance at being in Robert's presence had evaporated. She now thought of him as an older friend or maybe a distant relative, like a great-great-uncle.

"Young woman, I move as orderly as I can, considering my state of being."

"It must be difficult to move at all." She certainly had sympathy for his situation—dying so young and being stuck at the location where he died. Maybe they could do something to make his life, or existence, easier.

"I except my situation for what it is."

Sunny leaned forward. "You seem like a smart guy.

And you got a bum deal being murdered and so young. Maybe my sister and I can help you."

"Help me? Why? How?" His arms fluttered in front of his transparent body.

Maggie suddenly rounded the corner and stepped into the living room. "What are you doing in here in the middle of the night?"

"I was talking to Jason on Skype then Robert arrived."

Maggie turned to her left and lamely waved a hand. "Hey, Robert."

"I was just telling Robert I think we should help him . . . here at the Inn," Sunny said with a slow nod to Maggie.

Maggie sat on the arm of the chair Sunny occupied. "I think that's a wonderful idea."

Robert's image transitioned backward a bit, into the bookshelf. "I don't understand."

Maggie started to rise and Sunny placed a hand on her thigh to stop her. "Are you happy here, Robert?" Sunny asked. "I mean, as happy as a dead man can be. Would you rather be at the cemetery where your body was buried?"

"Heavens no, I don't want to be around all those dead people." He moved out of the bookcase so his entire body was visible. The look on Robert's transparent face was priceless.

He didn't want to be around *dead* people? The irony of the situation was almost laughable. Sunny snuck a glance at Maggie. Her sister had something on her mind for sure.

"I don't blame you one bit," Maggie said. She smiled. "I've been thinking about something that involves you, Robert."

"Me?"

"Would you like to stay at the Inn and the Barn as our resident ghost?"

"What does that mean?" He hovered a step closer.

"It means we'd like to advertise that The Blue Barn Inn is haunted. Use it as a hook to entice guests to stay with us and to use the Barn for events." Sunny noticed that Maggie maintained a cool and calm demeanor while speaking to Robert. She didn't want to spook him. *Spook* him? She bit the inside of her cheek to keep from chuckling at the unintended pun.

Robert's form shuddered then became deadly still. "I see. Use me as a hook. Would you use my name?"

"That's up to you," Maggie said.

"We could make it a mystery," Sunny suggested. She was glad they were finally talking about this with Robert. "We'd provide information about you dying here but say that it's never been confirmed so the story is just that. And—"

"And we can make it a love story because of Grace," Maggie said. "We could call it 'the story of the ghost who cries at night' or—"

"I don't cry." Robert lifted one translucent eyebrow.

"We know that." Maggie spoke in a gentle tone. "It's just a story to get people interested in staying here."

"Don't you think people would be interested in why you're so sad?" Sunny asked, genuinely curious. "I know I would. Who doesn't enjoy a love story?"

Robert swayed from side to side for a couple of seconds then turned in a slow circle. Sunny watched him with her mouth open. This had to be the weirdest, strangest situation she'd ever encountered. Geez, she needed some space. She shoved against Maggie's hip.

"Stop pushing me," Maggie said.

"You're crowding me," Sunny countered.

Maggie gave up the chair and stood. "Whatever."

A loud boom circled the room and a trail of blue smoke followed the sound then evaporated. "Ladies, did you like my trick?"

Maggie slowly returned to her previous spot on the armrest of the chair.

Sunny blinked, her stomach on a roller coaster ride. "I . . . crap, that was awesome. What other tricks can you do?"

"Sunny, that's rude," Maggie scolded her sister. She turned to the ghost and smiled. "You did that noise and smoke by yourself?"

"Of course. I've had a lot of time to work on my magic tricks over the years."

"Magic tricks?" Sunny swallowed hard. This conversation was getting too weird even with the awesomeness of a ghost doing tricks.

"We're getting off track," Maggie said. She smiled and pulled her ponytail tighter. "Robert, do you agree with our idea to advertise you as a resident ghost?"

He moved a step closer to them. "On one condition."

Sunny scratched her nose. A strong smell of cinnamon hovered around her.

"What condition?" Maggie asked.

"I want to know about my Grace."

Sunny grinned; this was one smart dead man. "We've been curious about Grace as well."

"We've been doing some research," Maggie said next. "We're not done yet but we'll let you know everything we've learned about Grace when we're finished."

Robert stared at them.

"There's one more thing." Maggie decided to share an idea she'd had for a while. "I'd like to add a small memorial for Grace in the backyard near the new gazebo."

"What kind of memorial?" Robert seemed less translucent.

"I'd hoped you could help with that since you knew her so well."

"Does that work for you?" Sunny said a small prayer that they wouldn't anger a ghost who had magic tricks up his sleeve.

Silence.

Robert seemed frozen for several seconds then he raised his left arm and pink smoke shot out from each finger.

Both Maggie and Sunny jumped from the chair. Maggie wrapped her right arm around her sister. The instant they touched, Robert disappeared and the pink smoke flew with him. The air smelled like vanilla.

"Holy crap, that ghost knows his tricks," Sunny exclaimed.

~~*

As soon as the kitchen gleamed after the morning

cleanup, Maggie headed to Adams Nursery. She wanted to talk to with Hank about the fire and an idea for helping teenagers in Brenham. The nursery's customer lot was empty when she parked so hopefully Hank would have time to talk.

An employee called him for her and he soon jogged into the entry area and stopped in front of her.

"Hey, Maggie, what can I do for you?" He gazed at her with a smile that reached his eyes.

"Do you have a few minutes to talk?" She looked around as a couple of customers walked in the front door. "Privately."

"We can go to my office. Follow me." He led her through a scratched wooden door to a short hallway and then around a corner. They stopped as he punch a button for a stainless steel elevator.

"This is a surprise," she commented as the door opened.

"My mother had the offices revamped after my father died." A few moments later they stepped into another modern hallway. "My office is at the end. Would you like coffee, a cappuccino, water?"

"No thanks, I'm good." She walked through the double doors he opened at the end of the hall. The office was impressive—dark wood floor, light walls showing off framed botanical prints and watercolors of flowers with a sitting area to the left. The desk was a kidney-shaped piece of thick glass with only a beautiful bonsai tree gracing the glass.

Hank headed for the comfy looking chairs and sofa. "Let's sit over here."

She followed and settled on the beautiful yellow couch while he sat across from her in a yellow and cream plaid chair.

Hank crossed his legs. "Okay, this is private. What's up?"

"Remember the fire at our Barn?"

"Of course. Did you catch the bad guy?"

"You were right, it was part of a gang thing. A teenager named Danny Brown started the fire and he is the nephew of the contractor doing the Barn's remodel."

"No kidding? Now you know why the Barn was targeted."

"Danny didn't know. Picking the Barn was a random choice."

"That's plain old bad luck."

"We're past it now. But this has given me an idea that I thought might interest you." She hoped she hadn't judged Hank wrong. His prominence in Brenham would help so much. "I'd like to propose a program to the police, the courts, and the schools offering a program for teenagers that gives them jobs."

"I assume you're talking about teenagers that are at a high risk for gang involvement?"

"Exactly. I've talked to Danny. He's not a bad kid, just trying to fit in, find his place."

"And our involvement would be limited to providing jobs, right? We're not equipped to give a teenager therapy."

Maggie chuckled. "Believe me, they wouldn't want it from me. I thought you and I could encourage other local business owners to hire these teenagers. We could have a get together at the Barn after the first of the year to talk about our ideas."

"The chamber of commerce might like this idea. In fact—"

"What idea are you talking about?" Mildred Adams marched across the floor. "What are you doing here, Miss Todd?"

Hank rose and pointed to the chair next to him. "Have a seat, mother. This might interest you."

"Nice to see you, Mildred." Maggie displayed her most polite smile.

Mildred wiggled into the chair and glared at Maggie. "Now what is all this about?"

Hank jumped in before Maggie. "Maggie and I are starting a program to hire at risk teenagers."

Mildred frowned. "Together? I'm not sure that's wise for us to get involved with the Todd family."

"Why is that?" Maggie's patience with this woman had hit the empty point. "In fact, Mildred, why is it that you're so nasty whenever I'm within spitting distance? Is it me or is it you?"

Mildred's eyes widened and her lips thinned into a grimace. "You have a lot of nerve coming to my nursery and—"

"Mother, enough!" Hank raised a hand. "Maggie is not your enemy. She's a guest here."

His statement hit Maggie in the face. "Mildred, I apologize for my question . . . it was rude. But I would like to know what you have against my family." Mildred's eyes narrowed and her mouth crumpled. Did she believe the apology? Maggie crossed her fingers; this "feud" was stupid. Both Maggie and Hank remained silent and observed Mildred.

After a few moments, she seemed to deflate—her stiff demeanor relaxed and she folded her hands on her lap. "I've always believed it was my job to defend Grandfather Herbert, rather than make fun of him like other members of our family. What he did was almost a hundred years ago and none of the current Adams family can be blamed for it."

Maggie leaned forward. "That is so true. The shooting was so long ago."

"What about the ghost of Robert Graham?" Hank asked.

Maggie swallowed and prayed she wasn't about to make a mistake. "He resides at The Blue Barn Inn. He's decided to stay there rather than go to his grave." She stole a quick glance at Hank, then Mildred. Neither seemed angry. "He's agreed to become our 'resident ghost.' Meaning we'll market the Inn as possibly being haunted and every once in a while he'll do something to keep the rumor alive."

Mildred smiled slowly. "I like that. Good use of a marketing hook." She turned to Hank. "Can we conjure up a ghost for the nursery?"

"Yeah sure, Mom. Maybe a lime tree that died from frostbite."

Chapter Twenty-One

November 24, Tuesday

Alex sighed, pushed his fingers through his too long hair and used his shoulder to shove open the glass door to the Starbucks down the block from his condo. He'd forgotten all about asking his favorite private investigator, Bob Blair, to do a background check on Grace Edwards. That is until Bob's phone call thirty minutes ago.

He grabbed a cup of black coffee and threw his butt in a chair across from the door. He barely had a chance to get the cup to his lips before Bob walked in and joined him at the small square table.

Bob nodded before digging in a battered briefcase. "Interesting person, this Grace Edwards." He placed a blue file folder on the table.

Alex had to admit his curiosity was now roused. "What did you find?"

"It's quite a story. I have everything detailed in the report."

"Thanks. I assume she's deceased."

"That's right, died 20 years ago at age ninety." Bob looked at his watch and frowned.

"Something wrong?" Alex asked.

"I hate to cut this short but I need to get to the airport."

Bob was already out of the chair before Alex spoke. "No problem. I'll call you if I have any questions."

"Thanks. My wife will divorce me if I'm late picking her up." Bob stuck out his hand for a quick handshake then hurried to the door and rushed down the sidewalk.

Alex drained the coffee cup as he rose and tossed it in a trashcan. He retrieved the blue folder and headed back to the condo to read Bob's report. He figured he'd need an easy chair and a cold beer for the task.

Two beers and two hours later, Alex had finished reading and analyzing Bob's report on Grace Edwards.

The man was a freaking PI genius.

Grace had enjoyed quite the life. He couldn't have been more surprised. Maggie would be over the moon with all this information.

Hmm, Maggie . . . maybe he should switch to scotch. He checked his watch. Yep, it was happy hour time.

He pulled out his cell phone and called in an order for his favorite cheeseburger and fries. They didn't usually deliver but he knew the owner and their teenage son would bring his food. The kid loved his video games.

He poured a finger of Macallan scotch in a crystal glass and walked to the windows overlooking the balcony. He remembered Maggie out there asking about the park across the street. They'd made love for the first time that night. God, it had been great. He'd really thought they had a chance as a couple.

He sipped the scotch. Meeting her had been such a surprise. Yeah, the surprise had been his once he saw Maggie's boyfriend in the hospital. She sure as hell played him.

Or did she?

Thinking back to that day in the hospital, she didn't seem all that attached to the boyfriend. They hadn't walked in holding hands. She'd seemed genuinely happy to see him. And she did talk about taking him back to the Inn the next day. Maybe her supposed "boyfriend" was simply an ex trying to make one last play for her. Alex rubbed a hand over his jaw.

Damn it. If that was the case, he sure as hell had fallen for the ruse.

Could he have acted like a bigger fool by jumping to such a stupid conclusion? Probably not, considering the manner in which he'd left the Inn and Brenham.

Yep, he'd screwed up.

Bob's report was the perfect reason to contact Maggie.

But, hold on. Maybe he'd been looking for a reason to create a distance from Maggie. It hadn't been all that long after he'd broken his two-year engagement that he met her. Maybe he'd jumped into things too fast.

He had some serious thinking to do.

It was finally time to think like a fully functioning adult. He drained his glass as the doorbell rang. He'd turn on the TV while he ate his burger and fries.

That would keep his mind off Maggie and his wayward heart.

~~*

The day had flown by after grocery shopping and prep for the Inn's Thanksgiving dinner, and Maggie finally had a minute to herself. She'd made a cup of pumpkin spice tea and retired to her bedroom. The time to write the letter to Alex had arrived, as she'd be crazy busy the next three days.

She set the tea on the bedside table then changed into the pink long john pajamas she'd had since college. The weather app on her phone said the temperature was falling to forty degrees overnight so she wanted to be prepared. She grabbed a pad of paper and a pen off her desk and slipped under the covers after plumping the pillows behind her.

Pen in her hand, Maggie stared at the paper with her mind blank. She'd read several of the love letters in the book her mother had given her. They had inspired her at the time but right now she felt deflated.

She reread her earlier notes and wiggled her fingers, enticing creative thoughts to enter her body. After closing her eyes, she pictured Alex's handsome face and the sexy grin that so often graced it. Yeah, he was a keeper.

Her eyes flew open. She had blown it. Big time. Huge.

Those thoughts then increased the pressure to write an outstanding love letter to Alex. She shook out her hands and sipped her tea. *She could do this.*

Maggie began to jot random thoughts on the pad of paper—the first time I saw you, a fairytale entering my life, security in knowing your character, new joy in my life, hopes for the future, my heart aches, a growing love

. . .

Love?

Maggie drank her tea as she considered Alex and love in the same thought.

Was it time to dig deep and filter through all of her feelings about Alex? If not, why was she trying to write a love letter?

She began again and wrote her thoughts in complete sentences. After twenty minutes she had a decent draft. She'd look at it again in a couple of days. Her goal was to personally deliver it to Alex in Houston on Saturday. She had plenty of time to finalize the words and write it on pretty paper.

Maggie turned off the lamp and snuggled under the bed covers. She'd had a good day and a good night. Although talking to Robert, "the ghost" as she thought of him, was on the strange side. She hadn't quite acclimated herself to actually conversing with a spirit, i.e. dead man. She couldn't help but wonder if he found it as strange as she did.

~~*

Robert watched Maggie from the entrance to her bedroom, out of her direct sight. He'd used his mind skills to push thoughts into her head. He figured that was the least he could do for her as she'd given him the gifts of belonging and purpose.

She cut off the light from the lamp on the bedside table and turned over, away from him. He liked Maggie. Conversing with her wasn't all that strange to him. He'd endured much worse in the house and barn since his death.

Ah, 1922, the year that all his hopes and dreams died, right along with his body. The same year he had planned to propose to Grace and then announce their engagement to the good folk of Brenham. That is, until that atrocious Herbert Adams decided he wanted Grace for himself. That man had set out to permanently eliminate any competition. A single bullet to Robert's heart had done the trick. And the horse barn of Grace's family home had become his place of death.

For weeks Robert had planned to propose to Grace on that particular night in February, a week after Valentine's Day. It was the one-year anniversary of their first date. Letting her know he was ready to pledge his life to her was important to him. How Herbert discovered his plans he didn't know. It sure as hell didn't matter now.

But still, it was so sad. Robert and Grace had a wonderful relationship. They were soul mates for sure. He closed his eyes and allowed his mind to remember his love affair with Grace and the speech he had planned to say to her. Had it taken place, most assuredly they would have been on the back porch of her parent's home . . .

"My dearest Grace, from the first time I saw you at the church supper, I knew you were destined for me. In that instant, you captured my thoughts and my heart. Your beauty is breathtaking and your sweet disposition fills me with contentment and joy. I can't imagine my time on earth without you by my side."

At that point he had planned to take the ring out of

his pocket and kneel on the floor in front of his sweetheart. Then he would say . . .

"Grace, holder of my heart, will you do me the honor of becoming my wife? I love you beyond the moon and the stars and want you to be mine until the oceans run dry."

He groaned at the unfairness of it all. Damn Herbert Adams to hell.

After several minutes he had himself under control and studied the sleeping Maggie. She was a good girl. She had been kind to him, and surprisingly, didn't appear to be afraid of him. The lady had gumption. He went back to the Barn, hoping Maggie would find her happily-ever-after, even if he and Grace didn't. He'd say a prayer for her and Alex, one thing he could still accomplish after the end of his human life.

Chapter Twenty-Two

November 28, Saturday

Now that Saturday had finally arrived, Maggie itched to jump in her SUV and leave for Houston to visit Alex. However, preparing the morning breakfast for her guests took priority. After the food was served, Sunny offered to clean up the kitchen and Maggie quickly agreed. Sunny made sure she was on her way to Alex's condo in less than ten minutes.

With her letter to Alex safely tucked away in her purse, she considered what might happen once she reached her destination. Truly, she had no idea if he'd even let her in the door of his home. Yet she was determined to try, knowing she'd never forgive herself if she chickened out now. Todd women were not weaklings.

The drive to Houston was uneventful and surprisingly quick. She pulled into a visitor parking spot at Alex's building a bit before noon. Maybe he'd be willing to go to lunch. She walked purposefully into the lobby and met the same doorman as before.

"I'm here for Alex Brady."

"Hey, I remember you," he said with a broad smile. "I never forget a face . . . you're Maggie, right?"

"That's right."

"Mr. Brady isn't home right now. He left an hour ago."

Damn. "Do you know when he'll return?"

"No, ma'am. You're more than welcome to wait for him." He pointed to an area with a long couch and square chairs on the side of the lobby across from the elevators. "I'll make sure he knows you're here the second he returns." He winked at her.

Maggie took that as her cue to retreat to the seating area. She settled into the corner of a beige and pink striped couch and pulled out her cell phone. She might as well listen to music while she waited. She plugged in the ear buds and selected one of her favorite playlists of easy listening songs. She closed her eyes to listen.

Someone shook her shoulder and wrenched Maggie from a dream about a dragon slayer on a white horse. Blinking and pushing hair out of her eyes, she glanced around her. Oh crap. She'd fallen asleep in the lobby of Alex's building. Heat rose from her toes to her face.

Alex leaned over her. "Are you all right?"

"Yes . . . yes, of course." She righted herself on the sofa and fluffed her hair with her hands. Licking her lips, she sat up straight and turned to Alex. "I know I should have called first, but I'd like to speak to you."

He gave her one last scrutinizing look and straightened. "Sure. Come on." As she rose from the couch he placed a hand on the small of her back and led her to the bank of elevators. Maggie kept her mouth shut and her head down as they rose to his condo.

Once inside the door, he pointed to the living room.

"Have a seat. Would you like something to drink?"

"Mm, a glass of water." Maggie moved to the end of the plump brown couch and sat pertly on the edge of the cushion. Now that she had arrived, her anxiety level spiked dangerously. She clenched her fists, willing her nerves to calm.

Alex came in holding two bottles of dark beer and handed one to her. "Sorry, out of bottled water. This is from a new brewery by Blanco."

"Thanks." She watched Alex flop into one of the chairs. He took a long pull on the beer then faced her.

"You wanted to talk to me?"

She sipped the beer, too preoccupied to pay attention to how it tasted. "I'd like to know why you left Brenham so suddenly."

"Maybe that's personal."

That comment was not what she had expected. He must still be angry. "Maybe it would be beneficial to our conversation if you were honest about why you're so angry with me."

He stared at her for a moment then carefully placed his beer bottle on the coffee table. After another moment, he produced a barely-there smile. "You want honesty? Fine, that's what I'll give you."

He rose and walked to the windows overlooking the balcony. Maggie studied him as he stood—his stance military straight and his shoulders powerfully square. He passed his fingers through his hair before spinning around and walking to the end of the sofa.

"I thought we might have a chance at a real relationship. That was shot to hell when your boyfriend showed up at the hospital after my accident."

"He isn't my boyfriend. We broke it off months ago in LA."

"Then why the hell was he hugging you?"

She flinched at that—hugging, really? "Where did you see him hugging me?"

"Jesus, at the hospital, in my room. He hugged you, saying he was convincing you to go back to LA."

Maggie took a long pull of the beer then set the bottle on the table. She leaned back in the sofa and crossed her legs. *Men are clueless.* "And you believed that crap he said?"

Alex backed away from the couch and crossed his arms. "You didn't give me any reason not to."

Now she was irritated. She'd told Alex more than once that she'd broken up with her LA boyfriend before she'd arrived in Brenham. Did he have male memory loss? "Alex . . . I explained this to you before. Why in the hell would you take Michael's word about a relationship and not mine? You know me, not him."

He looked at her with a blank face. Perhaps he was thinking about his tendency to jump to stupid conclusions. "You're right."

"Don't you realize he was playing with you? He made one last ditch effort to convince you that we'd rekindled something that died months ago."

Alex's eyebrows drew together. "Yeah?"

"Yeah."

"Hmm." He walked around the end of the couch and retrieved his beer. He tipped the bottle to his lips as he went into the kitchen. He returned empty-handed and again stood near the couch.

"So . . . can we try again?" Maggie prayed he could get past this.

"I'm not sure." He had no emotion on his face. It reminded Maggie of a canvas with only a masculine oval sketched on the surface with charcoal. Her stomach twirled.

"Why aren't you sure?" She meant her words and truly couldn't understand him being so unsure. Why in the world would he allow Michael to come between them? Alex was much too smart for that.

He blew out a heavy breath. "I . . . I need time to figure out my own mind, where I'm headed, what I want. I—"

"Of course, I understand." There was no need for her to stay any longer if Alex didn't know what he wanted. Maggie wasn't going down that road again. She dug in her purse for the letter. She'd written it by hand on nice stationery with a matching envelope—girly, yes, but from her heart. She rose from the sofa.

"You're leaving."

"Yes." She handed him the envelope. "Please read this."

"Okay."

Maggie walked to the condo's front door and turned back to Alex who had followed her. "Let me know if you change your mind. You know where to find me." She opened the door, stepped into the hallway, and turned back to Alex. "Take care of yourself."

"You, too." He barely managed to speak above a whisper.

She made her way to the elevator, struggling to hold back the tears. Maggie repeated the words "I will not cry" as the elevator descended and then opened in the lobby. Somehow she made it to her car without a single sniffle.

By the time she started her SUV, her reserve bottomed out. She sat there for several minutes, sobbing uncontrollably, trying to stem the tears with fast-food napkins pulled from the center console. After several minutes, she backed out of the parking spot and exited onto Dunlavy with I-10 West and then Brenham as her destination.

~~*

The second the door closed, Alex headed to the kitchen and tossed the envelope on the counter, not yet ready to open it. He pulled a box of leftover pizza from the fridge—sustenance before tackling Maggie's letter. He placed the pizza in the microwave and popped open another beer while the pizza warmed.

Leaning against a counter, he thought about Maggie and the "situation" as he now termed his dumb ass move of leaving Brenham and the Inn. Why the hell had he done that without having a talk with her first?

Was he afraid of committing to her? Not that he knew of. They hadn't exactly reached that stage, but she *was* the type of woman he could get serious about. She was the polar opposite of his flighty and high maintenance ex-fiancée. Maggie was down-to-earth and solid—a woman who worked hard and was dedicated to her family. So why the hell had he hightailed it back to Houston at the first sign of conflict?

The microwave dinged and he carried the plate and beer to the living room. He clicked on the television and found a college football game to watch while he ate.

He chewed the pizza, slugged down beer, and reconsidered his own actions. Maybe he wasn't emotionally ready for another relationship. He swigged the beer and contemplated further.

Was he emotionally bankrupt? Had his ex-fiancée sucked him dry? No, damn it, he was fine—just a little confused or maybe shell-shocked at meeting someone as fantastic as Maggie so soon after his break up. He stuffed more pizza in his mouth. Yeah, that was it. He needed to get his head straight and realize his good fortune regardless of the timing.

He emptied the beer bottle. How did he picture his future? Obviously, he'd complete the Ph.D. program and obtain a university teaching job. He'd rather live in a small town than Houston any day, a small town like Brenham. Live in a big two-story house with a long porch in front, a massive fireplace between the kitchen and the living room, and plenty of bedrooms for kids and guests. He couldn't imagine living alone for the rest of his life. Yeah, he did want a wife and kids, a real family.

That admission had him heading to the kitchen for Maggie's letter. He fingered the envelope, trying to summon the gumption to open it. He took a deep breath, blew it out slowly, and opened the envelope. He pulled out two sheets of light blue paper decorated with flowers along the left side. Girly stationery, but he appreciated that she'd taken the time to handwrite the note.

Dearest Alex,

I remember the moment I first met you—I was sitting on the Inn's kitchen floor and you pulled me up without laughing. I appreciated that. I know it sounds like a romance novel, but that moment was the beginning of the rest of my life. Somehow you managed to take my breath away.

I know that life is full of trials and that we cannot always get what we want, but I do know that the relationship we've started to build is the real thing and it's what I want to pursue.

Honestly, I don't understand why you left Brenham so abruptly. Although I now realize it was a mistake on my part to take Michael with me to the hospital to see you. He made you think something was going on and that was a fabrication. He must have realized it was pointless, because he left for LA in the middle of the night.

Alex, you've made me feel secure in myself and you've helped me figure out what I want to do with the rest of my life. I know you don't even realize that. I plan to open a catering business in Brenham and with any luck, start a family. I hope you know just how much you mean to me and how much your presence in my life makes everything that's important worthwhile.

In fact, my love, my heart beats only for you.

My best to you — Maggie

Alex sat on the couch without moving, the letter in his hands. He read it a second time, shook his head, then folded it slowly and stuffed it back in the envelope. He had some serious thinking to do. But if the warm fuzzy in his gut was any indication, he already knew his heart.

In time, his brain would catch up.

~~*

Maggie sat on her bed with a glass of wine in her hand. She'd managed to avoid Sunny when she returned back to the Inn from Houston and had made a beeline to her bedroom and a nap. Six hours later her cramped position on the bed roused her and she went to the kitchen.

The reality of her visit to Houston slammed into her chest. But she didn't cry. Her tear bucket was empty. She sipped her wine and decided she wouldn't think about Alex . . . ever again. The late night news would keep her distracted. The remote wasn't on the nightstand so she bent over the side of the bed and found it on the floor. She righted herself and wasn't alone.

"Hey Robert, what's up?" He stood in the doorway to the office.

"I know this isn't proper, me being almost in your bedroom, but I had to make sure you're all right."

"Why do you ask?" Maggie had no desire to discuss her heartbreak with a ghost.

"I know you don't want to talk with me about Alex, but I am concerned."

Of course he was concerned—he's the world's sweetest ghost. Tears threatened again but she held them off with a slow calming breath. "Thanks, Robert. I'm okay, sad right now but I know it'll get better. Alex is confused about what he wants."

"You've been crying."

"Yeah, goes with getting your heart broken." She

sipped her wine, misery once again overwhelming her.

"Are you being overly dramatic?"

What? And she'd just thought he was sweet. "No. This is real life. I'm hurt by Alex."

"How did he hurt you?"

"He didn't want to get back together." She finished off the wine. "Said he needs to figure out where he's headed."

"Doesn't he deserve a chance to do that?"

Damn, now Robert was taking Alex's side and making complete sense. "I'm so confused."

"Relax, Maggie. Have another glass of wine and watch the evening news." Robert stepped closer to the bed. "Give Alex some time."

"I gave him time before I went to Houston."

"I know," Robert said as though he were talking to a petulant third-grader. "But you know how men are."

Maggie smiled in spite of her misery. "Tell me, how are men?"

"Slow." He pointed to his head. "Slow and stubborn but eventually they come around."

"So I need to be patient?" She prayed she knew the meaning of patience.

He nodded. "And have faith. Your prayers will be answered."

Maggie blinked and Robert was gone. Damn. Faith and patience. Why not? She had nothing to lose.

Chapter Twenty-Three

December 13, Sunday

With breakfast over and the kitchen in order, Maggie checked her notebook for her to-do list. When she'd worked at her marketing job in Los Angeles she'd often complained about her crazy schedule. That was nothing compared to managing the Inn and preparing for the completion of the Barn's remodel, not to mention Dustin and Emma's wedding in a week.

Today, she needed to tweak a couple of appetizer recipes and the green beans. Last week she'd held her very first menu tasting with Dustin and Emma and they'd requested a change to three items on the menu. Nothing major but enough of a change that she wanted to test her recipes one last time. Hopefully Sunny would be back from church in time to be the official taste tester.

The renovations to the Barn were three days off-schedule, thanks to the sluggish scheduling of city inspections. Jim had worked around it as best he could but he wasn't a magician. He had added extra hands, including Danny, to his already tight crew to make up the time.

To top off the construction being behind, the appliances for the Barn's new kitchen were on backorder.

They were supposed to be delivered on Wednesday, a week after the original delivery date. She prayed nothing got in the way of their installation. She had enough on her plate right then. No way could she prepare the volume of food needed for a wedding buffet in the Inn's kitchen.

Retesting these recipes would be a distraction. Something to keep her mind off the fact she hadn't heard from Alex in the two weeks since she'd left his condo in Houston. Either she had totally misread their "relationship" or he was doing the soul searching he said he needed to do. She had to respect that but it was still frustrating as hell. She hoped he'd at least read her letter.

Maggie shook off her frustration and opened the refrigerator. She had work to do. She pulled out asparagus, garlic, Parmesan cheese, and butter. The first task was to roast the asparagus so she turned on the oven and grabbed a cookie sheet and parchment paper out of the pantry.

Dustin had asked for the Asparagus Roll Up appetizer to have more garlic. She didn't agree with him but it was his wedding so she was tweaking the recipe by adding garlic juice to the butter/parmesan spread. This was a quick recipe so once the asparagus had roasted, it took no time to get the rolls prepared and in the oven to brown.

The second adjustment was to a recipe for stuffed mushrooms with more garlic as well. She mixed the filling, spooned it into the mushroom caps, and set them in a skillet on the stove.

She worked on the green beans next. Dustin wanted

pancetta with them, rather than regular bacon. Maggie had a sneaking suspicion he would be the cook in the family. She had the beans ready to go when the timer dinged for the roll ups.

She grabbed an oven mitt and pulled the baking dish from the oven. It smelled wonderful. Catching a movement out of the corner of her eye, she turned quickly, nearly burning her other hand by grabbing the dish.

"Be careful," Alex said while taking a couple of steps toward her.

She set the dish on the counter and turned to him. "What are you doing here? How did you get in?"

He shrugged and grinned. "I didn't return my key when I left."

"Hold on." She adjusted the oven temperature for the green beans then placed her hands on her hips. "Okay, that answers that. Why are you here?"

"Hmm, to talk with you?"

She narrowed her eyes. "You don't sound very convincing. Why are you really here?"

"I want to complete my lease of the Brazos Suite."

"I see."

"Working on my dissertation hasn't been going all that well at my condo." He moved toward her but stopped a couple of feet away. "It's been lonely."

"Really?" Maggie's heart began the slow burn for a rocket launch.

"Really." He stepped closer to her. "In fact, all I could think about was you."

"Did you read my letter?"

"Uh-huh." He raised his hand and stroked a finger down her cheek. "Thank you." He took one step forward and wrapped his arms around her. "Thank you for being so honest."

She sank into his arms, relishing in the firmness of his chest against hers and the familiar spicy scent of his cologne. She wrapped her arms around him and hugged Alex tight. Now *this* felt like home. "Thank you for coming back to Brenham."

He pulled back and gently kissed her. "How could I not when I left my heart here."

The rocket fired and Maggie pulled him close, hugging him tight before she took a step away from him. "Would you like to taste my appetizer? We can talk later as I hear Sunny's car pulling into the back." She kissed him quickly. "You know how it goes."

He nodded and smiled. "That I do. What is this you want me to taste?"

She explained about Dustin and his desire for more garlic in the appetizers. As she scooped a serving for Alex, Sunny and Tyler entered the kitchen via the hall door.

"Hey, Aunt Maggie, whatcha cooking?" Sunny said. She stopped a few feet from Alex. "Oh . . . you've returned."

"That I have."

"Good." She turned to Maggie. "I'm putting Tyler down for a nap. Alex, do not move an inch until I get back." Sunny gathered Tyler in her arms and hurried to the back stairs.

Maggie grinned as she put the green beans in the

oven. "I think she might have a couple of questions."

"That's okay. I don't blame her." He took a bite of the asparagus roll up and chewed. "This is good. Garlic taste is okay, not too strong."

"Whew, good. One down, two to go." Maggie wondered if Alex might be her good luck cooking charm, which suited her just fine.

~~*

Sunny hurried down the stairs after tucking Tyler in for his morning nap. It was a bit later than usual but that was okay. Getting off schedule seemed to be the norm these days. In fact, ever since Alex had left, things around the Inn had been a little chaotic. And now he was back.

She burst into the kitchen as Alex stood behind Maggie with his arms wrapped around her. She giggled as she cooked something on the stove. The picture of them, so loving toward each other, tweaked an ache in Sunny's heart. Jason was a very affectionate man and she missed his kisses and hugs.

"I'm back," Sunny chirped, throwing off the loneliness for her husband.

Alex slowly swung his head in her direction and smiled, real friendly like. "Hey there, Sunny. I've missed you."

Yeah, he didn't want any problems from her and she wouldn't give him any. Alex was a good guy. At least her sister was smiling after two weeks of moping and acting like Miss Glum. That being said, as the little sister, who said she couldn't have a little fun with this?

"Really? I hardly noticed you were gone other than not having to clean your mess of a room." Sunny stuck her nose in the refrigerator and missed the pointed look Maggie threw her. "Anything in here for lunch?"

She took her time grabbing a carton of yogurt and two sticks of string cheese. Then she noticed the roll ups on the counter and popped one in her mouth. "I like these, more garlic this time?"

Alex had backed away from Maggie and was pouring coffee. "Would you like a cup, Sunny?"

"Sure." She grabbed the dish of appetizers and set it on the table. She sat so she could view Maggie at the stove. "Why are you back, Alex?"

He placed a mug on the table in front of her. "I missed you and Maggie."

Sunny fluttered her hand in front of her face like a southern belle moving a fan. "You did? That surprises the hell out of me." She sipped the coffee and watched his face. She could tell he wasn't quite sure how to take her comment and kept his mouth shut. Alex stumped for words. Priceless.

Maggie frowned and was about to speak so Sunny decided to fess up. She raised her hand. "Hold on, I'm teasing you. I'm very happy you've returned. Are you here for good?"

"He's here for as long as he wants," Maggie said. She placed a plate with the stuffed mushrooms on the table. "Let me know how these taste."

Alex joined Sunny at the table. "I hope it's for a long time. One day at a time." He stuffed a mushroom in his mouth and chewed. He looked at Maggie. "I've changed my mind. I'll be here forever if you keep making these mushrooms."

Sunny winked and he grinned at her.

"Okay if I move my stuff back to my old room?" he said, watching Maggie.

"Sure," she said. "I'll help you."

"No need. You keep cooking and I'll see you later. I need to get my head around my dissertation again." He rubbed Maggie's arm then left the kitchen.

Sunny spoke first. "Oh, my God. What a surprise. Did you just die when he walked in?"

"It was a shock, a good one though."

"I bet. Are you two in an official relationship now?" Sunny didn't want to get too nosy, just nosy enough that she knew the details.

Maggie opened the oven door and removed a baking sheet layered with green beans. "This is the last recipe I had to tweak for the groom. Will you taste it for me?"

"Of course, smells great. Will you answer my question?"

Maggie plated them and brought them, along with a couple of forks, to the table. "I don't have an answer for that yet. We didn't have a chance to really talk before you got home."

"Sorry about that." Sunny speared a bite of green bean and bacon. "Mm, I like this."

"Thanks. I had to switch pancetta for regular bacon." Maggie sat across from her sister. "Anyway, I'm thrilled Alex is back. We still need to have a long conversation and I'm sure we will when I get a chance to breathe. For now—I'm happy."

Thirty minutes later, Maggie put the last dish in the dishwasher, turned and found Robert watching her from the corner.

"Robert, is everything okay?" She was still a bit unnerved every time he appeared out of the blue.

"I saw Danny working with your contractor."

"Danny is Jim's nephew and he's helping to repair the damage created by the fire."

"Good idea. I have a suggestion for the memorial you mentioned, the one for Grace."

She smiled. Robert really was a nice guy. "What's your idea?"

"Grace loved angels. She had a real pretty necklace with one hanging on it. And her favorite flower was a yellow daisy."

"Hmm, how about a garden statue of an angel with daisies planted around its base?"

"I like that." He smiled slowly and floated above the floor. "You'd put it in the back garden?"

She liked that idea. "We'll put it near the new gazebo, with a memorial plate below the statue with Grace's name. How does that sound?"

"Good. Thank you."

"I'll do it after the first of the year. You can help me pick out the right statue."

"I would be honored." He disappeared into the ceiling, no smoke or flash.

Maggie had her mouth open. A ghost's fading through a wall or a ceiling hadn't yet become an everyday thing for her. She'd simply work on becoming acclimated to a resident ghost at The Blue Barn Inn.

~~*

It was almost nine that evening before Alex felt

comfortable calling Maggie. He'd debated about it for over an hour then bit the bullet and dialed her cell. She answered on the third ring.

"Are you busy?" he asked.

"Not really."

"Are you up for some company?"

"Uh-huh."

"Okay if I come to your room?" He'd never been there before but hoped it would make her feel more comfortable.

"Of course. You know the way?"

"Leave a light on." He brushed his teeth, slapped cold water on his face and a sprinkle of cologne. He locked the door to his room and tiptoed down the hallway through the kitchen to the door to the Inn's office. He rapped his knuckle on the dark wood.

Within seconds, the door opened and Maggie appeared in the doorway, a light from behind illuminating her figure. He sucked in a breath. She wore some type of yellow pajamas that were skintight and exposed her very toned stomach and butt. Oh yes, he was *definitely* home.

She stepped to the side. "Come on in. I made a hot toddy for us."

"What's that?" He stepped inside and then followed her. They went through a small office to the bedroom.

"It's a hot drink with bourbon, lemon, and honey. Very tasty on a cold night." She pointed to the chair. "Have a seat." She handed him a mug then sat on the corner of the bed.

"Thanks." Alex settled in the chair and tasted the

drink. "Not bad. I swear you have a recipe for every occasion."

"Not every occasion," she replied, a slight smile touching her lips. "Sometimes I'm too busy to cook."

Alex chugged his drink and it warmed his belly. "We need to finish our conversation."

She nodded. "I believe you said something about leaving your heart in Brenham."

He swallowed hard. Maggie didn't miss a thing. He set the mug on the dresser as he rose. He settled next to her on the bed, staring at the herringbone pattern of the carpet.

"I need to explain myself." He threaded his fingers with hers and squeezed gently. "I jumped to a ridiculous conclusion about you and that LA guy while I was in the hospital. I'm sorry for that."

"I understand."

"Actually, it—" Maggie started to interrupt him but Alex raised his free hand to silence her. "It forced me to look at what I'm doing with my life . . . where I want to go, who I'm going with."

"I see."

"What I'm trying to say is that you're important to me and I want to continue to get to know you." He scooted around on the bed until he faced her. "I hope you'll be willing to take it day by day and see what happens." Alex knew he sucked at flowery words. But he prayed Maggie would see beyond that and give him a real chance. He wrapped his arms around her and whispered. "You matter to me."

She hugged him tight. "Ditto."

He pulled back and cupped her face with his hands, enjoying the view of her glowing eyes and the smile that played on her lips. "You are so beautiful." Alex couldn't contain his need for Maggie any longer. His mouth lightly captured hers and he enjoyed her moan of pleasure as he increased the pressure of his lips.

Their passion quickly escalated and his hands slid down her sides to circle her waist. He breathed in her scent, instantly intoxicated. Maggie's aroma, her taste, and the way it felt to have her in his arms—this was something he wanted forever. This was home.

"Just so you know," he said quietly. "We'll be busy for the next few hours. You okay with that?"

Maggie gazed seductively at Alex through lowered lashes. She quirked an eyebrow while one corner of her mouth tilted upward in a sexy little grin. "You know me. I'm happiest when something is keeping me busy."

Home just got a little spicy.

Chapter Twenty-Four

December 22, Wednesday

Maggie sat at the kitchen table, a coffee cup before her, and a huge grin on her face. Life was grand . . . and then she remembered her current issue and the smile vanished. It wasn't a problem exactly, more of a conundrum. She looked at her watch. Where was Alex?

He'd promised that morning they'd finally talk about Grace. She'd been after him for the details since he'd returned and he'd kept putting her off. And finally, today was the day.

He'd been so busy in the ten days since he'd returned to the Inn that she hadn't seen him other than an occasional breakfast or dinner, and sleeping together a few nights. He'd finally gotten his groove on with his dissertation and was writing like crazy. Of course, Maggie had been busy with the completion of the Barn remodel. The appliances had arrived just in time to prepare the buffet for Dustin and Emma's wedding last Saturday.

Ah, the wedding. The newlyweds were probably drinking wine at a piazza in Rome right now. The whole event had turned out so well. It went off without a hitch, other than a very pregnant bridesmaid who nearly fainted during the vows. The buffet received many compliments and the Barn had glittered like a shining star. The whole event proved to Maggie that she had been on the right track with the bank loan and the remodel.

Of course, she learned her lesson about the amount of food to prepare for a buffet. In fact—

The front doorbell rang. She looked at her watch. Curious, she hurried to the foyer and opened the door.

June and Roger stood on the porch, arms circling each other, and smiles radiating.

"You're here," Maggie exclaimed. "I didn't expect you until later this afternoon."

"We're so excited, we couldn't stay in Houston any longer," June said.

"I don't blame you." Maggie hugged June first then Roger. "Come on in and we can get your things."

Roger pointed to duffle bags and suitcases on the porch behind them. "We have them right here."

"Okay then, let's get you to your room." Maggie picked up a suitcase and a duffle. She did not want Alex's mother carrying luggage. "I booked you in the Lavender Room as you requested. June, would you grab the keys off the table?"

June led them up the stairs with Roger behind Maggie. She really liked Alex's mother. They'd had some nice conversations talking about the wedding festivities. Roger seemed like a nice man. The couple was proof that a person was never too old to find new love.

June opened the door and they set the bags next to the bed. The room was tidy and spotless, ready for its new guests.

"I'll let you guys get settled. Let me know if you need anything." Maggie walked out the door and turned back. "Are you hungry?"

"No," Roger said. "We had a big breakfast on the way." His hand rested on the edge of the door and Maggie knew that was her cue to leave.

"I'll see y'all later."

She made her way back to the kitchen and decided to make an Italian cake for Christmas Eve. Her parents had arrived last week to help with the wedding and were now out shopping with Sunny and Tyler. That suited her just fine and assured her she'd have the peace and quiet to make this delicate dessert. It was one of her own recipes and delicious.

She grabbed her iPod and speaker from the bedroom and turned on her favorite playlist. The music kept her company while she prepared the cake. Once the three cake pans were out of the oven to cool, she slid in a cookie sheet to toast pecans for the top of the cake.

Finally, the vanilla layers were cool enough to frost with her favorite cream cheese frosting. She loved to frost cakes and added pretty swirls to the top as her hips swayed from side to side. She looked up and nearly dropped the knife; Alex stood a few feet from her.

"How long have you been here?"

"Not long, but long enough," he replied. "You really get into frosting a cake."

"It's fun." She cut off the iPod and started to sprinkle the pecans on the top of the cake. "Your mother and Roger are here."

"Already?"

"I think they're excited."

"Yeah, probably." He moved around the counter and gave her a loud kiss. "It's time to talk about Grace. I want this over with before things around here get too crazy again."

"I agree." Maggie set the cake on the back counter. "How do we do this?"

"I need to get the report in my room. I'll be right back." Alex hurried out of the kitchen while Maggie wondered how they could make contact with Robert. Maybe go to the Barn?

Waiting for Alex, she started to wash the cake pans in the sink. Something brushed against her back and she whirled around.

She blew out a hurried breath. The ghost of Robert Graham hung out of the cabinet next to the pantry. It looked plain weird but she'd keep that opinion to herself.

"My dear, I believe you and your friend have something to share with me."

"That's true. He'll be here shortly."

After a beat Alex strolled back in the kitchen carrying a blue file folder. He halted when his gaze landed on Robert. "Whoa."

Maggie held out a hand to Alex. "Sweetheart, this is Robert Graham. I believe he's eager to learn what you've discovered about Grace Edwards."

"No problem." He threw a glance at Maggie, his face a little green. "Do you mind if I get something to drink first?"

"Of course not," Maggie said, chucking to herself.

"Sit at the table and I'll get it. What would you like?"

"Scotch."

Maggie blinked but understood perfectly. This was Alex's first in-person exposure to a ghost. Right, like she was an old hand at it herself. She retrieved two glasses and the bottle of scotch from the liquor cabinet. She added a couple ice cubes to each glass and poured two fingers in each. She handed a glass to Alex and joined him at the table.

She nodded at Robert then smiled at Alex. "We're anxious to hear what you've learned about Grace."

Alex opened the folder, glanced at Robert and slugged down half the liquor in his glass. He coughed and picked up the report the PI had prepared. "She had a good life. Not exactly what you'd expect if she had married you, Robert, but good nonetheless."

"Where did she go?" Robert had moved further into the kitchen.

"It looks like she left Brenham a month after you died, right after her eighteenth birthday. She didn't finish high school. She took the train to Los Angeles. She must have had money to fund her trip as she rented a room at a boarding house once she got there."

"She had money from a trust when she turned eighteen," Robert said. "That's why she could leave. What did she do in California?"

"She lived there until she died in 1994. For many years she worked in the movies, first in a few silent movies and then in the talkies."

"She was an actress?" Maggie asked.

Alex nodded. "Apparently she was a good one, but

she never took on major roles. She was more of character actress who stayed in the background."

"She always loved to act in high school," Robert said softly. "Did she have a family? Was she happy?"

"She married when she was thirty-two, to a man who also worked on movie sets. They had two kids and several grandchildren. She had a good life."

"Was she in a movie we'd know?" Maggie asked. All this information was a surprise. She hoped it would put Robert's heart and mind at rest knowing that Grace had been happy.

"Actually she was," Alex said before draining his glass. "She performed in *Casablanca* as a bit player in all the scenes at Rick's Café."

"How cool," Maggie exclaimed. "I'm impressed."

"What's that, Casa . . . what?" Robert asked.

"It's a movie made in the early 1940s with Humphrey Bogart and Ingrid Bergman. It's a wonderful love story."

"It's one of the best films in movie history," Alex added. "You should be proud of Grace."

"I've always been proud of my Grace. She was exceptional." Robert retreated back into the cabinet. "Thank you for telling me about her. I'll be your official ghost for the Inn." With that he disappeared.

"There's more about her kids and grandkids," Alex said.

"I think he learned what he needed to know," she concluded.

The back door slammed and laughter filtered into the kitchen.

"We're being invaded," Alex said with a sexy grin.

Maggie rose. "Nah, it's just the tribe returning from shopping. We'll need to let Sunny know what happened with Robert."

"I'm sure she'll be curious about the report." Alex rose and took their glasses to the sink.

Maggie bumped his side playfully with her hip. "You know, Grace's story would be a great plot for a book."

He raised both hands. "I have no time to add romance author as another career."

She grabbed his hands and wrapped them around her back. "Too bad, you could write the love scenes like a pro."

Chapter Twenty-Five

December 24, Thursday

Christmas Eve had been a fantastic day. The temperature had dropped to the low thirties and the fireplace in the Inn's living room had been burning consistently, adding to the holiday atmosphere. Sunny sat in a chair by the hearth and watched her father play with Tyler and his new fire truck from Alex. They were all taking a break after a huge dinner before Maggie's fabulous smorgasbord of desserts, including her new tradition of twenty-four days of cookies. Sunny had gained five pounds just from cookies all month.

Alex and Maggie were putting a jigsaw puzzle together at the dining room table with June and Trudy while Roger "watched" a movie on TV, with eyes closed and snoozing softly. Sunny's gaze landed on each face around the room and her heart grew with pleasure and contentment. June and Roger got along wonderfully with her parents, who'd accepted Alex as though he were already an official member of their family attached to Maggie. Her heart expanded with fondness for each of them.

She'd had a conversation with Maggie earlier in the day about Sunny taking over as the Inn's manager so that

Maggie could concentrate on starting her catering business. They'd ended their conversation with a hug, both shedding tears of joy, while excited for the future. Sunny was happy that her big sister had nixed her idea of going back to California to stay in Brenham—Texas ruled.

She rose to get a cup of coffee when the bell rang at the front door. "Are we expecting anyone, Maggie?"

Maggie shrugged. "Not that I know of."

Sunny went to the door and looked out the side window. Then her heart dropped to the floor and she began to scream and jump in front of the door. "Oh. My. God. He's here. He's here."

She threw open the door and launched herself at her husband, who stood on the porch wearing a sly grin. Jason caught her and wrapped his arms around. Their lips crushed together in a long, breathtaking kiss. Sunny couldn't believe he was here, in Brenham, on Christmas Eve. She hugged Jason with all her strength.

Maggie walked to the door and cleared her throat. "Hey guys, in or out. You're giving the neighbors quite the reality show."

Jason Monroe stepped back from his wife and pulled her over the threshold. "Hey, babe . . . surprised?"

"Surprised? I'm having a heart attack right now." Sunny quickly wrapped her arms around her husband again and hugged him like there was no tomorrow. *Thank you Lord, for this gift.*

Bob appeared with Trudy and placed Tyler in Sunny's arms, then shook Jason's hand. "Good to see you, son. I'll get your bags." Trudy gave Jason a good hug as well.

"Thank you, sir, ma'am. It's good to be back." Jason smiled at Tyler. "Do you think he remembers me?"

Sunny smiled at her son, her eyes blurred with tears, and holding back a sob. "Tyler, remember Daddy? He's come home to us."

Tyler raised his little arms toward Jason. "*My* Daddy."

Jason took his son in his arms and hugged him tightly. "Hey little man. You can't believe how much Daddy missed you and Mommy."

Sunny wiped her eyes and glanced around to see everyone else doing the same. Nothing like a soldier coming home to bring on the water works.

Jason reached out for her and she entered the warmth of his embrace. She and her son with her husband—she couldn't ask for a better Christmas.

Once the initial shock of having him home wore off, she introduced him to Alex along with June and Roger. "These two lovebirds are getting married in the Barn on Sunday."

Jason beamed at the older couple. "A wedding, huh? Looks like I arrived just in time. I love a good bachelor party."

Alex ribbed Roger. "Oh, yeah. I say we have an all day poker game on Saturday."

Roger slid his hands together. "Great idea. Are you in, Jason? My sons will be here that morning with their families. Great way for the men to get out of the way."

Sunny grabbed her husband's hand, pulled him toward the hallway. "Excuse me, but nobody's taking my man off for a day of poker. You'll have to party hardy without him." She grinned seductively at Jason. "Come on babe, it's time for Tyler's night-night time. Then mama's gonna collect her Christmas present."

Alex jabbed Maggie gently in the side. "Hmph. Looks like Jason will be playing poker of another sort for the rest of the evening."

Sunny threw him a mischievous grin. "You got that right."

Sunny walked up the back stairs with Tyler in her arms and her husband following behind her. Oh yeah, this was one excellent Christmas Eve.

Chapter Twenty-Six

December 27, Sunday

Weddings, regardless of the size, location, or eloquence, were wondrous affairs.

Maggie had been on an emotional high since her first cup of coffee that morning. This wedding day was special, and the nuptials were personal for her since they involved Alex's mother. It was pure joy for Maggie to have the event at the Barn.

Of course, being the practical gal she was, it gave her additional experience in hosting such an event. June's wedding was much more intimate than Emma's and different in flair and pace. Every bride had her own style. And it was good for the Barn's reputation to gain experience in hosting large and small events.

Alex nudged her arm, as she watched the bride and groom take their first dance as husband and wife. She sighed. Their dance was awesome. The Barn sparkled and so did the bride who wore a light pink tea-length dress with rhinestones over the bodice. Her silver sandals floated over the dance floor.

"Your mom is beautiful," she whispered to Alex. "They're superb dancers."

He chuckled. "My mom's a pro, she had a dance

studio for years."

"No kidding? I should hire her to give dance lessons for the happy couples."

"If the lessons are in Houston."

"Right." Maggie watched them move in perfect unison. "Maybe we can convince June and Roger to move to Brenham."

"Probably not." He wrapped his arm around her waist. "They aren't small town folks like you and me."

"Uh-huh," she said as she leaned against him. "We had to discover we like small town Texas. Maybe they will, too."

Alex chuckled. "Nah, you know that old saying about a leopard changing it stripes, or was it a tiger changing its spots?"

"No clue," she teased. Other guests had joined June and Roger on the dance floor. Sunny and Jason finally had time together as the babysitter had taken Tyler to bed. They danced like it was their first time. Jason had told them he was home for good. The Army had given him an early discharge, budget cuts or something. Sunny was beyond happy, more like bouncing off the walls with joy.

Maggie wiped a tear from a suddenly moist eye. There was so much happiness and enjoyment at the Barn tonight. This was exactly what she'd envisioned when she first spoke to Larry Lamb about the bank loan.

Alex tugged on her hand. "I need to talk with you for a minute . . . privately. Okay?"

"Of course, let's go back to the Inn. I can get away for a few minutes."

Alex grabbed two glasses of champagne from the bar and followed Maggie out the front door of the Barn to the back door of the Inn. They ended up in the living room. The lamps were low and a fire burned behind the safety screen, setting a seductive mood.

They both settled on the sofa and Alex handed Maggie a glass.

"Thank you. It's good to sit down for a bit. I need to invest in more comfortable shoes for these events."

Alex set his glass on the side table and pulled her legs over his thighs, taking off her heels. "Massaging a lady's feet is one of my special talents."

"Oh yeah?"

"Yes ma'am." Alex worked on her left foot first. "I'm sure you know those high heels aren't good for you."

"But they make my legs look good in a short skirt."

His hand slid up her calf. "You look good in anything—short skirts, long skirts, jeans, nothing at all."

"Thank you, kind sir." Maggie would fall asleep if he kept rubbing her foot and leg. "You need to talk with me?"

"Yes." He laid her foot on the sofa and rose. He picked up his flute and walked to the fireplace, his back to Maggie. She sipped champagne while she wondered what was on his mind. His return to Brenham had made her so happy she couldn't even imagine what he might be thinking.

Alex turned to her. "First, I want you to know how happy I am. Second, thank you for giving my mother such an amazing wedding. I'm sure she'll never forget it."

Delight buzzed though Maggie. "It was my pleasure. June is a beautiful bride." She swung her legs around and patted the cushion next to her. "Come sit by me. I don't like you so far away."

Alex's slow grin set her nerves to humming.

He put his empty flute on the table and settled next to her. "I need to get your opinion on something."

"All right." She stroked her finger along his muscular forearm.

"A week ago I received a call from that producer in California. The one I told you about who was interested in making a movie from one of my video games."

"I remember. You said the two of you couldn't agree on the right adaptation." Maggie had a sinking feeling this conversation wouldn't end well.

"Exactly." Alex intertwined her fingers with his and set their hands on his thigh. "Well, they've come around to my way of thinking and—"

She tried to tug her hand from his but he wouldn't let go. "That's wonderful, I—"

"Shh." He placed a finger over her lips. "Don't jump to any conclusions until I'm finished."

"Okay." Maggie nodded and blew a slow breath, preparing herself for bad news.

"What I was saying is that I think the movie is going to happen. But first I need to talk with the producer in person and look at the script summary."

"Of course, that makes sense."

"I know this a lot to ask," Alex said while he rubbed the top of her hand with his thumb. "Could you fly to LA with me on Tuesday? It'll be first class all the way."

"What?"

"The meeting is on Wednesday."

"Huh?" For some reason, Maggie's ability to speak had temporarily departed. He wanted her to accompany him to California? He wasn't ditching her for Hollywood?

"I thought we could go to Las Vegas on Thursday morning, that's New Year's Eve, and stay for a couple of nights." He leaned over and kissed her. "You know that rock band from Sugar Land, Topped Off, is playing at Caesar's Palace. I'm sure we can get concert tickets. What do you think? I really want you to go with me."

Maggie swallowed hard. "Will you be moving there?"

"What? No. The only place I'll be moving to is a new house in Brenham."

"You're buying a house here?"

"I thought we should do it together." He wrapped both arms around her. "But I don't want to get ahead of myself. What do you think about taking a few days away from the Inn?"

Maggie released her breath in a slow, relieved sigh. Why had she assumed Alex had bad news? She obviously needed to put past experiences behind her.

"Stay in LA for a couple of nights then fly to Vegas for a couple for nights, all first class. Hmm." She tapped her chin, pretended to be considering his suggestion for about five seconds. She leaned in suddenly and kissed him. "I would love to go with you."

"Excellent." He pulled her close and she settled

against him. They sat there, her head resting on his chest, watching the flames dance, alternately licking upward then ebbing low. The flames were kind of like life. Steady, constantly moving up and down, and in need of new fuel to stay alive. In her life, that fuel was love.

"By the way, Mr. Brady, I love you." She said it without thinking and without analyzing the pros and cons of whether it was the smart thing to do.

Alex pulled back from her and she saw a tiny fireplace reflected in his eyes, the flames of life. "Miss Todd, I love you." He kissed her. It was gentle and sweet and tender.

"Um, excuse me."

Maggie pulled away from Alex at the gravelly voice. She turned around and their ghost stood behind the sofa close to the front foyer. "Good evening, Robert."

"Sorry to interrupt, but I wanted to say thank you." His body outline was surprisingly clear.

"Thank you for what?" Maggie had no idea what was on his mind.

"For including me here." His arm swept in front of him. "Ever since I've been stuck in the barn, I've felt like an outsider. Always dodging the humans. Now, that has changed because you've given me a role here."

Tears welled immediately and Maggie brushed them away. What a nice thing for a ghost, er, someone to say. "You're welcome. I'm glad you're here with us." He floated backwards with his hands in front of his chest. She quickly realized the meaning of her words. "I didn't mean it like that. I—"

Alex grabbed her hand. "What she means is that

we're all happy you feel more comfortable around here. Just don't be scaring the guests for fun."

A deep rumbling vibrated the living room and she realized it was Robert laughing. He was shaking and waving his arms around. "Robert, it's not that funny."

"Oh, yes it is." He stopped moving. "I promise I'll be on my best behavior . . . most of the time." He evaporated with a scent of lavender left behind.

"I think you've created a comedian," Alex said as he wrapped his arms around her. "Now where were we? Oh yes, I was saying how much I love you." He gently kissed her and ran the tip of his finger along her jaw.

Her arms tightened around him. "I'm so very happy."

"Once this wedding is over, I plan to make you really happy." He nuzzled her neck and his hand brushed up her side.

"The wedding!" She wriggled out of his arms, put on her heels, and jumped upright. "The cake. Come on, Alex." She pulled him up. "We need to cut your mom's cake. I can't believe I forgot."

"Oh, baby, I'll make you forget all kinds of things." He grinned wickedly.

She laughed. "You are so bad. I'm holding you to your promise of making me *really happy* afterwards." She grabbed his hand and pulled him toward the back door of the Inn.

"And I promise I'll love you for the rest of our lives."

She glanced at him as they exited the door and winked. "To the end of time, my love."

* * * * *

Maggie has graciously agreed to share three of her original recipes. Enjoy!!

Chocolate Chunk Coconut Bar Cookies

Ingredients
>1 cup/2 sticks unsalted butter, softened
>1 cup packed light brown sugar
>½ cup granulated sugar
>2 eggs
>1 teaspoon vanilla extract
>2 ½ cups all purpose flour
>1 teaspoon salt
>1 teaspoon baking powder
>½ teaspoon cinnamon
>12 ounces of chocolate chunks, your preferred variety of chocolate
>1 cup sweetened coconut

Directions
>1. Preheat oven to 375 degrees, grease a 15X10 jellyroll pan.
>2. In mixing bowl, combine butter and sugars and beat by hand or with a mixer. Add eggs individually, beating after each egg is added. Add the vanilla extract and beat thoroughly.
>3. Whisk together flour, salt, baking soda, and cinnamon in a separate bowl until combined.
>4. Stir flour mixture into butter/sugar mixture one-third at a time and mix well. Add chocolate chunks and coconut and mix together.
>5. Spread dough evenly in jellyroll pan. Bake 20-25 minutes until golden brown. Let cool before cutting.

Servings: 24-36 cookies depending on how you cut them.

Tomato Bacon Basil Tart

<u>Ingredients</u>
    1 sheet refrigerated pie crust
    1 ½ cups shredded mozzarella cheese, divided
    2 plum tomatoes, thinly sliced
    ½ cup mayonnaise
    ¼ cup grated Parmesan cheese
    1 tablespoon prepared pesto
    ½ teaspoon freshly ground black pepper
    5 pieces of bacon, cooked and crumbled
    1/3 cup fresh basil, chopped

<u>Directions</u>
1. Preheat oven to 425 degrees.
2. Fit pie crust into an 11-inch tart pan, going up evenly along the sides. Prick bottom with a fork. Bake 6-8 minutes or until lightly brown.
3. Once crust cools for a bit, spread with 1 cup of mozzarella cheese and top with the sliced tomatoes.
4. In a small bowl mix together the mayonnaise, Parmesan cheese, pesto, and pepper. Spread evenly over the tomatoes.
5. Sprinkle with crumbled bacon evenly over the crust.
6. Combine remaining mozzarella cheese with the basil and spread evenly over the crust.
7. Bake 10-12 minutes until filling is bubbly and crust is golden brown.

<u>Servings</u>: 6

Maggie's Yummy Hot Toddy

<u>Ingredients</u>
   1 ounce/2 tablespoons of your favorite bourbon
(Maggie's favorite is Jack Daniels)
   1 tablespoon honey
   2 teaspoons fresh lemon juice
   ¼ cup boiling/hot water

<u>Directions</u>
   1. Pour bourbon, honey and lemon juice in your
favorite mug. Add water and stir until the honey is
dissolved.
   2. Enjoy.

<u>Servings:</u> 1

Thank You!

Thank you for reading **Crazy for Home**. I grew up in small towns and have an ongoing love affair with them and of course, with ghosts, nice ghosts that is. I hope you enjoyed Maggie and Alex's story along with the resolution of the "life" of Robert Grant. Like Robert, I think I'd rather exist around the living rather than the dead. The next Texas Ghost Stories book, *The Dancing Maiden*, will be out the beginning of 2016.

If you know a ghost who you think would be an inspiration for a Texas Ghost Stories book, please contact me via my website at www.karensueburns.com. Like any writer, I'm always looking for and thinking about story and character ideas.

Also, if you enjoyed **Crazy for Home**, please take the time to leave a review via the vendor where the book was purchased. Reader reviews are one of the best ways for writers to gain new readers and gain feedback about their work. Thank you if you do post a review. Also be sure to let me know via my website or on Facebook. I'd love to hear from you!

The first book in the Texas Ghost Stories is **The Liberation of Mr. Delaney** published in 2013: *When a heartbroken bookstore manager meets a charming ghost,* *sparks fly and the elimination of a decade old curse becomes crucial to their futures. Along the way a murder is solved, a family is reborn, and love once again proves its far-reaching power.*

Note: All of my heroines love to cook as I do. Please visit my website for some of our favorite recipes – www.karensueburns.com

Notes

www.ingramcontent.com/pod-product-compliance
Lightning Source LLC
Chambersburg PA
CBHW032207190626

46810CB00019B/2110